THE RIVER IS
ALWAYS WAITING

THE RIVER IS
ALWAYS WAITING

ATTRACTION IS SOMETHING

THAT YOU **FEEL**,

NOT SOMETHING THAT YOU **ARE**.

STEPHEN MEASURE

SILVER LAYER PUBLICATIONS

Silver Layer Publications
P.O. Box 1047
Chino Valley, AZ 86323
www.silverlayer.com
www.stephenmeasure.com

Editing: Kathryn Tilby
Cover design: Barry Hansen
Book design: Marny K. Parkin

Library of Congress Control Number: 2013953941

ISBN: 978-1-940778-00-6 (hardback)
ISBN: 978-1-940778-01-3 (paperback)

Last Updated: June 14, 2017 (copyright page)

For those who choose to resist

. . . Sufficient unto the day is the evil thereof.
Matthew 6:34

Part One

The Unexpected Answer

Chapter One

THE OAK TREE, STRONG FOR CENTURIES, WOULD STAND no longer; roots reached wide and deep across the mountainside, but days of rain had reached even deeper, the soil saturated and weak, the strength of the roots left with no foundation, nothing to grasp. Everything cold, wet, dark. The world was slipping; yet the rain continued its steady drumming, water running down trunk and branches, flying off leaves that twisted in the wind, painted glass wind chimes clattering as they fought against twine, slick and tight. The ground pooled where it did not flow, everything mud and water, moving down, held back only by old roots and stubborn stones; but those too would come. Nothing stands forever. Its core breached, its resistance crumbling, the hillside shifted, slowly—soon.

Below, a light shone onto the hill from a solitary cabin, where Alice sat alone trying to read *The Screwtape Letters*. An odd book, perhaps, for a girl her age to read, but she loved it—especially the parts she understood—because the story fascinated her: letters from a devil to his nephew, each letter teaching the younger devil how to lead people into mistakes. And reading the letters made Alice feel like a detective examining captured evidence, or a spy scanning through the stolen plans of the enemy, an enemy whose attack plans were all there, right there in the book, one devil to another: if the man does this, then make him think that; if the man thinks this, then push him one step further—always one step further—one step further toward a mistake.

Alice had been reading the book for the past two days. With no TV in the cabin and no other electronics to entertain her, reading was one of the few things to do while it rained outside. She had the Narnia series as well, which was a better fit for her age, but she had read those books twice already in the cabin and wanted to try something else. Her reading had been slow since she stopped regularly to ask Dana what a word meant, but tonight it was going even slower than usual. Although she had hoped to finish a chapter before Dana returned to the cabin with Simon, Dana's dinner date, she hadn't finished a single page yet.

The couch was comfortable and, though it was dark outside the cabin, there was plenty of light inside. The problem was the rain—not the steady drumming on the roof, which she had grown used to by now, but the sharp tap that hit the roof every now and then, drawing her attention to the ceiling and making her lose her place in the book yet again.

Just a large rain drop hitting off rhythm, just a harmless drop of water—Alice knew that—but alone in a cabin, high in the mountains, surrounded by darkness, reading *The Screwtape Letters,* she saw the same image each time the tap struck—a devil, prowling across the dark roof, striking the shingles with a cold, bare knuckle, searching for a weak spot to get through, to get her. *TAP!*

Above the kitchen cupboards that time. Alice glanced over, but all was still, the dishes quiet in the sink, the counters cleared, everything clean and waiting. She sighed and closed her book. Trying to read now is pointless, she told herself. Besides, Dana should be back with Simon any minute now, shouldn't she? Alice leaned forward on the couch, looking across the room at the clock on the microwave. Twenty minutes, she thought. Dana said it would only be ten. What is taking so long? Are they still talking? Has Dana told Simon about me yet?

The food sat hopeful on the table, the plates empty and ready to be filled. Maybe I should cover the food somehow to keep it warm, Alice thought. Dana had bought groceries and supplies before they drove up the mountain three weeks ago; but Alice, never having cooked or taken care of food before, didn't know what she was supposed to cover it with. I guess if the food gets cold, then it serves Dana right for being late, she told herself.

Three weeks in the cabin, with Dana seeing Simon for half that time, the two of them meeting most days for hikes. Dana should have told

Simon earlier, Alice thought. She shouldn't have made him believe that she was here by herself. Yes, Dad asked us to keep it a secret, but who is Simon going to tell? Besides, Simon probably won't even recognize me. Why would he?

She hoped Simon wouldn't be upset when Dana finally told him. It's not like I'm her kid, Alice thought, so it shouldn't be a big deal, right? But guys are jerks—that's what Dana always says. Is Simon different? Dana sure acts like he is. Well, if he isn't a jerk, then he won't mind me being here.

The light flickered for a moment. Alice looked up at it, worried that the power would go out. Is the wind stronger tonight? she wondered. Reaching over to the side table, she pushed the wind chimes to one side, making room to set her book down. There were three wind chimes there. Paint now dry—blue, green, and yellow—they were waiting to be hung on the oak tree up the hill. She hoped it would stop raining soon. Wind chimes should hang in the breeze, not sit on a table, she thought. Dana had said they would run out of wind chimes soon, that they hadn't brought enough to paint a new one every morning, that there were too many mornings left before they would return home. But Alice figured she could always repaint some of the older ones. They might need it anyway, she thought, after this storm. She wondered how they were doing up there in the rain. Had any fallen off the old oak tree? On the phone her father had said that the weather channel was calling it the worst storm to hit the area in years. He told Dana to be careful. But Dana is always careful, Alice thought.

The tap struck again, above the dinner table this time, next to the overhead light, softer than the last tap but louder than the normal rain. Alice wondered if it sounded different because the drop was bigger, or if it just hit the roof in a certain way. Or, maybe—no, she told herself, that's silly. There's no need to get scared over nothing.

Everything on the dinner table was set so nicely: plates, cups, and silverware arranged just right, although it did seem strange to see three places set instead of two. The third placemat hadn't been easy to find either. Dana had panicked when she realized there were only two in the kitchen drawer. She found a third, but only after digging through the closet. It didn't match the other two placemats very well; but Dana said that Simon wouldn't notice, making Alice question why, then, Dana had worried so much about it.

She drew her legs up beneath her to sit cross-legged on the couch and wondered what Simon would think of the cabin. It seemed comfortable to her—simple, but comfortable. Dana was worried, though, especially about the ugly painting by the door. Modern art, it belonged to Alice's mother but was put in the cabin so her father could get it out of the house. Too big to fit anywhere else, the painting had been hung by the door, covering the window that used to be there. When they first got to the cabin, Dana had tried to take it down and hide it somewhere so they wouldn't have to look at it every day, but the frame was screwed tight to the wall. And, knowing that Alice's mother had expensive taste, Dana didn't dare risk damaging it because, whether Alice's father defended her or not, that was a sure way for Dana to get fired. So the painting remained, and Dana could only hope that Simon wouldn't notice. But Alice didn't think he would, not with Dana there.

She wondered what Simon would be like. Back home, Dana went on dates occasionally; but they were always first dates, never second ones, and she always returned home unimpressed. However, there was something solid about Simon, Dana had told her, something different. She said that boys didn't grow into men anymore, that guys in their twenties still acted like teenagers. But she said that Simon wasn't like that. Alice wasn't sure what that meant. I guess I'll find out soon, she told herself.

The light flickered and went out. Alice's breath caught as the darkness pressed in. There was a pounding above, as if the devil were frantic to reach her before the light returned. Alice pulled her legs up against her chest and hugged them tightly. Then the room was back, the light coming alive with a sudden click, the pounding retreating to the roof, only the rain. Alice blinked at the light, her eyes unsure, and sat silent another moment before letting out her breath.

The one time the power goes out, she thought, and Dana, of course, is gone. She crossed her legs again beneath her. And what if it hadn't come back on? The dark here isn't just dim like it is in the city. It's completely black. Where did Dana put the flashlight? Probably in one of the kitchen drawers.

The tap struck again, this time above the couch. How close was that to the power line? Alice asked herself. No, stop being ridiculous. Dana will be here any minute and then I'll get to meet Simon and we'll all be laughing and everything will be fine. Any minute now, I'm sure.

Except Dana seemed to always be late whenever she went anywhere with Simon, every time, since the first day they met. That day, Dana and Alice had planned to hang their latest wind chime in the oak tree once the paint dried, and Dana had gone for a short hike while they waited. But the short hike turned slowly into a long hike; so, tired of waiting, Alice walked up to the tree by herself. She had already hung the new wind chime when Dana finally arrived, her hands in the pockets of her blue jacket.

"I met a strange man today," Dana said, the smile on her face telling Alice that "strange" didn't mean bad.

And they talked a little about Simon, the man Dana had just met, as Alice sat with Dana beneath the oak tree, the chimes sounding softly above them, colors moving in the breeze, Dana pretending to not care that she'd met him, Alice knowing that Dana was only pretending. And the first thing Dana did when they returned to the cabin was dig through the bathroom to see if she had brought any makeup. We're staying in a cabin—of course she didn't bring makeup, Alice thought. Not that Dana needed it anyway. Alice's mother might have to cake it on to look pretty, but Dana looked great with or without makeup. Her blonde hair didn't come from a bottle either.

"Why do you dye your hair?" Alice had asked her mother once as she watched her apply a final layer of makeup while looking in the mirror.

"Oh, Alice, your father would never marry a redhead," Alice's mother said. "A successful man like him wants to marry a pretty girl—a blonde."

She said this without even looking at Alice, only placing her hand briefly on Alice's shoulder before turning absently and gliding out of the room, leaving redheaded Alice unsure whether her mother had meant to insult her or simply didn't notice.

Dana, though, was furious when she heard what Alice's mother had said. "Why that stupid, stuck-up—"

Alice jumped to her feet, off-balance, as the cabin door flew outward, the night's darkness revealed for an instant before Dana hurried through the door, slammed it shut behind her and flipped the deadbolt into place. Then, turning her back against the door, she sank slowly to the ground, soaking wet, face in her hands, her body shaking.

Chapter Two

Where is Simon? Alice wondered before realizing what a stupid question that was. Feeling awkward, she stood there watching Dana, who sat sobbing by the door. Alice had never seen Dana cry before. Not after any of her failed dates. Not when Alice's mother yelled at her. No, Dana never cried—not until now. And Alice wasn't sure what to do. I need to do something, though, she told herself, but what can I do?

She remembered, then, when she was younger, only a toddler, crying in the night, her father away campaigning, her mother unwilling to hear. She remembered the feeling of unfamiliar arms wrapping around her, the arms of her new nanny, still just a teenager herself, hugging her tightly; and she remembered the song Dana had hummed to drive the loneliness away.

Not knowing what else to do, she sat down next to Dana and put her arms around her. She didn't know what to say, so she just sat there, feeling Dana's sobs grow quieter and wondering what went wrong.

It's probably my fault, she thought. Simon probably got mad that I'm here. I wish Dana had told him earlier. But he seemed like such a nice guy. How could he do this to Dana?

The cold wetness of Dana's coat was gradually working its way into Alice's shirt. Dana's hair was dripping as well. Where did she leave her umbrella? Alice wondered. She needs to get out of that coat and get warm or she'll get sick. Unwrapping her arms, Alice reached for the top button; but Dana batted her hand aside and then stood and walked to the closet. She opened the door and tried to take off her coat, but its bottom buttons didn't cooperate.

"Stupid!" she yelled, ripping the still-buttoned coat up over her head and throwing it down on the ground. Then, laying her hand flat against the wall, she leaned against it, facing the floor, not crying anymore though her eyes were still red. She stood there silently, staring at the ground, as if she could find an answer there if she looked hard enough.

Alice stood up but didn't move away from the front door, debating whether she should give Dana space or not. And what should I say to her? Alice wondered. Dana liked Simon so much. Surely they could work this out—whatever it had been—couldn't they?

"Maybe it was just a misunderstanding," she said, more hopeful than believing.

But Dana just shook her head, drumming her fingers on the wall and giving no clue about what she was thinking. She stood there another moment without speaking; then she raised her head and looked at the kitchen table, seeing the food all prepared, cold water in a pitcher, three plates waiting to be filled. The sight drove her into a frenzy. Jumping from the wall to the table, she snatched the large glass platter of food and hurried it to the garbage can, where she dumped it in with an angry grunt.

Alice stepped forward, worried at Dana's outburst and grasping for something to calm her.

"Simon will come back and work things out, Dana," she said. "I just know he will. Maybe even tonight. He'll come make things right. You'll see."

The platter shattered when it hit the ground, glass spilling across the floor as Dana, frozen and facing away from Alice, asked in a distant voice, "What did you say?"

But Alice was staring at the glass that littered the floor. Was this more than just a breakup? she wondered. Then she saw Dana's blank expression, now turned toward her, and realized that Dana had asked her a question. "I just thought," she stumbled, unsure what to say. "Well, he knows where the cabin is, now, right? Don't you think he might come back and want to work things out?"

Dana's face went pale. She stepped toward Alice, crunching glass with her boots as she pointed at the bedroom. "Go pack your things. Now. We're leaving tonight." Then she turned to the closet.

But Alice didn't move. "What do you mean, leaving tonight?" she asked. "I thought my dad wanted us to stay here for another three weeks."

Dana reached into the closet and pulled out two coats, one for Alice and another for herself, her wet one still lying on the floor. She threw them both onto the back of a chair and said, "We can't stay here anymore, Alice. It isn't safe. Your father will understand."

He won't understand if it turns out to just be some stupid argument between you and Simon, Alice thought, and she said, "Unsafe? Why? Because of Simon? People fight all the time, Dana. Just look at my parents—"

But she stopped talking when Dana turned toward her and Alice saw the fear in Dana's eyes. It wasn't just an argument. Something was wrong. The cabin walls suddenly felt thin.

"Go in the bedroom and pack," Dana repeated, purpose and direction making her face less pale and her voice more calm. Then she returned to the closet and dug through it once more while Alice stood and watched.

It was the pounding on the roof that drove Alice to the bedroom. Things not only prowling above but lurking now in the darkness around the cabin, stalking from tree to tree. Would Simon be among them? No. Alice shook her head. Stop being stupid, she told herself.

But she went quickly to her small dresser and took out her clothes, placing them in piles on her bed. Dana entered the room, then, dragging their two suitcases behind her. She placed one on Alice's bed and threw the other onto her own. Then she started loading it with clothes, ripping them out of drawers and throwing them into the suitcase.

The taps on the roof were more frequent now, a sign of growing agitation. Alice moved her clothes into her suitcase and then turned to consider the handful of books that lay on top of her dresser. Dana had bought the books—the Narnia series by C. S. Lewis—for Alice on their way out of town. Dana knew nothing of Narnia and was not religious herself, but she knew that C. S. Lewis was; and, above all, she knew that Alice's mother would definitely not approve. So, the memory of her parting argument with Alice's mother still fresh in her mind, Dana had bought the books eagerly after stumbling across them while getting supplies for the cabin, her sense of right and wrong guided mainly by learning what Alice's mother considered to be right and then doing the exact opposite.

But right or wrong, owning the books had bothered Alice at first. While the little love that existed between Alice and her mother flowed in only one direction, there was enough of it to make Alice feel uncomfortable to know that she was reading something her mother would not want her to read. But, when she started the first book, she sensed something that convinced her to continue reading whether it made her uncomfortable or not, some meaning inside that she knew would make the effort worthwhile, like a medicine that, though sour, was also good for you. Some books are like that.

However, now she needed to decide if she dared take the books home or not. She loved both Narnia and *The Screwtape Letters,* but she knew that taking them home could create problems for Dana, who was supposed to keep her away from those kinds of viewpoints. Mother would be furious, Alice thought. She might even try to fire Dana. Would Dad stop her?

"If you're done with your clothes, then grab all the stuff from the bathroom," Dana said, still loading her suitcase. "I put a bag there by the doorway."

"Okay," Alice told her, delaying her decision until later. She picked up the bag on her way into the bathroom. It was a small, simple room, the doorway facing a sink and mirror, the shower on the left, a toilet somehow squeezed into the middle. She assumed the toothbrushes were garbage and left them there, but she stuffed the toothpaste and hairbrushes into the bag before squatting down, opening the cabinet beneath the sink, and loading its contents into the bag.

Closing the cabinet, she started to rise when she lost her balance and tipped backward, catching herself with one hand on the cold bathroom tile, which rattled. Did I break it? she wondered, turning around to get a better look. No, she thought. It isn't cracked. The tile looks fine. Then what? She placed her hand flat on the tiles. The entire floor was vibrating. The tapping on the roof grew frantic.

And then she heard it, a low noise, seeming to come from the bedroom. She stood and walked out of the bathroom, looking around and trying to pinpoint where the sound was coming from. The window, covered by drapes, faced the hill behind. The noise was coming from there.

"What are you doing?" Dana asked as Alice walked across the room and threw back the drapes to look at the hill.

But Alice could see nothing through the window except darkness and her own reflection. The noise, though, seemed to be getting louder, a distant rumbling, moving closer.

"Do you hear that?" Alice asked.

"Hear what?" Dana said. "Is someone outside?" And suddenly she was by Alice's side at the window.

The rumbling grew louder. Now, a dull roar. "Can't you hear that?" Alice asked.

Dana's reflection nodded in the window.

"What is it?"

"I don't know, but I don't like it. Can you see anything?"

"No. Can you?"

"No. Maybe we should turn off the light—Wait . . ."

The window started rattling as the roar split into sounds—the cracking of wood, the crashing of rocks. The darkness in the window flowed toward them.

"Run!" Dana screamed, grabbing Alice and pulling her toward the door. Alice stumbled, but Dana yanked on her arm, sending her flying through the doorway. She hit the ground hard, her breath forced out in a squeak.

A door slammed and the roar hit the cabin, everything in motion, glass shattering, wood cracking, the world lurching, someone screaming—three painted glass wind chimes hung in the air before crashing to the floor—darkness washing over, chasing all light away, full of commotion. The walls closed in and the roar was all around and the air was gone and the cabin was a coffin and the coffin was too tight and she couldn't move and she couldn't breathe and the devil pounded nails in the lid and she was buried underground—and Alice would scream if only Alice could breathe—and the devil pounded nails in the lid and her coffin was too tight and Dana was there, holding Alice, speaking softly, the coffin now a cabin, the walls retreating, still dark, commotion all around; but Dana was humming, quieter than the groaning, calm, the air returning. Alice took a breath. She clung tight to Dana, the two of them lying on the cold floor of a cabin, not a coffin.

"It's okay, Alice," a voice said to her, a hand rubbing her back. "It's okay."

No, it's not okay, Alice thought as the wood creaked all around her and taps struck angrily against the roof.

"Just breathe," Dana's voice said. "It's okay, Alice. Relax. Your heart is beating so fast. Just relax. It's going to be okay."

They rocked a little, side to side, there on the floor, Dana whispering soothing words to Alice until the creaking grew softer, quieter now than the rain.

"What happened?" Alice asked.

"Shh . . . It's over now." Dana still rocked her.

"But what was it? What happened?"

"It must have been a landslide or something. I think it knocked out the power. But it's over now, and we're okay. Does anything hurt?"

"Not really."

"Your pants are wet," Dana said, sitting up and feeling along Alice's ankles.

"Am I bleeding?" Alice asked, the walls feeling closer.

"No. It's cold. Just water. The floor is wet."

And the walls retreated. Alice let out her breath. She heard a single angry tap above, followed by the steady drumming of the rain.

"We need to get off this floor," Dana said. "Where's the couch?"

Alice felt Dana leave her. Alone. The darkness weighed on her, thickening.

"Shh . . . Alice, it's okay. Just breathe. That's right. Just breathe. It's going to be okay. Let's get you off the floor now. Look, here's the couch. See? Right here. Sit down right there. That's right. I'm sitting right here beside you. Now breathe. It's going to be okay, Alice. Just breathe."

Dana held her on the couch, as they rocked back and forth in the darkness. "It's going to be okay. But, oh, you're so cold, Alice," Dana said, rubbing Alice's arms. "You need your coat. I'd better find the flashlight."

Alice's grip tightened around Dana.

"It's going to be okay. Do you want to stay here in the dark all night? No, I'll just be a minute. The flashlight's in the left kitchen drawer. I know right where it is. You just let go of me for a minute and then it won't be dark anymore, okay? Now just let go and don't worry—everything's going to be just fine. I'll get a light on. Just give me one minute, maybe thirty seconds."

Alice nodded uselessly in the dark and let go of Dana. Then Dana was gone. But she kept talking as she walked across the room, muttering a curse when she ran into a kitchen chair and laughing a little at the sound of crunching glass.

"I never liked those plates anyways."

Hearing Dana and knowing she was there kept the walls away from Alice and the darkness from choking her even though the cabin continued its quiet, mournful creaking. Dana was rummaging in the drawers.

"So, not that drawer, but I'm sure it's right here in the next one. Let me see. Let me see. Yes!"

Light filled the room with a click, much dimmer than the ceiling light but enough to drive the shadows into corners.

Dana carried Alice's coat back to the couch and helped her put it on after shining the flashlight all over her to check for injuries.

"Better, right?" she said then scanned the rest of the room with the light.

Glass covered the floor from broken wind chimes and plates and cups that had fallen from the table. The water pitcher had spilled, its contents dripping over the table's edge and mixing with the cold, dark water spreading toward the couch. Then they heard a low groan to their side. Dana whipped the flashlight toward the bedroom door, which was bulging outward, the roof leaning slightly toward it, water and mud spilling through an inch-wide gap along the door's bottom. Creaking loudly, the door bulged farther, whatever filled the room now straining against the latch.

Alice had a vision of the door bursting open and debris filling the room, smothering and crushing them.

"Oh, no you don't," Dana told the door, handing the flashlight to Alice and rushing to the table, throwing chairs out of her way. She grabbed a bulky leg and dragged the table toward the swollen door, plates and utensils falling with every step, some shattering, some bouncing away across the floor. When she reached the door, she let go of the table and moved behind it. Then, lifting hard, she toppled the table onto its side, the top resting against the bedroom door and holding it in place. Dana considered her handiwork a moment before adding the four chairs, leaning them up against the base of the table for support.

The groaning faded away. Alice looked above her, expecting a tap of frustration but heard only rain. The table was solid wood, an antique. She hoped it was heavy enough to hold. Dana, though, seemed satisfied, already turning her back on the door and looking again around the room.

But as Alice held the light on the table, she caught a flicker of movement on the opposite wall. Swinging the beam in that direction, she tried to catch it.

"What is it?" Dana asked.

There was nothing there, just a wall. However, with the light shining now in that direction, Alice saw movement in the other. She swung the light back, catching nothing again. Back and forth the light went, Alice seeing something move but only outside the light, the darkness advancing then retreating as she chased it with the flashlight's beam. And then she realized: it's the walls that are moving.

"Alice, what's wrong?" Dana said, standing now by her side.

Alice dropped the flashlight. She covered her face in her hands. The walls can't move if I can't see them, she told herself.

"What's wrong?" Dana repeated, putting her hand on Alice's arm.

But Alice just shook her head.

Dana picked up the flashlight. "How about we get out of here?" she said.

Alice nodded in reply, hands still covering her face. She heard Dana walk across the room, smashing glass with each step, then silence for a moment, only rain and creaking wood.

"Yeah, I figured it would be dead," Dana said.

Alice looked up to see Dana holding the telephone to one ear.

"What about your cell phone?" Alice asked, hope holding the walls in place.

Dana shook her head. "I haven't kept it charged because there's no signal up here anyways. So, it's just been sitting in the car this whole time."

She shone the light back on the bedroom door.

"At least, it better be in the car because otherwise . . . " Dana paused and then asked, "Alice, where are the car keys?"

They both stared at the bedroom door. A small trickle of mud oozed past one side of the overturned table.

"Oh, no," Dana said, setting the light on the counter and tearing through the kitchen drawers. "Please, no. That would be bad, so bad."

She went through drawer after drawer, not finding the keys.

What will we do if we don't find them? Alice wondered, her panic returning. Walk home? All the way down the mountain? By ourselves? We didn't even bring a backpack. But then she remembered something. "Dana," she said, "didn't you bring your purse?"

"You're right!" Dana said, carrying the flashlight to the closet. She peered inside for a moment, rearranging the boxes she had moved in her earlier search for Simon's placemat, and then emerged triumphant, leather purse in hand. Opening it quickly, Dana searched through the contents, an anxious look on her face, and Alice let out a sigh of relief when she heard the welcome sound of metal clicking on metal. Dana pulled out the keys. "Hah!" she said. "See, it's going to be okay."

And for a moment, Alice thought it would be. She stood up, excited, already seeing them in the car, already imagining them driving down the mountain. I'll get to see Dad tomorrow, she thought with excitement, and I'll get out of this cabin. Never again, she told herself, looking over at the bent bedroom door. I'll never stay in a cabin again.

Dana scanned the room as Alice walked up beside her. Then she shrugged. "Let's just get out of here," she said, putting on her coat.

Purse over her shoulder, she guided Alice toward the door before stopping and telling her, "Okay, I want you to wait in the doorway a minute while I go and make sure the way to the car is clear."

Alice didn't like the thought of waiting alone, but she nodded anyway. The rain fell steadily, and she realized they would get wet; but then they would be in the car, driving away from the cabin and from what crept above. Except they'll see me, won't they? Can they stop us? she asked herself. No, I'll run from the cabin, and Dana will be there, and everything is going to be okay.

Dana undid the deadbolt, turned the knob, and pushed on the door. It didn't move.

"Oh, come on," Dana said, putting her shoulder into it and shoving. It still didn't move.

"What's wrong?" Alice asked as Dana put more and more pressure against the door, causing a small line of darkness to grow between the door and its frame. The door stopped after an inch and would move no further. Dana stepped back and kicked it. It bounced back toward them, slamming shut.

"Something's blocking it," Dana said.

She opened it again, the inch it would go, and shone the light through the small slit.

"I think a tree might be in front of the door. Here, hold this," she said, handing the flashlight to Alice.

Then Dana pushed, using her full weight, her boots sliding along the floor as she tried to open the door even a little bit wider. But it wouldn't budge.

The dancing above returned. Sharp taps, excited yet angry, here and then there across the rooftop, as if leaping around from one side to the other.

"How are we going to get out?" Alice asked. "Are we trapped here?" Already, the walls were closing in again.

Dana knelt in front of the door, peering again through the slit. "I don't know," she said. "I don't think I can move this tree."

And the phones don't work, Alice reminded herself. We're going to be trapped here forever, aren't we?

Dana stood and closed the door. The cabin had an electric heater—no power meant no heat—and already the night was getting chilly. She looked around the room, and Alice saw the uncertainty in her eyes. The dancing continued above them.

How long before someone rescues us? Alice wondered. Her father was supposed to call in a few days. But what if he forgets? she asked herself. He's busy with the election. What if he forgets?

The walls a little closer, the air a little thicker, the dancing a little louder, Alice shivered from the growing cold and stared at the wall, willing it to stay in place. Her mother's painting stared back, the ugly, ugly thing. If it wasn't there, Alice thought, then there would be—

"Wait," she said. "There's a window behind my mother's painting!"

Dana looked from Alice to the painting, hope appearing in her eyes.

"Is it still there, though?" she said. "I've never seen the shutters opened."

She walked to the large frame and felt along its edges. The painting was screwed down tight, all corners flush against the wall. Dana experimented by pulling on an edge, but it wouldn't move at all.

"I don't think we have a screwdriver," she said, more to herself than to Alice.

And, standing there, the fingers of one hand resting on the frame, Dana stared at the painting for a moment.

"Screw it," she said and walked to the kitchen drawer, returning with a large knife.

Alice saw the brief image of her mother's makeup-perfect face twisted in anger; but they had to get out of there, and she could almost see them climbing out the window and driving away in the car, the warm blow of the heater on her face as she left the cabin far, far behind. She held the flashlight high and watched as Dana, gripping the knife with both hands, raised it to the top of the painting and punched through, the canvas giving a sharp jerk. Dana pulled the knife downward, cutting a slit along the middle from top to bottom. Then, setting the knife on the floor, she grabbed one side of the canvas and pulled hard as she stepped back. The fabric tore easily, revealing the wall behind and part of the window frame. Excited, Dana tore back the other half, the painting now reduced to an overpriced frame, rumpled canvas sheets hanging pretentiously from each side, the hidden window made visible, all boarded up on the inside.

You are going to die here, Alice. You will never get out.

"No," Dana groaned, feeling at the boards.

But Alice could already see how tight they were. She knew Dana wouldn't be able to pull them out.

"Oh, come on. Come on."

Alice heard the words, but the image was getting hazy, the air so thick, the walls so close, the dancing so loud. And all around, stalking, all around the cabin—no need to come in, for she would never get out. The flashlight dropped to the floor. "Hey," a voice said, but the air was too thick, and the walls were too close, and the dancing—everything went dark.

She woke on the couch, her head in Dana's lap. "Shh . . . " Dana said. The light from the flashlight was dim. The rain was quiet. She heard no dancing above. "Shh . . . " Dana said again. "You just rest now. We'll find a way out in the morning. Sunlight always makes things better. We'll find a way out. Just rest."

Alice wanted to believe her, but the walls seemed so close.

"Turn off the light," she said.

"Okay."

Now in the dark, Alice could pretend there were no walls around her. She lay on the couch, facing away from Dana, who was rubbing her back. Alice wondered what time it was and how long it would be before dawn. She wondered if she would see her father again. She wondered if her mother would miss her. It seemed so quiet now without the rain and the tapping. She wondered where they had gone and if they would return. She thought they would. What they had started—this was only the beginning.

"Shh . . . " Dana told her and then started to hum. And Alice was a toddler again, frightened, missing her father, held by her young nanny, and falling asleep to the unsteady humming of a gentle lullaby.

Chapter Three

SOMETHING WAS POUNDING ON THE ROOF; SOMEONE WAS
yelling. Alice woke up confused and cold, unsure what had happened to her blanket. Heavy footsteps ran above. Then, feeling Dana
beside her, Alice remembered.

"Dana, are you in there?" a man shouted, muffled through the ceiling.

There was a faint trickle of light shining down from someplace above,
a small crack somewhere in the roof, giving enough light to show a dim
outline of the room. Dana stirred at the voice.

"What?" she mumbled and sat up, pulling Alice with her. She started
to stretch but stopped with arms extended as her eyes opened and she
saw the room.

"Dana!" the voice called louder this time. "Are you in there? Are you
okay?"

She jumped up off the couch. "We're here! We're in here! Simon,
we—" Dana stopped, turning to Alice with wide eyes. She put a hand
on Alice's shoulder.

"I'm going to get you out of there," Simon called from above. "Let me
try to clear the front door."

Footsteps ran across the roof as Dana and Alice listened below—
Dana standing, hand still on Alice's shoulder, Alice sitting, legs held
tight against her chest. It was quiet, then, for a moment, the only sound
the distant chattering of birds, less vocal than usual this morning. Then,
wood was being dragged in front of the cabin, and they could hear a man's
voice—Simon talking to himself—muttering something they couldn't
make out. Dana walked to the front door. She opened it as far as it would

go, only a crack, but even that small slit seemed to fill the room with light, the tree blocking the door now a dark silhouette against the gray light coming through the narrow opening. The tree looked too big for one man to move. Which tree is it? Alice wondered. How many others fell?

The sunlight from the door's opening, as weak as it was, was strong enough to change the mood of the room. Alice scooted over on the couch to sit in the light, still hugging her knees tightly—the dull beam brought no warmth—but being in the light made everything seem just a little bit firmer, the unreal feeling from before now fading away.

She felt foolish, sitting there in the light, at her imagination the night before. To have thought the walls were moving or devils were dancing on the roof. It all seemed so silly to her now that day had come. But daylight or not, she did feel better glancing from wall to wall and seeing them stay in place. That, she liked. The car isn't far from the cabin, she told herself. Just get through these walls, just get through the door, just get away.

Dana stood quietly by the doorway, her arms folded, listening to Simon work outside—wood scraping on wood, the deep thud of rocks, the shuffling sound of moving dirt. And she kept glancing at the slashed painting, its frame still on the wall, as if she were debating what to do with it. Then Alice realized that Dana wasn't actually looking at the painting itself; no, Dana was looking at the floor in front of it—at the knife she had left there the night before.

The noise outside stopped and the door moved back and forth, hitting again and again against the fallen tree, which didn't budge. Then the door stopped swinging and there was silence for a moment.

"Dana, I can't move this tree without chopping it up first," Simon said, an eye and an inch of face appearing through the door's crack. "I'm going to run back to get my hatchet. I won't be long."

"Why don't you just get the ranger?" Dana said, but Simon's face was already gone. She drew near to the opening and called after him, "Wait! Simon, just get the ranger. Get the ranger, Simon!"

Dana stood there for a moment, waiting, but there was no reply. She kicked at the ground, sending something rattling over to the couch, a small piece of glass, blue, part of a wind chime. Alice bent down and picked it up, holding it in her hand. It reminded her of calmer times, quiet days spent alone or with Dana, safety. She stuffed it into a pant pocket. Dana was closing the door, about to shut the sun outside.

"Please, leave it open!" Alice said, not wanting to lose the thin strip of sunlight—shadows gathered in the corners at the thought of the sun going away. The walls might not move, but Alice knew that they wanted to.

"Okay," Dana told her, letting go of the doorknob.

Alice shifted on the couch, not looking in the corners.

"How long will he be?" she asked.

"I don't know. Thirty or forty minutes."

"Can he get us out?"

Dana didn't answer. She picked up the knife and took it to the kitchen, where she laid it flat on the counter, hilt out, not far from the doorway.

They waited, then, and ate a small breakfast to pass the time. With no power, Dana couldn't make the usual pancakes, but she found some cereal, which they ate dry—the milk had run out weeks ago—scooping the cereal out of bowls with their hands, not bothering with spoons. Alice wasn't hungry, but she ate a little anyway. She didn't want Dana to worry.

Scouting around the room, Dana found Alice's book, *The Screwtape Letters,* and handed it to her. One corner was damp and another bent, but the book was otherwise in good condition. Dana's purse, however, wasn't so lucky. Water dripped from its soiled bottom when she lifted it off the wet floor. Sighing, she took out her wallet and keys and put them in her pocket, leaving the ruined purse on the ground.

And Alice dreamed as they waited. A simple dream, her in the car, window rolled down, arm resting on the windowsill, feeling the sunlight, warm sunlight, the air rushing past, not stale air, not damp, cold, yes, brisk but free, free air, running past her face as the wheels were spinning and spinning, taking her far away, where there were no more shadows, and no more walls, and no more devils that—

"Listen, Alice," Dana said, standing again by the door as she waited for Simon to return. "When he gets the door open, we're going straight to the car. Do you understand me? I don't care what he says. I don't care what he does. We're leaving right away. Do you understand?"

Alice nodded. Stupid to fight, the two of them, she thought. It's obvious they like each other. But just get me out of here. Just get me home. She tried not to notice how the shadows were twisting in the corners; they seemed so slippery. A gargoyle sat silently on the cover of her book. Do they sleep in the day? she wondered. Will they try to stop me when I leave? No, everything will be fine. They'll come back to an empty cabin. Let them dance then. They can dance over an empty cabin.

The first crack of the hatchet brought Alice back to the room and she jumped, almost dropping her book onto the floor. She hadn't heard Simon return.

Dana walked closer to the door, peering through the slit, but Simon was chopping on the side of the doorway she couldn't see. He struck again and again, the hatchet hitting with a rhythm. Alice could almost picture him striking the tree then pulling his arm high then striking the tree then pulling his arm high, again and again and again. Then the chopping stopped. Alice rose from the couch, hoping Simon was done. She glanced in the corner and was happy to see it empty. Putting her book into her coat pocket, she walked over to stand next to Dana, both of them watching the door and waiting for it to open.

But it didn't open, and the tree didn't move. Silence, nothing but Simon's heavy breathing—chopping like that must have been tiring, Alice thought. She heard him walk up to the door.

"Dana, this tree is thick, and I'm no lumberjack," he said. "How about I just chop through the door? I mean, your cabin is trashed anyway. You should see the back of it—totally smashed by the slide and buried. And chopping this tree will take me forever."

Dana glanced around the room behind her, staring for a moment at the upturned kitchen table and the door it held in place. "Okay," she said. "Do it."

Alice cheered her answer, although she said nothing aloud. Home, she thought as she glanced into the corner again. It was still empty.

"Alright," Simon said. "Then move back. I don't want to hit you."

Dana obeyed, pulling Alice far to one side until the two of them almost stood in the closet. Simon closed the front door, making the cabin more dim than Alice expected. But the walls held firm as the door shook with the first hit of the hatchet, which struck again and again, metal finally showing through the door, only a tip, then the full head, light streaming through the hole, growing larger and larger.

"Okay," Simon called. "I'm going to try to kick it in now. Make sure you're far back."

Dana gripped Alice's hand. "Be ready," she said, her stance prepared to run.

With a loud crack, the door flew inward, turning on its latch for an instant before flying backwards, a man staggering through the doorway in a blur of flannel and jeans and the cool gray of metal.

"Go," Dana said, already pulling Alice to the door. They rushed through the doorway and scrambled over the large tree. The light so bright, Alice couldn't see where they were going, rocks where there had been no rocks, branches in their way, ground no longer level. But Dana pulled Alice along, the two of them almost running. And then the car was there and Alice felt the sunlight and she felt the brisk air—just like in her dream—but the wheels were not spinning and the car was going nowhere: it had been smashed by a boulder, flipped onto its side.

If I dye my hair blonde will it make Mother love me? Simon stood in the doorway, fastening the hatchet to his belt. "Where are you going?" The pretty girls are all blonde. The pretty girls are blonde, like Dana. They stood, the two of them, staring at the bottom of the upturned car— Simon and Dana—not looking at each other, not talking to each other. Mother never hears when I cry.

Something was watching her. Alice turned to face the cabin and finally saw the damage the slide had caused. The hill, no longer behind the cabin, now surrounded it; the cabin's roof and front door stuck out of a mountain of tree limbs and rocks and freshly moved soil. Everything was different; nothing was the same. And through the cabin's open doorway, darkness looked out. Silently, it watched her. Alice shook the haziness from her head.

"You're lucky. Imagine if it had hit your cabin," Simon said to Dana.

"What are we going to do?" Alice asked.

"Lucky," Dana said, staring at the overturned car. "Lucky."

"Dana, what are we going to do?" Alice asked again.

Dana turned toward Alice, her eyes as uncertain as the night before. Simon kept looking at the car. Clouds hung low and dark over the mountain, the day's light—once seeming so bright—now only gray.

"What are we going to do?" Alice asked. "Where are we going to go?"

Dana looked over the car at the trees that stood behind it. "There are other cabins around. We'll go and get help."

But Simon shook his head, "The other cabins are empty, Dana. The Stones, the Taylors—they've all left. And no one is in the rentals this late in the season."

"So, we'll just use their phone then and call for help," Dana said.

Simon shook his head again. "The lines went down a half-mile below my cabin. This entire side of the mountain lost phone and power, not just your cabin."

"The ranger, then," Dana said. "I'm sure he's still here. Alice and I will go and get him to help us."

Simon shrugged. "Maybe he's still around. I don't know. I haven't seen him since he dropped by my cabin last week to warn me about the storm. He might be on the other side of the mountain, though. They're doing something with the campsites over there. He goes there a lot."

"He never came by to warn us," Dana said.

"Did he even know you were here?" Simon asked.

Dana didn't answer.

Alice could feel the cabin behind her. She needed to get away. "How far away is the ranger?" she asked Simon, who turned and looked at her for the first time. He seemed uncomfortable.

"Maybe a half-hour hike," he said. "That's cutting through the trees, though. Going along the road would take longer."

"Fine," Dana broke in. "So just point out the way and we'll go there."

Alice flinched at Dana's tone. We never even thanked him, she realized.

But Simon looked resigned, as if he thought he deserved it.

"I'm not going to just point you in a direction and have you get lost in the forest," he told Dana. "The storm isn't over, you know. You could freeze tonight."

"We'll take our chances."

He shook his head. "Let me show you the way."

Dana folded her arms, giving a look that Alice knew too well.

"Dana!" Alice said, feeling watched. "Stop it! Let's follow him. Let's get out of here. I want to get out of here."

Simon nodded and started walking off into the trees, not waiting for Dana to reply. "This way," he called over his shoulder.

The cabin sat behind Alice—totally still. Never again, she promised herself. I'll never stay there again.

Dana held her ground for a moment but quickly caught up when she saw Alice following after Simon. "This is a bad idea," she said softly.

But Alice didn't care. Already the cabin felt distant, the darkness no longer able to see her. Everything seemed fresh. The sunlight—even through the clouds—was welcome, and the air felt open. The dripping trees and the damp ground made the world feel clean, and birds were chirping in the branches above, driving away the unrealness that had hung around the cabin like a haze. She felt good stretching her legs and moving with a purpose. She felt good to be moving toward home. Maybe I'll see Dad tonight, she hoped.

Simon led the way, hatchet bouncing against his hip, followed by Dana, who kept herself always a little in front of Alice. They hiked like that for some time, uphill then downhill then uphill again. When they had first started, Alice felt like she could walk for hours; but as the hike dragged on, the mud pulling at her feet more and more, she became tired, and Alice and Dana began to lag behind Simon. It had grown silent, the birds now quiet, footsteps the only sound, Simon's far ahead, Dana's at her side. The light from above was now grayer. Had the clouds become thicker? she wondered. Everything was paused, waiting for something to happen.

Simon stopped, then, to let them catch up. He turned, looking back at them, and Alice saw a subtle shift to her right, deep within the woods. Stopping to stare, she caught the last movements of a shadow as it crept away, its vague outline merging with the darkness that hung beneath the trees. Followed me from the cabin. They don't sleep. They never sleep.

The cabin's doorway was open, calling her to return.

"What's wrong?" Dana asked, the sound of her voice making every-thing solid.

Alice blinked and turned to Dana. "I saw something," she said and pointed at the trees where the shadow had vanished. "Over there."

"Where?" Dana asked, looking at the spot where Alice was pointing. "Like an animal?"

Alice shrugged, unsure what to say.

"I don't see anything," Dana said. "Maybe it was a squirrel or a rabbit. We probably scared it off."

"It was bigger than a rabbit," Alice said but didn't bother trying to convince Dana. Maybe it was just my imagination, she thought as they started walking toward Simon, who turned and continued into the for-est. But what if I'm not imagining things? she wondered. What then? Why are they following me? What do they want?

She didn't know, but she remembered that she had put *The Screwtape Letters* into her pocket, and she realized it could hold the answer some-where inside. That's what the book is about, isn't it? she reminded her-self. Except it's old, and things are even less clear now than they were back then. The answer is probably still there, though, she decided, if I search for it. She glanced at the woods to her side as they walked, but all she saw were trees.

Simon got far ahead of them again because Alice was too tired to walk quickly; but then he stopped, giving them a chance to catch up to him as he stood looking down into a ravine, his shoulders slumped.

"What is it?" Dana asked. "Where is the ranger's cabin?"

Simon pointed downward, and it was then that Alice noticed how fresh the cliff looked. The drop-off had the same churned look as the hill that had collapsed onto her cabin. She edged closer to look over the side and saw a smashed cabin spread out at the bottom of the hill.

"What happened?" Dana asked.

"It's like the whole mountain is coming apart," Simon said.

And it felt that way to Alice, too, as if everything strong were collaps-ing. Nothing stands forever.

Chapter Four

WHAT ABOUT THE RANGER?" DANA SAID. "IS HE DOWN there? He could be hurt."

Simon shook his head. "I don't see his truck anywhere. He must be on the other side of the mountain. Lucky for him."

"Lucky," Dana repeated.

Simon kicked a rock over the cliff. It rolled, loose dirt following after, and hit the cabin's wall with a thud.

"What now?" he asked.

Dana studied the slide and the dirt road at its edges. The cabin had been built overlooking the ravine, but the ground all around it had fallen below, carving the steep half circle that lay in front of them and cutting the dirt road in half, each side of the road stopping abruptly at the ground's edge, the rest of the road lying somewhere below with the cabin.

"We'll wait here for the ranger," she said. "I'm sure he'll come back soon."

"It might be a while," Simon told her.

"That's fine. We'll be safe here. We don't need to take up any more of your time."

Simon nodded but didn't move. He stood there awkwardly, looking down at the cabin, as if he wanted to say something else to Dana.

But Dana ignored him. She led Alice away from the edge of the slide, where they found an overturned log they could sit on. Eager to read, Alice pulled her book out as soon as she sat down, already searching for an answer.

Then, still not looking at either of them, Simon spoke to Dana. "I'm going to hike around and look for the ranger," he said, and he walked away into the trees after getting no reply.

Dana sighed after he left, tension vanishing from her face, and she slid down to sit on the ground and lean her back up against the log. Alice, however, kept reading. It was hard going, the writing thick and strangely formal, nothing like her recent raw experiences; but the answer had to be inside the book. She had to know what they wanted.

The day wore on as they waited. Dana fell asleep. Alice's head started to sag too, but someone had to keep watch—they could be anywhere. She worked out a system where she would read one paragraph and then look up and scan a part of the woods around them. Then she would read the next paragraph before looking up again to check somewhere else, turning around on the log at times to keep everything in view, her eyes open for any creeping while Dana slept.

The world was gray, Dana's breathing the only sound; and it seemed, at least to Alice, as if it should be raining. Still, she continued her vigil, understanding little that she read but keeping a close eye all around. Everywhere, that is, except the cliff in front of them, because she didn't imagine, not at first, that something might crawl up the loose slope to reach her.

But then she thought of the darkness that had looked out from her cabin. And if her cabin held darkness, then couldn't they all? And wasn't there a cabin below? And couldn't something come up from there? Right now, couldn't it be climbing up toward them?

She jumped down from the log and spun in a complete circle to scan the woods before sneaking toward the edge of the slide, her eyes focused. The cliff looked wrong, grass growing right up to the edge before suddenly stopping, and she expected to see a hand reach up from below at any moment.

The ground was soft as well, each footstep sinking in, and Alice was forced to walk more slowly the nearer she came to the drop-off. But she edged closer until finally she was able to peer over the side, where she saw the cabin below, silent and empty. She scanned the hill leading down to it as well but saw nothing except loose, damp dirt. Then the ground beneath her began to sag toward the drop-off.

"Alice! Get back!"

Dana grabbed Alice's hand and pulled her to safety. "What were you thinking?" she demanded, leading Alice back to the log.

Alice sat down, picking up her book and laying it in her lap. "I was checking on the cabin."

"The cabin?" Dana said. "What do you mean, 'checking on the cabin'? It's not going anywhere! You could have fallen over the edge, Alice. You need to be more careful."

Dana sat down beside Alice, who put her book back into her pocket. Then, hearing wood snap, they both turned in alarm; but it was only Simon hiking up toward them. His hatchet no longer on his belt, Simon leaned on a dark walking stick as he climbed up the slope. He was talking to himself—Alice could hear a quiet murmur—but he stopped as he drew closer.

Dana spoke quickly to Alice before Simon could hear, "So, I was thinking. If the ranger doesn't show up anytime soon, then we might need a place to stay tonight—"

No, I'm not going to stay in a cabin again, Alice thought.

"—and I think the rental cabins are kept stocked. So, they'd at least be a safe place to stay until help arrives."

Not in a cabin. Never again, Alice told herself. I just want to go home.

Simon approached them, a determined look on his face; but Alice's attention was drawn instead to the figure that lurked in the brush beside him. She yelled and fell off the log.

"What?" Dana and Simon both asked.

"Something's there!" Alice said, and Simon charged in the direction she pointed, his walking stick held tightly with both hands.

But seeing nothing, he turned back to Alice and called, "What am I looking for?"

"It was right there!" Alice said, standing up and pointing at the spot in the brush.

"What was, Alice? What did you see?" Dana's voice was soft, as if she were talking to a little kid.

Alice shook her head. "Nothing," she said, knowing they wouldn't believe her even if she told them. Whatever she had seen was already gone. Or maybe it hadn't been there in the first place.

Simon stomped around the area for a few minutes before returning. "It might have been a deer or something," he said.

But Alice knew he was only humoring her. She sat back down on the log, looking away, not speaking to either of them.

Dana stared at Alice for a moment; then she turned to Simon. "Did you see the ranger?" she asked.

He shook his head. "No, but I hiked up to look at the road that goes around the mountain. It's washed out, Dana. I don't think we'll see him for days."

Dana slumped against the log, her obvious disappointment making Alice realize the situation they were in—no phone, no car, no ranger. How are we going to get home? she asked herself.

"Dana," Simon said. "You can't just wait here until he gets back, and I don't have a car either—I hiked up the mountain on foot, remember? But why don't you stay at my place until help arrives? The storm is supposed to last a few more days. We might be on our own for a while."

Dana glared in response.

Simon lowered his eyes. "I can stay outside in a tent," he said. "You two can have the cabin to yourselves."

Dana shook her head, refusing his offer, but Alice knew better. Dana likes Simon, she thought. She might be mad right now, but she likes him, and he'll convince her eventually, and then she'll make me stay in his cabin. But I won't—they'll find me there. No, I won't. I'm going home.

"I don't want to stay in Simon's cabin," she told Dana.

Turning her back on Simon, Dana looked down at Alice. "We'll just stay in one of the rentals, instead," Dana told her.

"What are you going to do, break in?" Simon asked.

Dana ignored him.

"And after you break in, then what, Dana? How many days will you be waiting for help to get here? What will you eat?"

"The cabins are stocked."

"Now? We're going into the off-season, Dana. That's a bad bet to make. Don't do this. My cabin has plenty of supplies. Stay there until help arrives."

"Then we'll go back to our cabin," Dana said, and Alice saw her cabin again, its doorway opened wide.

"Come on, Dana," Simon said. "Your cabin isn't safe to stay in. It's halfway buried, the roof is caving in, and the door is gone. Be realistic. You can't stay there. Just use mine. Please, let me help."

"That's not an option," Dana told him. "Alice and I will be fine in our cabin—"

Alice, Alice, Alice, you will never get away.

And seeing the open doorway, Alice remembered what had looked out. "No!" she yelled. "I want to go home! No more cabins! I won't stay in a cabin! I want to go home!"

Dana turned back to her, speaking softly again: "Alice, I know last night was bad, but it'll be okay. I'm sure help will get here soon."

"No, I'm not going to just sit here and wait. I want to go home. I don't care if I have to walk all the way. I'm going home—by myself if I have to."

Then Simon broke into the conversation, "But what about the animal you saw? I mean, my cabin would be safer, don't you think?"

Alice jumped to her feet. It wasn't just an animal, she thought. "No!" she said, "I'm going home! I'm going home right now!" She started walking around the edge of the slide toward the road.

Simon and Dana followed after, Dana talking about how cold it was, telling her it would be better to stay in a cabin and wait for help. But Alice wasn't going to be reasoned with. No more cabins. Looking out the doorway at me. Never again. "I'm going home," she kept repeating.

"Stop it, Alice. This is crazy!" Dana said, grabbing Alice's shoulder to keep her from walking any farther.

"I'm going home," Alice said again, struggling to break free. No more cabins. Never again. "You can't make me stay."

"But you don't even know the way!" Dana said.

And Alice realized that Dana was right: she didn't know how to get home. But Simon had hiked up the mountain—he knew the way. Alice pointed at him. "But Simon does! He can take me!"

"No, Alice," Dana said. "That's a really bad idea."

"Shut up, Dana. Just shut up," Alice said, her agitation bursting out. "I don't care about your stupid fight and I don't care if you're mad at him either—because I'm going home. I'm going home, and Simon is going to take me there."

She held out her hand for Simon. Dana batted it down.

"No, Alice," Dana told her.

But Simon wasn't arguing. He just stood there, watching Dana. Alice reached for his hand again. "Simon will take me," she repeated, knowing by the way he was looking at Dana that he wouldn't say no.

"No! You're not going alone with him!" Dana growled, grabbing Alice's hand to keep it away from Simon's. "Okay, fine, Alice. If you're going to be so stubborn—then, fine. We'll all go." And she faced Simon, standing between him and Alice, her eyes flashing.

But Simon didn't return her anger. His face was slack, his expression sad. "Okay," he told them. "I'll show you the way."

We never even asked him, Alice realized. We never thanked him, we never asked him, and he just took it all without complaining. He really does like Dana, she thought, that's why I knew he'd say yes. Alice felt guilty about how Dana was treating him—about how they both were treating him—but she couldn't worry about that right now. Right now she needed to get away.

"Which direction do we go?" she asked Simon, not giving either of them time to change their mind.

He leaned on his walking stick, glancing at Dana as he thought for a moment. "We need to stop by my cabin first," he said. "It's a good two-maybe-three-day hike down the mountain at least. We'll probably meet help on the way—I mean, I hope we do. But we'll need enough supplies to last all the way, just in case."

Simon paused, then he asked: "But are you sure you want to do this? We might find help sooner by walking toward them, but we also might end up hiking all the way down the mountain by ourselves. Dana, you know that there's another option."

And Alice saw the doubt in Dana's eyes. She could tell that Dana didn't like the idea of walking down the mountain, but the other option—staying in Simon's cabin—Dana seemed to like even less.

Alice grabbed Dana's hand. "Let's go," she told Simon.

He nodded, not arguing, and turned, leading them down into the trees. Dana and Alice were close behind, Alice's hand tight in Dana's grip. They walked through trees for a while, always downward, and then they turned onto a dirt road, which they followed for a few minutes before climbing up the small shoulder and heading down a wooded hill. Alice was tired from all the walking that day and the little sleep she had had the night before, but she didn't complain, afraid to give Dana any reason to change her mind.

The hill became steeper the more they descended. Alice almost lost her footing a few times on the loose ground—the memory of the landslide returning each time she felt the ground begin to sag—but the trees grew close together on the hill, and she was able to stop each fall by grabbing a branch to steady herself.

At the base of the hill, they saw a cabin ahead in a small clearing, with a creek flowing between the hill and the cabin. Simon led them a little way upstream, where a wooden bridge had been built over the creek.

It was strange finding a bridge over such a small creek. Even as swollen as it was, the creek would have been easy to cross by stepping from stone to stone. And the bridge looked new, its boards polished and decorated with freshly carved patterns. They walked across it, and then Alice noticed a phrase cut into the final board. She looked back to check and discovered the same words carved into the first board as well: "The river is always waiting." Alice stopped Dana and pointed out the words to her.

"What does this mean?" Dana called to Simon, who was already halfway from the bridge to the cabin.

Simon turned and saw Dana pointing at the phrase carved into the board, the two of them looking at him expectantly. Then he glanced at

Alice briefly before turning back toward the cabin. "Well, it is, isn't it?" he said over his shoulder.

Alice and Dana shared a confused glance. Then Dana shrugged and they followed after him.

The cabin had a porch that ran along the front, all of it sheltered by a heavy wooden awning. The porch was empty except for a large chair that sat to the left of the doorway. As they got closer, Alice saw that the chair was made of chopped logs, each polished and decorated with carvings like she had seen on the bridge. Small pieces of wood lay scattered around the chair, their bark stripped. They appeared to be works in progress, although she couldn't make out any of the designs.

"You didn't happen to bring a cell phone with you, did you?" Dana asked Simon as they reached the porch and he opened the door, leaning his walking stick against the frame.

"No," he said. "I came here to get away." Then he asked her if they were going to wait inside or outside.

The question alarmed Alice; but, thankfully, Dana told him they would wait outside, and the two of them sat down on the porch steps, Dana placing herself on the step between Alice and the cabin's door, while Simon went inside to pack. Trees ringed the other side of the clearing. It was late afternoon, the sky now a darker gray.

"You know we're going to get poured on," Dana said, looking up at the clouds. "I'm surprised it hasn't rained already today."

But Alice didn't care. It could rain all day and all night so long as she was walking closer to home. She worried for a moment that Dana might try to use the rain to talk her out of hiking down the mountain, but Dana just sat quietly, keeping her thoughts to herself.

Then Simon came back to the doorway as if to ask them a question; and when he looked down at them, something emerged from the trees.

Alice screamed. Simon grabbed his walking stick and leaped off the porch, running in the direction she had been looking. He jogged in and out of the trees, but it was gone and he found nothing even after looking up through the tree branches.

Am I the only one that can see them? Alice wondered. Ignoring the look Dana was giving her, she pulled out her book and tried to read, feeling desperate to understand what they wanted. It's not just my imagination, she told herself. I know it's not.

"Did you see anything?" Dana asked Simon when he returned.

"No," he said, giving Alice a curious look as he went back into the cabin. He came out a moment later and handed Dana a walking stick, different from his own, white rather than dark.

"Maybe you should have this—just in case," he told her, glancing up at the trees once more before returning to his packing.

The walking stick was beautiful, covered with elaborate carvings: two images of the moon at its top, one full and one half; a hand grip carved below the moons; and long wavy lines running from the hand grip almost to the base, like falling rain or thin bending clouds. It was tall, probably reaching almost to Dana's shoulder, and smooth and polished as well. But it seemed unfinished, the lower section still not decorated.

Dana ran a finger along the carvings, seeming surprised at the craftsmanship. While the chair and other woodwork around the patio looked skilled, this one looked like a masterpiece, the product of much time and effort. Then Dana looked at its base, and her eyes grew wide. Alice could see a small carving there but couldn't make out what it was.

"What's on the bottom?" she asked Dana, putting away her book.

But Dana only shook her head and set the walking stick down on the porch, placing it so Alice couldn't see the hidden carving.

"Alice," Dana said. "What do you keep seeing out there?"

"I don't know," Alice said, disappointed that Dana would so obviously change the subject. I'll bet Simon was making it for her, she thought.

"Well, if it is some kind of animal, then I don't think being scared is going to help," Dana told her. "They can sense fear. You don't want to encourage them by showing it."

"Okay," Alice said, although she wished that Dana hadn't said "if." Dana wouldn't have said that if she believed me, Alice thought. I'm not just imagining things. Am I?

Then Simon came out of the cabin, carrying both a backpack and a larger hiking pack, and shut the door behind him. He wore a coat and was carrying his walking stick again, which Alice now noticed was as decorated with carvings as Dana's, although it was gray rather than white and had an ugly black mark that ran down its length from top to bottom like a scar. His hatchet was fastened again to his belt. Alice hoped that meant he believed her, at least a little bit. Dana, however, looked uneasy when she noticed it. She rose to her feet, standing between Simon and Alice.

"You take the smaller pack," Simon told Dana and handed it to her. "It just has a sleeping bag and a flashlight. It shouldn't be too heavy."

"I can carry more than that," she said, taking it from him.

"That's okay," Simon told her, lifting the hiking pack up onto his back. The pack had a rolled up tent and sleeping bag attached to its bottom. "I've got it."

"Only two sleeping bags?" Dana asked.

"Yeah, that's all I could find in the cabin," he said. "You and Alice will need to share one. Is that going to be okay?"

"And only one tent?"

"I can sleep outside."

Simon walked past Dana down the steps, then turned around to look back over his cabin, pausing for a moment as if saying good-bye. Dana put on the other backpack.

"Are you ready?" he asked.

She nodded, grabbing Alice's hand, and they followed after him to the edge of the clearing, where a dirt path began between the trees.

As they left the clearing, Alice glanced back at his cabin—the empty chair, the creek, the bridge. She remembered the engraving: "The river is always waiting." Why had he carved those words into the bridge? she wondered. What did the phrase mean? Was it important? Then they were walking on the dirt road, the bridge hidden by the trees. Soon the cabin was out of sight as well.

They hiked along the road without speaking, Dana always at Alice's side, grip tight on Alice's hand but eyes fixed on Simon, who walked ahead of them, Simon looking from side to side into the trees, the hatchet swinging with each step. Alice, however, now doubted that he'd be able to see anything even if something were there.

At peak season, the road was well-traveled with visitors driving to and from their cabins, but it was rarely used now that summer was ending, and weeds were already growing in the tire ruts. The day began to fade. They continued on.

After an hour of walking, Simon suggested they stop while it was still light enough to set up camp, and Dana agreed. They turned off to the left, but not before Dana gave one last look of regret back up the road. The cabins all lay in that direction.

There was a small level area near the road. Well-covered by trees, it seemed like a good spot, so they stopped there. Simon set up camp while Dana and Alice sat on a stump nearby, Alice reading her book, Dana watching Simon rest the hatchet against a tree and then put up the tent. It was small, at most a two-man. He had it up quickly and then unrolled one of the sleeping bags inside, leaving the other attached to his pack. Then he pulled out an electric lantern and turned it on before the gray day changed all the way into twilight. Dinner was MREs and water bottles.

Is this what we'll be eating the entire time? Alice wondered as she watched Simon open their food. But, meal in hand, she realized how hungry she was—not having eaten since breakfast—and wolfed it down, unsure if it tasted better than she had expected or if it was just her hunger. It probably doesn't matter either way, she decided.

Simon left camp to gather wood, vanishing into the darkness, a darkness that had grown thicker, but a darkness that did not move—that was the difference from the night before. Were they out there now? Alice asked herself. Were they watching her, waiting? Then she remembered what Dana had told her. It really doesn't help to show them that I'm scared, does it? No, she decided. If they are there, then they are there. If they are there, then let them think I'm not afraid. Let them see me reading. Let them worry that I'll know soon.

But, although she could pretend she wasn't scared, she couldn't pretend she was any closer to understanding what they wanted from her.

The book was hard to read without Dana's help—and she couldn't ask Dana for help when Dana doubted her—so, even after all her reading today, she had learned very little. Still, hard to find or not, she told herself that the answer must be in the book and she had to find it.

Simon returned with an armful of wood and began to construct a fire. Alice, feeling the cold despite her coat, huddled up against Dana, watching him.

"Isn't it all wet?" Dana asked Simon, more words than she had said to him since leaving his cabin.

"Yeah," he said. "Too bad I didn't pay more attention in Boy Scouts."

He was leaning small damp branches together like a teepee under which he wadded some sheets of paper. Then he pulled out a box of matches and lit the paper. It burned, giving a brief hope of warmth, but the fire went out without starting the wood. He tried a few more times with more paper, but while the wood would start to smoke for a moment, it never caught fire.

"Sorry," Simon said, spreading out the failed fire with his foot and putting the matches back into his pack. "Maybe I'll find some dry wood tomorrow night and we'll have a fire then."

Alice closed her book and put it away. It was too cold to read anymore, and she was tired. The answer would have to wait until tomorrow. Dana suggested that they go to bed and Alice agreed. They stood up and went to the tent, Alice getting in first after Dana unzipped it.

"Good night," Simon said.

Dana stopped, holding the tent flap, and looked over at him. "Aren't you going to go to sleep too?" she asked.

"I will in a little bit."

She studied him for a moment and then, setting her walking stick down in front of the tent, she went in, zipping the tent closed behind her. Alice had already taken off her coat and shoes and was getting in the sleeping bag. It was cold, but she knew it would get warmer as soon as Dana joined her. However, rather than getting in, Dana sat down on top of the bag, looking out at Simon's shadow through the tent.

"Aren't you coming to bed?" Alice whispered.

"Shh . . . Just a minute."

They watched as Simon moved around camp, and they heard him rummaging through his hiking pack, speaking softly to himself. Then he got up and left the camp, not taking the lantern with him.

"Where is he going?" Alice whispered.

Dana said nothing.

"Did you bring a flashlight in here?" Alice asked.

"Yes, it's by the foot of the sleeping bag."

"Good."

Simon returned several minutes later, unrolled his sleeping bag, and turned off the lantern. The sudden darkness weighed against Alice as it had the night before. For a moment Alice felt as if she were back in the cabin, and panic crept up on her at the thought of being trapped. But there were no walls here, and then Dana was in the sleeping bag, and then everything was okay. Dark, yes, but okay.

Had Simon seen something, Alice wondered, out there alone in the dark? No, he would have told us if he had, wouldn't he? Maybe nobody saw anything, maybe not even me. Maybe it was all just my imagination. Or maybe they really are out there, watching and waiting.

Thunder rolled above the mountain, an announcement that the storm would now continue, and the thought occurred to Alice—what if it's not just me that they want?

End of Part One

Part Two
Some Build Bridges

Chapter Five

DANA WOKE AS A FLASH FILLED THE TENT, THE GREEN OF the roof's fabric visible for an instant before returning to black, thunder booming in the night. She heard no rain. Another flash, bright white, exposed the open tent flap. Alice was gone.

Scrambling from the sleeping bag, Dana stumbled out of the tent as thunder spread across the sky. The air cold and the ground hard, her coat and shoes left in the tent, she hugged her arms and strained to see through the heavy darkness that surrounded her. Lightning flickered above, showing the tops of silent, gray trees before fleeing the chasing thunder. Dana remembered the flashlight then; twisting around, she grabbed it from the tent and clicked it on, then swung the small beam back and forth across the empty campsite.

"Alice!" Dana yelled. "Alice!"

But there was no reply. The night was silent, filled with light and then dark again. Thunder crawled behind the clouds, its sound soon dying, leaving her alone once more.

"Alice?"

Dana heard a low grumble: Simon, still in his sleeping bag.

You know what he is, Dana. Alice is gone. What did he do?

Growling, Dana jumped on top of Simon, yelling and shaking him awake: "Where is she? What did you do to her?"

"Who? What?" Simon mumbled, blinking at the flashlight.

"What did you do to her? Where did you take her?"

"Who? Alice? She's gone?"

Simon sat up, knocking Dana backward, but she bounded back on top of him, pressing him to the ground as she straddled his sleeping bag.

"Did you think I forgot?" she yelled. "I know what you're attracted to! How could you? What did you do to her?"

The hatchet leaned anxiously against the tree. Dana grabbed it and waved it in his face. "If you hurt her—"

Simon stared at the gray metal, his face white in a flash of lightning, thunder crackling after.

You need to make him pay, Dana. Make him pay for what he did to her.

"I'll kill you," Dana said, the blade pressed onto his cheek. "Do you hear me? If you did anything to her, I'll kill you."

Then Simon looked up at her, walls down, eyes drawing her in, and she saw something there she hadn't seen in any other man. "I've never hurt someone like that, Dana." His voice was cold and hard. "If I had, I wouldn't be here."

And Dana fled into the night, screaming for Alice. Rocks and roots dug into her feet as she hurried through the trees, the light from the flashlight frantic, the hatchet still in her hand. She swiveled her head back and forth, desperate for a glimpse of red hair, but all around she saw only gray, trunks reaching from the ground like grasping fingers, branches above illuminated by bright bursts of lightning before returning to darkness, thunder an ever-present background.

"Alice!" she yelled again, "Alice!" But there was no reply.

Then Dana's foot caught as she ran, and she fell forward, her face smashing hard into the ground, her arms spread out in the dirt. And lying there, without even looking, Dana knew she had stumbled over Alice—the body already cold.

"Alice?" she whispered.

Thunder burst above, holding her flat upon the ground until its grip loosened and she could raise her head. Then, full of dread, she held her breath and shone the flashlight at her feet. Only a log. Dana leaped up, grasping the hatchet and flashlight, and ran farther into the woods.

"Alice!"

She didn't know where she was going, running this way and that, hoping to see Alice but finding only trees and brush. Then a lightning flash stopped her, the hatchet and flashlight falling to the ground as she almost lost her balance, the world soaked in an eerie surge of light, a figure visible for an instant, standing among the trees.

And then it was black again, the flashlight now useless on the ground, its beam shining only a few feet before blending into darkness, the thunder murmuring above. Dana turned to her side but saw only vague outlines within the black. The cold air dug into her. Slowly, she squatted down, eyes fixed on the dim shape, watching for any movement as she picked up the flashlight and turned the faint beam toward the figure: Alice, facing away from her, not moving, silent.

"Alice!" Dana yelled, running toward her.

But Alice did not answer.

"Alice?" Dana asked and slowed as she drew near.

But Alice just stood there, not turning, wearing no coat, only shirt, pants, and socks. She should be freezing, Dana thought. I'm freezing. She shivered.

"Alice, are you okay?"

Dana walked closer as thunder sounded and lightning filled the night once more. But Alice did not turn, and Alice did not speak—only a hurried whisper, growing louder as Dana approached.

She paused behind Alice, close enough to touch her, except—something held Dana back. The whisper had grown into a murmur.

"Alice?"

Dana crept around to face her. Alice stood still, eyes closed and arms to her sides, nothing moving except her lips. Mumbling something that Dana couldn't hear.

"Alice?" she whispered, inching closer.

But Alice didn't move, not even opening her eyes, only standing there, mumbling to herself. And as Dana came closer, she heard what Alice was saying, the same phrase repeated over and over again.

"They want him to forget. They want him to forget. They want him to forget. They want—"

"Alice!" Dana cried, shaking her shoulders. "Alice!"

She wrapped her arms around Alice, hugging her, stopping the mumbling through a tight embrace. Alice has never sleepwalked before, Dana thought. What's wrong with her? She's so cold. Dana rubbed Alice's back, trying to warm her.

Then she heard a noise to her left and saw a large shadow. Grasping Alice tighter, she aimed her flashlight and found Simon staring back at her. Light shining in his face, he said nothing but dropped a bundle to the ground, turned, and walked away. Dana looked down at what he had left—their coats and shoes.

She shivered, a mixture of cold and guilt—his expression had been so empty. Guiding Alice to the pile, Alice's eyes only half open, Dana helped her put on her coat and shoes. Then she put on her own, feeling warmer though the cold still stung. She shone her flashlight in the direction Simon had left but saw only trees. Already gone.

Alice stood there silently, eyes blank, not really awake at all. It's a bad time to start sleepwalking, Dana said to herself. We need to get back to the tent and into the sleeping bag before she gets sick. How long has she been out here anyways? How long has she been standing here talking to herself?

Dana grabbed Alice's arm, ready to lead her toward the camp, but then she realized that she didn't know where they were. Lightning illuminated the area, bathing the surrounding trees in a white light that quickly faded. She didn't recognize anything. The sky was a uniform dark. Somewhere up there, thunder was grumbling.

Then a soft light appeared in the distance. Simon had turned on the lantern back at their camp. And, seeing the light and knowing its source, Dana thought for a moment of going in the opposite direction, maybe finding a cabin, somewhere safer, somewhere away from Simon. No, she told herself. We'd just get lost and freeze.

She led Alice toward the light, not bothering to talk, Alice, sleeping more than walking, stumbling at times, Dana, holding her steady, the light growing larger, the lightning settling down, the thunder more distant. But the sky still showed no stars, and Dana wondered how much longer the storm would last. Probably the entire way down the mountain, she told herself.

When they were close enough to see the tent, the light flicked off. They continued forward, emerging from the trees into the small campsite, Dana's flashlight shining on the tent. Simon was in his sleeping bag, his back toward them.

Dana led Alice to the tent, looking over at Simon before she entered, wondering if she should say anything, ashamed at having accused him of something so horrible. But what can I say? she asked herself. With what he told me last night, with Alice gone, what was I supposed to think? He is what he is whether I wish he was or not.

Simon is nothing more than what he wants, Dana. Have you ever known a man to be more than that? No. That is all they are. That is all they will ever be.

Dana shook her head and went inside, zipping the tent closed behind her. Then she helped Alice out of her coat and shoes and guided her into the sleeping bag, where she soon joined her, their shared heat driving away the cold.

The thunder and lightning gone, alone with Alice in the darkness, Dana started to drift back to sleep. But then she heard a noise outside the tent. Muscles tightening, she wrapped her arms around Alice. However, fear changed to guilt as the sound became clear: the short, sharp gasps of muffled weeping.

Chapter Six

IN THE MORNING, A DULL GRAY LIGHT FILLED THE TENT. Dana woke as Alice was stirring, and they got out of the sleeping bag together and quickly found their coats and shoes. The air chilly, their coats were cold but grew warmer once on. Dana watched Alice, who seemed normal this morning as she quietly tied her shoes. Nothing like the night before, which seemed almost like a dream now that the sun was up. But Dana knew it had happened. She just hoped it wouldn't happen again.

We could be in a cabin right now, she thought. Even without power it should be warmer than this. And don't some of the cabins have propane heaters? Alice's didn't—it only had electric heat—but Dana thought that the rentals might. Now, instead of being warm in a cabin we're going to freeze hiking down the mountain, she thought, regretting that she had agreed to go. But what could I have done? she asked herself. Dragged Alice into a cabin and sat on her until help arrived? Besides, Simon was right. I don't know if there would be any food there, and I don't know how long we'd be waiting for help to show up. We could have stayed in his cabin, though, she reminded herself. Except that hadn't seemed like an option then, knowing that Simon would be there. Of course, Simon is with us now, she thought. But I couldn't just take Alice all the way down the mountain on my own, could I? And we're moving toward help—doesn't that make it better?

Besides, it's not like Alice gave me a chance to think things through yesterday, Dana told herself. She's never been like that before, so unreasonable. Something must have gotten to her. The way she acted when she walked off by the ranger's cabin—ignoring everything I said—it was like talking to a statue. Anyways, this is the way it is, Dana thought. We're hiking down the mountain, cold or not. So I'll have to make it work. She hoped, however, that help would find them soon.

Unzipping the flap, they went outside. Clouds hung heavy, but there was neither rain nor lightning, only a thick silence, everything muted by the weight above. Even the birds were quiet. There were always birds singing in the morning. Well, not this morning.

Alice danced from side to side to shake away the cold, and Dana was tempted to do so as well, but she would feel silly, knowing that Simon might be watching her. His sleeping bag was already rolled up and put away, but she didn't see him in the campsite. He's probably off in the trees somewhere, she assumed, but she didn't want to worry about him right then.

Breakfast had been left on the tree stump: a bottle of water and a couple of granola bars, the same kind of granola bar that Simon had often shared with Dana on their hikes. She sat down on the stump next to Alice and ate the familiar bar, remembering the times she and Simon had spent together. The mountain had so many beautiful things to see— especially the Double Waterfall. That had been her favorite. And after she had told Simon how much she liked it, it seemed as if no matter where they hiked he always found some way to walk past it. Then, if she wasn't already too late getting back to Alice, they'd usually sit down there inside the lower fall and look out through the water. It had been such a peaceful place, resting there beside him. Many times she had wondered what he was thinking as he sat there quietly. Now, maybe, she knew.

And now, knowing it was over, Dana could admit to herself that she had been starting to feel something, something she had never felt for a man before, something she had been afraid to face while she still dreamed of its possibilities. But those dreams were obviously dead now, something replaced with nothing—making her almost wish that he hadn't told her what he had told her or that she hadn't heard what he had said.

No, she told herself, I don't wish that. I'd rather know the truth. He is what he is. It's better for me to know it now than to find it out later. Later might be too late.

"Why is Simon sitting over there?" Alice asked. Her book, *The Screwtape Letters,* sat open on her lap as she pointed to a tree outside camp.

Dana looked and saw Simon sitting on the ground among the trees, facing away from them toward the road, his head leaned back against a gray trunk. Has he been there the entire time? she wondered, surprised to see him so close. He hadn't said a word all morning. Which is good, Dana thought, I can't talk to him now anyways. After what I said last night, after what I did, what am I supposed to say?

"Do you remember sleepwalking last night?" she asked Alice, not wanting to think about Simon.

"When did I do that?"

"The middle of the night. You don't remember it?"

"No. I don't even remember any dreams from last night."

Does that make it worse? Dana asked herself. Alice standing there asleep like that, mumbling some crazy thing to herself, and now she doesn't even remember? We should have stayed in a cabin, Dana thought. At least there Alice wouldn't wander off into the night.

"What's wrong with Simon?"

Dana froze. How could Alice possibly know about that?

"What do you mean?" she asked.

"He looks upset."

"Oh," Dana said, feeling relief at Alice's innocence but also guilt at what had happened the night before. "I said something to him last night while you were asleep."

"Something mean?"

"Something unfair."

Dana glanced at Simon again. He does look upset, she thought. And that made her feel worse. Whatever he is, he hasn't done anything wrong, she told herself—but I have.

"When did you say that?" Alice asked.

"When you were sleepwalking."

"What did you say?"

"Don't worry about it."

Alice grew quiet. She always hates it when I hide things from her, Dana thought.

"Well, you should apologize then," Alice said.

"I know," Dana told her, but Alice had already turned her attention back to her book and her breakfast, and Dana was happy to let the topic drop.

They finished eating and then went off into the trees to go to the bathroom. Dana hated going outside like that. It always felt so dirty and uncomfortable. And damp, she thought. We should have stayed in a cabin.

When they returned to camp, they found Simon taking down the tent, their sleeping bag already put away. He didn't say a word to them and didn't even look up as they sat down. Alice immediately pulled out her book and started to read again.

She seems so intent on that book, Dana thought. Is it because it's good or is it because she's bored? Or does it just help keep her mind off of what has happened?

Simon finished packing, putting the empty hatchet holder into his hiking pack rather than attaching it to his belt.

"Do you want me to go find your hatchet?" Dana asked, remembering that she had dropped it somewhere in the woods.

Simon wouldn't look at her. "Maybe it's safer to not have it around," he said.

The words stung.

Simon stood and put on his hiking pack. "Let's get going," he said, handing the backpack to Dana.

Alice kicked Dana's foot.

"Simon," Dana said, taking the backpack from him. "Listen, I'm sorry I said what I did last night. You're just trying to help, and I was wrong to treat you like that."

He looked toward the road, hands on the shoulder straps of his hiking pack. "It's okay," he said. "I get it."

"No, Simon. It's not," she said. "You've done nothing to deserve being treated like that."

Then Simon looked at Dana, meeting her eyes for the first time that morning, and he gave a short nod before turning, picking up his walking stick, and starting toward the road.

Dana put on her backpack and grabbed her own walking stick while Alice put away her book. They followed Simon back onto the road. Dana felt better after apologizing, though she wished his eyes hadn't looked so sad. But he is what he is, she reminded herself, knowing she couldn't trust him around Alice. Still, that doesn't mean I can't be fair, she decided.

No one spoke as they hiked down the road, Alice to one side, Simon to the other, Dana separating the two of them, the silence deepening the depressing mood set by the clouds and the cold. It didn't seem right to Dana to be walking like this with Simon, the two of them not talking. They had always had so many things to tell each other, but now not a word. She wished she could say something that would smooth things over. Her apology had helped, but it hadn't been enough to mend the gap she had created the night before. Having to spend the entire trip down the mountain like this is going to be miserable, she thought.

At least walking is warming us up, she told herself. Or maybe the day is just getting warmer. But looking at the clouds above, Dana didn't think that was likely. They looked as thick and dark as ever. I'm sure today it'll rain, she thought. Maybe even thunder and lightning as well.

Alice was unusually quiet. Dana watched her, noticing that Alice's eyes stayed fixed on the road ahead, not even glancing at the trees to either side. Is she scared of seeing something else, like she did yesterday? Dana wondered. Dana had suspected that Alice was just seeing things, but now she thought about it and scanned the woods as they walked. What if something really has been following us? she asked herself. What could it be? Something dangerous? She wasn't sure what kind of large animals roamed the mountain. Were there any bears here? She hadn't seen any. Maybe some kind of mountain cat? Simon would know. Dana decided to ask him—but only when Alice couldn't hear. Alice seems worried enough, Dana thought. I don't want to scare her more by talking about it in front of her.

The carved handgrip of the white walking stick fit her hand perfectly, and after an hour of walking it felt comfortable to lean a little against it. She thought, then, of the letters carved into its base: "DH." Was Simon making it for me? she asked herself. The possibility made her feel even more guilty than she had before. She had never known a man to put such time and effort into a gift for someone else, especially not for her. Alice's mother is lucky if Alice's father even sits through a meal with her, Dana thought, and, of course, there's my own father . . .

If only things were different, she said to herself as Simon walked silently beside her. But they aren't. He is what he is and that's just the way it is. Still, Dana was filled with regret as she held the walking stick and thought of the time and sacrifice it represented. If only.

"So, Simon, I saw the initials carved into the base of this walking stick," she said. Guilty or not, she wanted to know. "Were you making it for me?"

Simon glanced over and nodded. "Yeah. It wasn't ready yet, though." He pointed at the bottom portion, which was still uncarved. "I needed more time to finish it."

Dana eyed the uncompleted part. "What were you going to put there?" she asked.

He shrugged. "I hadn't decided yet."

With the silence broken, the mood felt less heavy. Even Alice perked up a little, looking at the walking stick with interest. But Simon said nothing else, and soon it started to rain. It fell lightly at first, but Dana looked up at the clouds and groaned. We're going to get soaked, she thought. Then, when the drops became more frequent, Simon led them under some trees off to the side of the road.

"I brought some ponchos," he said, "but we might as well rest here for a minute."

"Okay," Dana said and sat down next to Simon, their backs against a tree. Alice sat on a rock in front of them.

The rain became a downpour, and water ran along the road. The trees around them provided good cover, not perfect—a few drops still hit now and then—but it was better than standing out in the open.

"Will we get home today?" Alice asked, the first words she had spoken since breakfast.

"I don't think so," Dana said, but she turned to Simon.

"It'll take at least two days, maybe three," he said.

Alice nodded and looked at the ground. Did she realize how long of a walk it was going to be? Dana wondered, and how cold it would get? I didn't know it would be this cold, she thought. If I had . . .

Alice looked up at Dana again. "And my dad won't be mad about us coming home early?"

What a strange question, Dana thought. Alice didn't say anything about that yesterday. Is that what she's been thinking about this morning? Worrying that coming home early will cause a problem for her father? But what else would he expect us to do?

"I'm sure he'll understand," Dana told her.

Alice grew quiet again, her gaze back down on the ground, still not looking into the woods around them. She pulled out her book and opened it.

"Why would her father be upset if you came home early?" Simon asked Dana.

She thought quickly. "Oh, Alice's father is dealing with a political problem," she said, feeling Alice staring at her. "You know . . . good old boring politics." She forced a laugh. "He wanted to keep her out of it, so we came here."

Then, gaze locked with Simon's, Dana gestured toward Alice with her eyes and shook her head slightly.

Simon glanced over at Alice before looking back at Dana and nodding. He didn't say anything else.

They sat there for a while, rain coming down all around, Simon looking at the trees, Dana watching Alice read her book. It probably does keep her mind off things, Dana thought, glad that Alice had something to keep her occupied. She hoped Alice hadn't caught on to what she had said about her father. He didn't want Alice to know, and Dana wasn't supposed to say anything. Of course, she thought, if he doesn't want Alice to know, then maybe he should stop doing it.

But now, her secret no longer completely a secret, Dana could ask Simon something she had wondered before.

"And you, Simon?" she said, turning toward him. "You've been staying here a long time, haven't you? So, why are you up here, anyways? I never asked before because I knew you'd ask me the same thing."

Simon smiled slightly. "Yeah, I guess neither of us wanted to ask that question, did we?" Then the smile vanished as he thought for a moment. "It's hard to explain without you knowing, but I guess you know about that now . . . "

Dana shifted against the tree and glanced at Alice, who was still reading and not paying attention to their conversation.

"I guess you could say I'm taking a break from college," he said, "maybe a permanent one—I'm not sure. My generals are done, and I need to choose a major before I go back."

So, he's in college, Dana thought. He's never mentioned that before. Then again, neither of us ever talked about our life away from the mountain, not really. It's like we were living in a bubble together, hiking around and seeing the sights but ignoring the fact that we had a life away from here, both of us wanting to avoid the questions that talking about it would raise. College does seem to match him though, she said to herself. He seems like a smart guy, like he's educated.

"So, you need to pick a career?" she asked.

"Right."

Dana folded her legs beneath her and rested her elbows on her knees. Maybe I can help him with this, she thought, feeling like she needed to do something to make up for how she had treated him before.

"Okay, so what would you be happy doing every day?"

Simon picked up his walking stick, which he had laid beside the tree. Setting the base in the dirt, he held the walking stick up in front of him, tilting it a little back and forth as he talked.

"See, for me, that's probably not the right question," he said.

"Then what's the right question?" Dana asked. "As far as a career goes, isn't that what matters? Enjoying your work?"

Simon leaned his head against the tree, laid the walking stick against his shoulder, and raised his knees, his hands clasped together in front of him.

"Sure, but picking something I would enjoy doing isn't what's hard," he said. "What's hard is thinking of a job that I'll enjoy, that will pay well, and that . . . "

"That what?"

Simon looked up at the branches, the rain beginning to slow. He shook his head and spoke softly to himself. "What do I have to lose, right?" Then he turned back to Dana.

"The problem is that I need to avoid computers," he said. "That's what is hard. Because what kind of a job today pays well but doesn't use computers?"

After his pause, Dana had expected him to say something dramatic. But this seemed trivial. A little weird, maybe, but nothing to get so worked up about. Am I missing something? she asked herself.

"I thought only old people were scared of computers," she said.

"You don't understand."

Simon laid his walking stick on the ground beside him, put his hands behind his head, and leaned back into the tree. His elbow touched Dana's shoulder lightly.

"I'm not scared of computers," he said. "That's not the problem. What I'm scared of is what I might do if I use one again."

That still makes no sense, Dana thought. "I don't see—"

Simon looked off into the woods, shaking his head. "That's how it started, Dana. That's why I'm scared."

And Simon's confession from two nights before, spoken in anger and surprise, slammed into Dana. She looked again at Alice, mentally measuring the distance between Alice and Simon, wishing it were larger.

It. That's how it started.

Alice sat quietly reading her book. Dana felt cold.

"It's just better for me, you know, easier—staying away from computers. I don't want to even mess with it."

Dana folded her arms and moved slightly away from him so that his elbow no longer touched her shoulder. She thought about what he had just said. He's going to stay away from computers—for what, his entire life?—and all because it will help keep him out of trouble? But that's a good thing, right? If he's willing to make a sacrifice like that, shouldn't that make me trust him more? No, he is what he is, Dana reminded herself. Isn't he? If he feels that way—if he wants what he wants—then isn't that who he is? But if he's willing to bend his entire career, his entire life, in order to do the right thing . . .

"Forever? Really? For the rest of your life?" she asked.

"Yeah, I mean, just think about it. Lots of guys, maybe most, get in trouble on the Internet, but for me it could be worse—much worse. And you know why."

Simon glanced at Dana before staring off into the woods again, speaking more softly now, "Because who says I'd be able to stop next time?"

And hearing he had stopped made Dana feel a little more comfortable. She was also impressed by the lengths he would go to keep himself from facing it again. Maybe he could be safe for Alice, even with his attraction, she thought. But that only confused her. He wants what he wants, doesn't he? she asked herself.

You cannot trust him, Dana. He cannot escape an attraction. It is what he is. It is all that he is. He is nothing else.

When someone feels an attraction, Dana thought, doesn't that mean something about them? Like if a man likes other men—doesn't that mean he's gay? But what about Simon? What does his attraction mean about him, then?

I can't trust him with Alice, she told herself. That much is certain. But she did wonder. The look in his eyes the night before had scared her. No, not scared, she realized. It just surprised me. How can I even describe it? Depth? That sounds close, but an empty hole has depth, too, and empty isn't the right word for Simon. No, he's the opposite of empty. There's something there that I don't usually see.

The two of them sat quietly against the tree, neither wanting to say anything else. Eventually, the rain stopped and they returned to the road. Dana watched Alice as they started walking. Alice's eyes were fixed on the road once more. She considered asking Alice if something was wrong but decided to leave it alone for now. Probably just stress, she thought. Maybe it's better if Alice doesn't look into the trees anyways. It freaks me out when she screams like that.

As they walked farther down the road, Dana started comparing the walking stick Simon had given her to the gray one he carried himself.

"So, why does my walking stick look different from yours?" she asked him, looking at hers more closely. "I don't even remember seeing any trees this color."

Simon was silent for a while before answering. "I thought it fit you."

"Why?" she asked.

Another pause. "I don't know. Goodness, I guess."

Dana felt herself turning red. Goodness? Boy, did he misjudge me, she thought, almost dropping the walking stick in embarrassment. Goodness? And he had spent so much time carving it for her. But what about Simon? The question from earlier repeated in her mind. But what about Simon?

She gave a half-laugh, "No, Simon, you're the religious one, not me."

Simon's head jerked toward her, a surprised look on his face, his reaction reminding Dana that they'd never actually talked about this before. She only knew because she had seen him, not because he had told her. Wandering the mountain one morning, she had heard his voice and decided to follow it—he talked to himself sometimes, and she had tracked him by voice before. Except this time, finding him alone by the Double Waterfall and seeing what he was doing, she had said nothing, turning back quietly instead, not wanting to disturb him; wondering, as she left, if it had been about her—hoping that it had. But she had never told him what she had seen. It wasn't for her to bring it up.

"So, you should make yourself a walking stick like mine, too," she said, avoiding the subject. "That way we can match."

Simon's surprise lingered for a moment before he shook his head.

"No, this one is a better fit for me," he said, and he held it up for a few steps, its color as dark as the clouds looming above.

Dana didn't like the implication. If he matches the color of mine with goodness, then what did that say about his? she thought. Does he think of himself as tainted? Except he is, isn't he? she asked herself, and then she repeated her question once more: But what about Simon?

Alice stumbled, and Dana barely caught her elbow in time to keep her from falling. But Alice didn't seem to notice, her mind somewhere else.

"Watch your step," Dana told her. She got no reply except a nod.

Is it just stress? Dana wondered again. Seeing things, walking in her sleep, mumbling weird things to herself, not even watching where she's going. Was it really a good idea to let Alice walk down the mountain? Too late to turn back now, I suppose, Dana thought. But was it wise to let her be this close to Simon? Sure, he might *want* to keep himself out of trouble, but think of what he might do. Worse, think of what he might have already done. She hated to even consider it—but had he? Then she remembered what he had told her the night before as she threatened him with the hatchet. He hadn't ever hurt anyone like that. Good. But what about the second thing he had said?

"Simon, last night, what did you mean when you said you wouldn't be here if you had ever . . . you know."

Simon didn't answer. The silence stretched on, and Dana wondered if maybe he hadn't heard her. Then, when she was about to repeat her question, he finally spoke.

"Let's just say that I think it'd be better for me to hurt myself than for me to hurt someone else like that," he told her.

I wouldn't be here. That's what he said last night. I wouldn't be here.

"And that's what I meant," Simon continued. "It's there, I deal with it. But it's always just been something that I *could* do, something that—at worst—part of me *wants* to do, but never something that I've *done*. Do you see what I mean?" He lowered his voice. "I mean, to have given in

. . . to know what I had done . . . all that guilt. I couldn't do it. I couldn't live with myself."

It makes a difference that he's never acted on it, doesn't it? Dana asked herself. That must count for something, right? What if you feel an attraction but you never act? What would that mean? she wondered. Except, what would it be like to have it always there just waiting for you to slip? Maybe that's why he feels like darkness represents him better than goodness?

She looked at his walking stick again, noticing the streak of black that ran from top to bottom. It wasn't a natural mark—he had burned it purposefully into the wood. She glanced up at Simon and caught him watching her. He had seen her notice the charred portion, but he gave no explanation. Turning his gaze forward again, he walked on in silence, the blackened mark keeping pace with his every stride, as if it were a part of him.

So, he does think of himself as tainted, Dana said to herself. But that doesn't seem fair. It's not like he chose this, right? And if he never acted on it . . .

"Maybe you just think I'm good—or whatever—because you focus so much on the darkness around you," she said, "and seeing that darkness all the time just makes everything else seem good in comparison. Do you see what I mean? But if you keep the darkness outside of you and don't give in to it, then doesn't that make you as good as anyone else? Certainly as good as me."

Simon shrugged. "Maybe," he said, a hint of hope in his voice.

Except Dana wasn't sure she herself agreed with what she had just said. However, she wanted to believe it, and she thought it was something that Simon deserved to hear. Still, Dana asked herself, when someone feels an attraction, doesn't that mean something about them? But what about Simon? What does that mean about him?

Farther down the road, the hill to one side had collapsed and spilled across the way, blocking the road with a buildup of dirt and debris. Although it was only a small slide, it still reminded Dana of what had hit the cabin, and she glanced up at the clouds, dreading what else they had in store. Already, the rain was starting to drizzle again, accompanied by a cold breeze that kept growing stronger.

To avoid the slide, they had to hike through the trees above the road, where they came across a pair of logs well covered by overhanging branches. They decided to stop there for lunch, which turned out to be the same food as breakfast.

"This is going to be a long hike, isn't it?" Dana said, looking at the granola bar as she sat down next to Simon on one of the logs.

"We'll be dying for a cheeseburger by the time we get to the bottom," he said and smiled.

Dana smiled back, but Alice said nothing, sitting on the other log, not looking at either of them. Dana couldn't remember her being this quiet before. On the other hand, Alice hasn't seen her "animal" all morning, Dana thought. That must be a good sign, right? Unless, of course, there really is something following her.

Dana did a quick scan of the forest around them but saw nothing, and she reminded herself to ask Simon what it might be—if it was anything at all. Alice had already finished her lunch. She moved off the log to sit in front of a nearby tree, once again taking out her book and starting to read, the pages ruffling in the wind.

"She must really like that book," Simon said to Dana.

Dana nodded. Is it just an escape for her? she wondered. Then why won't Alice even look around? Dana glanced through the trees again. Maybe Simon will have some ideas about what Alice keeps seeing, or maybe he'll just convince me that she's seeing things. Except would that be any better? Dana asked herself. She shook her head, not wanting to think about it right then.

She wadded up the empty wrapper in her hand and relaxed beside Simon. It was strange—knowing what she now knew about him but still feeling this way around him. Her dreams of a future with him were gone now, of course, but the present at least could be comfortable. It was a good feeling.

"Thanks for showing us the way," she said to him. "I doubt we'd make it by ourselves."

Simon downed a gulp of water and wiped his mouth with the back of his hand.

"I just wanted to make sure you'd be okay." He set down his water bottle and adjusted his position on the log before saying, "Listen, Dana, I'm really sorry about how I reacted two nights ago."

Dana stiffened.

"I mean, it's good you know now," he said, "but I wish I hadn't yelled. I wish I had said it better. I'm sorry."

Simon leaned forward, running his hands across his face before clasping them together in front of him. "I was just surprised, you know?" he continued. "It's just—I've been so sheltered up here, not having to worry about it. I wasn't expecting everything to change so suddenly."

And, remembering that night, Dana could see how poorly she had handled it. I shouldn't have just sprung Alice's presence on him, Dana thought. I shouldn't have told him right before he was going to meet her. Of course, how was I supposed to know it would be such a problem for him?

Dana had been so excited that night, so eager to introduce him deeper into her life. Then she had learned this about him. If only things were different, she told herself, but they aren't.

"But you're okay with this, aren't you?" she said. "With being here . . . with us?"

Simon nodded. "Yeah, it's fine. I mean, you're here, so I'm not . . . by myself." He gestured toward Alice.

"But I thought you ignored it," Dana said, worried that she had gotten the wrong impression from him. "So, why would that be a problem?"

Simon folded his arms and stretched his legs out in front of him. "I've chosen to ignore it, yes, but that doesn't mean I should push my luck. It's not like this is just some one-time choice. That's not the way it works."

Dana thought about it and then said, "So, you're scared you would still give in?"

"I hope I wouldn't, but I also don't want to find out," he told her. "Why risk it?"

Then his voice shifted, a shadow of enthusiasm emerging. "I mean, imagine a married man who wants to be faithful to his wife, yet he chooses to spend time alone with a pretty co-worker on business trips. Now—just think about it—is that a good idea if he's trying to be loyal?" Simon shook his head. "Well, I don't think it is. Half of keeping a promise is staying away from situations where you are likely to break it. That's what I think."

If only every man thought that way, Dana said to herself. And that slight change in his voice when talking about something important—that was the voice Dana knew from him.

Simon looked down at the road. "You can't just assume you'll always be strong," he said. Then he pointed at the slide that had forced them up into the trees, "I mean, I'll bet that hill thought it would stand forever. Well, the rain had other ideas."

Dana considered the slide as rain fell lightly upon the mass of mud and dirt. Just a little trickle of water, she thought—well, a lot of little trickles of water—could pull any hill down. That's a good thing to remember, but it's a little pessimistic.

"It sounds like you expect everyone to fail," she told Simon.

He shrugged. "I'm really talking more about myself than others. But that's how life is. There's always something pulling us, wanting us to reject what we chose before."

Then Simon looked straight at Dana, his intensity forcing her to blink. "And I can't ever forget that, Dana. I can't ever be careless. I need to always be steady."

Dana turned away from his gaze, disturbed by the image she saw in her mind as he spoke: foul hands grasping for Simon, who resisted briefly before the hands clenched onto him and pulled him down—just like the hill had been brought down across the road.

"So, what do you think is pulling you?" she asked.

Simon was quiet. Then he nodded toward Alice, who was still reading. "Alice's book would answer that for you," he said.

Dana glanced at Alice and at the book in her hands. She knew little about *The Screwtape Letters* besides the words and phrases she helped Alice read now and then. She wondered if Simon had read it. He must have, she thought; otherwise, why would he say that?

Then Simon's enthusiasm returned. "But it's not only that. Lots of things in life pull us one way or another. And they're not all bad, either; some of them are good. But you need to figure out which way you're being pulled, and you need to fight back when you're being taken places you don't want to go."

"Like what exactly?" Dana asked him. "Bad friends? Something like that?"

"Sure, some friends are good and some friends are bad, and that does influence you, yes. But it's easier to understand what I'm talking about if you think about more noticeable, dramatic things, the kind of things that obviously change a person. Like winning the lottery and blowing all the money, or becoming a celebrity and getting all screwed up."

"Getting screwed up by becoming a celebrity? What do you mean by that?" she asked.

"Haven't you ever seen the movie about the body snatchers?"

"No, what does that have to do with it?"

"Never mind, I'll think of something else." He thought for a moment before continuing. "Okay, it's like this," he said. "Celebrity changes you— that's the problem. On the inside, you know? I mean, you might look the same on the outside, but you get all twisted up inside. Like a disease that rots away your core, leaving behind something shallow and sad, all wrapped up in a pretty shell."

His negativity toward celebrity shocked Dana at first, but then she wondered if he might be right. What would fame do to a man like Simon? she asked herself, imagining a proud mountain being pulled down bit by bit through erosion. What would he do if he fell? She didn't want to think about it.

However, she couldn't agree with his complete rejection of celebrity. Surely there are some celebrities who haven't let fame get to their head and gone bad, she thought.

"But, Simon, not all celebrities are bad people."

"Not all smokers get lung cancer, either," he said. "But anyway, I never said celebrities were all bad people. *Bad* isn't the right word. I just think that fame made them worse, not better."

Then he pointed at the tree behind Alice. "Think of a tree that grows under a shadow, forcing it to grow sideways to reach the sunlight. Now, that doesn't make it a *bad* tree, does it? I don't think it does. But, bad or not, when you see it leaning sideways, don't you wonder how much taller it could have been if it had grown straight up toward the sky?"

"Okay," Dana said, "but most people don't think being a celebrity makes you worse. Most people would die for the chance to be a celebrity."

"Yeah, well, so what?" Simon told her. "Who cares what people think? You shouldn't judge right and wrong, good and bad, based on what other people say."

"What do you mean?" Dana asked.

"What I mean is that morality isn't math," he said. "You can prove math through logic, but you can't prove morality that way."

"Why not?"

"Well, you can prove math because everyone agrees that a plus sign is a plus sign and a minus sign is a minus sign. But imagine if we didn't agree about that. Then you couldn't get anything done, right? And that's the problem with morality and logic. Logic needs a solid foundation if you want the right results, but morality is based on values, and the values that society builds its morals on top of are all subjective, so the foundation isn't firm—it's loose, like sand."

That sounded wrong to Dana. "But I don't think values are subjective," she said.

"Why not? Of course they are—at least, as far as society is concerned."

"Like what? Give me one example of a subjective value."

"Well, anything. Here, what about racism? Or, I guess, the belief—the value—that racism is wrong."

"So, racial equality?"

"Yeah."

"But you just proved my point," Dana said. "That's not subjective at all. Everyone knows that racism is wrong. Everyone agrees with that."

"Today, sure, but what about in the past?" he said. "People would have disagreed with you back then."

"So? What does that matter? They were wrong!"

"You think so. I think so. And I hope most people today think so. But people in the past would have thought that *we* were wrong, not them. Don't you see? You can't just expect that everyone will agree with your values—because they don't. And if you don't agree on what is a value, then how can you use logic to prove what is right and what is wrong? I mean, using the exact same logic, two people can reach two completely different conclusions."

This made Dana uncomfortable. She knew that people in the past had been wrong about things—that much was obvious—but it had never occurred to her that they would have thought they were right at the time, just like people today think they themselves are right. If people can think they are right when they're actually wrong, she said to herself, then couldn't people today be wrong and still think they're right? And if things are like that, then how could society's morals ever be stable? Dana thought of Simon, then, and his struggle. If nothing is stable, then what could hold someone like Simon in check?

"I don't understand why you're saying this," she told him. "What is morality based on if you can't use logic?"

"For society, I think it's based on persuasion and charisma—you know, who has the most pull, who has the most influence. That's how society chooses its morals, not with logic," he said. "And that's why the morals of society are so unreliable. One minute people say that an action is wrong, and the next they tell you that it's wrong to call that same action wrong. It's all so flaky. And that's why it's a bad idea to base your view of right and wrong—your morality—on what other people think. Their morals were different in the past. Their morals will be different in the future."

Dana hoped he wasn't saying what she thought he might be saying. "Wait. Are you telling me that you don't believe there is a real right and wrong?" she asked him. "That it's all just based on popular opinion? Because that doesn't fit the other things you've told me."

She looked at Alice, who was sitting and reading her book. Can I trust others to help me keep Alice safe? she wondered. The world seemed darker. She felt alone.

"No, I'm not saying that at all," Simon told her. "Of course, right and wrong both exist and also never change—an absolute right and wrong. But that's not what I'm talking about right now."

"It's not?" Dana said, relieved but confused.

"No, I'm just talking about what everyone else *says* is right and wrong. I'm talking about what people *call* right and wrong. And that can be a very different thing from what actually *is* right and wrong. I mean, at times our views are closer to the truth than other times, but usually at least something is out of whack. In the past we were better with sex and marriage, but today we're better with race. Up and down, moving forward in some ways but moving backward in others—hopefully more forward than backward, though it hasn't seemed that way lately—and always the only thing changing is what people *think* is right and wrong, not what really *is*."

Hearing that made Dana feel better, a little less alone. "Okay, good, so there is right and wrong. And it doesn't change," she said. "But, people's right and wrong—"

"What people *call* right and wrong."

"Okay, what people call right and wrong. So, that changes back and forth based on . . . popularity, I guess?"

"Pretty much."

Dana set her empty wrapper down on the log beside her and picked up her water bottle, thinking about what he had just said. A gust of wind caught the wrapper and spun it through the air into a nearby bush. She stood up and walked after it, bending over to grab it, but the wind hit again and sent the wrapper twisting in the other direction.

"Need some help?" Simon asked her.

"Very funny," she said, springing onto the wrapper before it flew away again. Then, the wrapper secure in her hand, she sat back down beside Simon, feeling a little embarrassed.

"Okay, fine," she said. "What you said makes sense, I guess, but how does it help to know any of that?"

"Well, at least now you know not to waste your time worrying about the crowd and what it thinks," he said, and then he pointed at the wrapper she clasped in her hand. "They're like that wrapper—flailing in the wind, blowing this way and that. We were talking about celebrity before, but who cares what they think about celebrity today, or anything else for that matter? They might think something completely different tomorrow. They're fickle. They jump around with no thought to rhyme or reason. You shouldn't tie yourself to something like that."

Are people really that aimless? Dana asked herself, remembering how the wrapper had bent and twisted in the wind when she chased after it. Then she considered the implications of what Simon had said. Does he think that people might change their minds about the attraction he feels? They've changed their minds about other attractions, right? Not that it would change the actual wrongness of acting on his attraction, but would people one day tell him it was okay? And would he like that change? Surely he wouldn't . . .

"So, what happens if someday the wind blows one direction and people decide it isn't wrong for you to . . . give in?" she asked.

Simon shook his head. "So what if they do? Why would I care? I mean, look, their view on sex is already screwed up as it is. According to them, it's all just a joke—just something to do for fun. So why should I be surprised if they change their minds further?"

Then he seemed to reconsider. "Okay, I guess I would care a little. I mean, we're screwed up enough as it is and I don't want things to get any worse. Still, when it comes to me and my life, well, I already can't depend on them—so I don't. I mean, today they expect me to resist but tomorrow, who knows? And I need a firm foundation to stand on. I can't just blow around aimlessly in the wind with the rest of the crowd."

Dana thought then of what she had seen by the Double Waterfall, but it wasn't for her to bring it up, and he seemed content to leave it unsaid—

"I need to go to the bathroom."

Alice was suddenly standing in front of Dana. "I need to go to the bathroom," she repeated.

Why doesn't she just go by herself? Dana wondered, startled by the interruption. Lost in their conversation, she had forgotten that Alice was even there. Then she remembered where they were, and she remembered what Alice kept seeing. She must be scared to go by herself, Dana thought.

And Simon sensed what was going on. "I'll find you a safe spot," he said, standing and walking off into the trees.

He found a small drop-off thirty feet away with brush blocking the view and enough tree branches overhead to keep off the rain. After looking around for a moment, he returned, satisfied that it was okay, and sent Dana and Alice there by themselves while he stayed behind, his back turned on the two of them.

I trust him, Dana realized, as she let him do this for them. Weakness or not, attraction or not, I think I still trust him. Maybe not to be alone with Alice—Dana understood what he meant about the risk that would be. But, given how unreliable most people actually were, Dana was happy to have someone as dependable as Simon around, someone who considered right and wrong to be more than just the opinion of the crowd, someone she could count on. As long as he stays the way he is now, she thought. But can he always stay this way?

"Who is talking to Simon?" Alice asked, hidden behind a bush.

Dana looked back in surprise, but Simon sat alone, facing away from them and staring down at the road.

"He isn't talking to anyone," Dana said. "Did you hear someone?"

Alice gave her a strange look and then stood up without answering. Is she starting to hear things now, too? Dana asked herself.

They returned, and Alice sat down and immediately buried her face in her book again, even more intent than before. Dana sat down beside Simon.

"Were you talking to yourself just now?" she asked quietly.

"I don't think so," he said, looking embarrassed. "But I don't always notice when I do. Why, did you hear me?"

"Never mind," Dana said, watching Alice. She'll be better when she gets home, Dana told herself. She just needs to get home.

"Do you like your book, Alice?" she asked.

"Yes," Alice said, not looking up.

Dana remembered, then, that Simon knew about the book.

"Have you read it?" she asked him.

He glanced at the cover. "Yeah, I read it when I was a teenager. It's a great book. Lots of good advice, if you know how to find it."

But why is Alice reading so much? Dana asked herself. What's going on inside her head? Then, glancing at Simon, she thought: I'd like to know what's going on inside his head too. Could he really stay the way he is today forever? What would help him stay that way? The crowd? Society? Right now everyone agrees that acting on his attraction is wrong, but will they always?

She looked down at the wrapper still in her hand and imagined it floating in the breeze, caught on a branch for a moment before breaking free and circling slowly to the ground. Where would it go next?

Society's opinion about sex has changed so much, Dana thought, and it's changed so quickly. It used to be something between husband and wife, but now it's just part of the dating game—if even that. And what about homosexuality? We used to consider it wrong to do those things, but now we celebrate it.

But what about Simon? What about his attraction? Couldn't it be accepted too one day—maybe even celebrated? Dana hoped not but wasn't sure what would keep it from happening. She thought about what people thought about sex. It seems like the only barrier today is consent, she said to herself. Anything else goes, anything at all. But everyone—well, everyone decent—agrees today that having sex without consent is wrong.

Dana turned back to Alice and watched as she read her book. Does Alice even understand any of it? Is she mature enough? Then the wrapper lifted off the ground in her mind, touched by a light breeze, and scooted to the side. Will people always think that consent is required? Dana asked herself. Will there always be an age? So many things have changed—will this?

Needing to understand, Dana dug deeper, and down in the midst of shattered assumptions she found an answer that she didn't want to know. Why wouldn't this ever change? she realized. Because sex is special? No, it's not special anymore, not to most people. To them it's trivial, and if it's just trivial . . . then what? What would prevent it from changing? Where is the foundation—does it even have one?

She opened her fingers, the wrinkled wrapper flat on her hand in front of her. It lay still for a moment, making Dana wonder if maybe the wind had stopped, but suddenly it lifted off, turning end over end as it flew away from her. And Dana understood then what Simon had told her before: there is no base, there is no anchor, there is nothing solid holding up the morals of society. Everyone thinks it is wrong because everyone thinks it is wrong. To the crowd, there is nothing else.

And, looking at Alice, Dana felt alone—just her against the world. Except I'm not alone, she reminded herself, because Simon is here. And to him it's wrong because it's truly wrong, not because of what the crowd thinks. It was funny, finding comfort in Simon of all people, given what she knew of him. But along with the bad she also knew the good. She knew that he was solid. She knew he wasn't tied to any crowd. No, she knew he was bound to something else, something she didn't understand, but something that held him in place. I just hope it holds him in place forever, she thought, not wanting to be alone.

And the wrapper floated far away, twirling and jerking helplessly in the wind.

"Simon, do you think it will ever happen?" Dana asked him.

"What? *The Screwtape Letters*? It's happening all around us."

"No . . . what we were talking about before. Do you think that society will ever change their opinion in that way?"

"Oh, that." He paused. "Well, I hope not."

But that wasn't good enough, not after what she had been thinking. "I hope that most people hope not," Dana said. "But what I want to know is, do you think it will happen?"

Simon shook his head. "It's hard to see. We're just so blind, you know? All these voices, screaming at anything that stands in their way, claiming that it's our attractions that define us, demanding that no one do or say anything to discourage them from their desires. And if that's the conventional wisdom, well, who knows where the bottom will be?"

And, as Simon spoke to her, Dana saw the same thing in his eyes that she had seen the night before. I've always seen it in him, she realized. It's one reason why he seems so different from other men, why he seems so interesting.

"I mean, we have this naive belief that we've reached the end of the line," Simon said, "and that society's morals will move no further. But, no matter what we think, the morals of society are going to shift again. They're going to move—they always do—and eventually they'll move one step further than we're willing to follow. And what will we do then?"

He shook his head. "We're just blind fools—that's all there is to it. So, no, I don't know if we'll fall that far or not. I hope we don't. I really hope we don't. But that's the best I can say."

Yes, it's more than depth, Dana thought, watching him explain himself. It's the complexity of his inner world. Most guys, nowadays, have less complexity than a toy fort, yet inside of Simon there is a cathedral. Self-contained—that's how to describe him. But how does he do it? I think I know part of it, she said to herself, but there must be more.

She picked up her water bottle and took a drink. What would it be like to marry a man like that? she wondered, dreaming her old dream for a moment. But then she remembered his attraction, and she slammed the dream shut. That's impossible, she reminded herself, setting her bottle back down. I couldn't live with that, not in a husband.

Still, she wanted his strength in her life. He was solid. She had always felt that way about him, as if the world were a little less blurry whenever he was around. Couldn't we still be friends? she asked herself. Even with what he is, couldn't I still be his friend?

The rain had stopped, and they decided to return to the road. Simon told Dana that if they kept up their pace they might be able to reach the main road before dark, so they all walked quickly, the cold wind biting through their coats.

Simon seemed happier now, not as happy as he had been before everything blew up, but content at least. And Dana felt good walking next to him again, like she had so many times before. Yes, we can be friends, she told herself.

And what about Alice? she wondered. Could it really have been an animal she saw, or is she just seeing things? I need to ask Simon what it might have been, she reminded herself. And what about her reading? It's good that she has something to do, but is she starting to go overboard? Could that be tied somehow to what she keeps seeing? Could it mean that something is wrong?

At least she isn't trying to read while she walks, Dana thought. And at least Simon says it's a good book. Maybe it just keeps her mind off things. Maybe I shouldn't worry about it.

"So, Simon," she said. "Not to spoil the book for Alice, but does it have a happy ending?"

Her question caught Alice's attention, and both of them looked at Simon, interested in what he would say.

With a small, clever smile, he answered: "I guess that depends on who you're rooting for."

Chapter Seven

THE COLD WIND CONTINUED ALL AFTERNOON, AND THE clouds swirled and grew darker. When Dana looked up, she could sense that something was coming. They picked up their pace, hoping to reach the main road before the day turned dark or the storm stopped them.

Then, rounding a corner, they came upon another slide that crossed the road, although this one was smaller than the last. Simon walked forward and tested the dirt with his walking stick to see if it was solid. The spilled ground gave a little as he walked upon it, but not much, and they decided to go over it this time rather than walk around.

As she stepped up onto the small slide, Dana thought of their earlier conversation in which Simon had used the example of the landslide to show how easily a person could fall. It's too bad more men don't think like Simon, she thought. If Dad had, maybe he wouldn't have betrayed Mom.

She wished that Simon could have met her father earlier in her father's life, back when it would have made a difference. But Simon would have been too young then, she reminded herself. Still, I wish my father could resist his urges the way Simon does.

But how does Simon do it? Dana asked herself. She thought she knew what he meant about having a foundation—though it wasn't something they'd talked about yet—but there must be more than just that. I'll ask him about it, she decided. That way, I can understand him better.

They continued a brisk pace and reached the intersection of the paved mountain road just as it was starting to rain. The rain quickly began to pour, driving them under a grove of trees for shelter, where they sat and stared at the main road, wishing they could continue on just a little bit longer that day, knowing that the more they walked the sooner they'd be home.

But the rain showed no sign of stopping, and they didn't want to get soaked; so, since it was already late afternoon, Simon decided to set up the tent and make this their camp for the night. *At least the wind has died down*, Dana thought, *so it won't blow apart the tent.* She worried, however, about all the rain. They'd already seen two slides across the road. *Will the rain cause more slides as we go down the mountain?* she wondered, wishing the rain would stop. *But wishing won't change anything*, she reminded herself. *We just need to deal with things as they are.*

Simon detached the tent from his hiking pack. He pulled the canvas and poles out of their bag and lay them on the ground next to each other. Dana took one side of the canvas and helped him spread it out.

"Ah, you decided to help this time?" Simon said to her.

"You obviously need the help," she replied. "It took you forever last night to put it up by yourself."

"And what if it takes me longer now because you're helping?"

They joked back and forth as they pushed the poles through their loops and pulled the tent up. Then Simon got out the stakes, which they pounded into the ground in case the wind returned. It would have been easier if they'd still had the hatchet, but they used rocks instead, and Dana was relieved that Simon never complained about her losing it.

Actually, I think it did take us more time with me helping, she said to herself. *But I'm not going to tell Simon that.*

"Shouldn't we have put down a tarp or something to keep the bottom dry?" she asked.

"Yeah, probably, but I couldn't find mine when I packed yesterday," he said, hitting the last stake firmly into place. "I must have lost it somewhere."

The trees provided some protection but didn't block all of the rain, so Dana and Alice got inside the tent as soon as it was ready, sitting in the front and facing Simon.

"We can make room for you, too," Dana told Simon, gesturing at the space next to her, the opposite side from Alice.

"No, that would be too cramped," he said.

He pulled out a poncho from his pack and put it on before setting both backpacks inside the tent to keep them out of the rain. Then he sat down on the ground outside. The light hadn't faded much; however, Dana could already feel the cold of night approaching.

But I'll take that over the wind this afternoon, she thought, remembering how it had dug through their coats. Alice pulled out *The Screwtape Letters* and started to read again.

"You know what would be nice right now?" Dana said. "A fire."

Simon nodded. "Yeah, but it'll take a miracle to find dry wood in a storm like this. Everything I found last night was wet, and you saw how that went."

"What's wrong? Have you forgotten your camping skills?" Dana said. "I think your cabin has spoiled you."

"Maybe you're right," Simon said, and he smiled. "We're all pretty spoiled nowadays. You know, I remember when I was a kid and my grandpa would take me camping. He knew all of that kind of stuff. Sometimes he didn't even use matches. He'd just use flint and steel, or one of those bow things that you rub in your hands."

"I'll bet your grandpa could have started the fire, rain or not," Dana said.

"Probably, but you're stuck with me," Simon told her, "so I hope your coat is warm."

"You're not even going to try?"

"Sure, I'll try if the rain stops. But don't get your hopes up. Not when it's been raining like this."

Then Dana caught a flicker in the clouds above.

"Wait, what was that?" she asked.

"What was what?" Simon said.

Alice set down her book and bent her neck out of the tent to look up at the sky and see what Dana was talking about.

"I thought I saw a flash, like lightning. But I don't hear any thunder," Dana said.

Then she saw it again, a bright flash within the clouds, illuminating a pocket of them with light before everything fell back to gray again.

"It's like it's inside the clouds," she said. "But where's the thunder?"

Simon shrugged his shoulders as he looked up at the sky. He seemed nervous. That made Dana feel nervous as well. Thunder rumbled above.

"How close was that?" Dana asked, but before Simon could answer they heard a giant boom and a crash, obviously near.

Simon jumped up and turned around to look for the source of the sound. He walked a few feet in each direction, looking off into the woods, but it was becoming dark and he couldn't see far.

"What was that?" Dana asked.

"I don't know," he told her, stopping in front of the tent opening. "But it sounded like a tree got hit."

He looked out over the road.

Dana could see nothing through the rain, and as it poured down she thought more and more about the landslide that had hit the cabin. She remembered staring at darkness and then seeing it rush toward her. At least Simon is with us this time, she told herself as she put her arm around Alice. But that lightning strike had been too close.

"Should we be under these trees?" Dana asked Simon. "Couldn't they fall on us?"

Simon squatted back down in front of the tent.

"I don't think we have a choice up here," he said. "Just keep low."

A streak of lightning arced down from the sky and thunder exploded all around them, followed by another, and another, the force of the repeated bursts shaking the tent. Alice huddled against Dana, face buried in her shoulder, arms tight around her, jumping at every boom. This is too much for her, Dana thought. The sky was full of light. The mountain was full of thunder.

Dana rocked Alice back and forth, telling her it'd be okay, and she watched Simon, who crouched protectively outside the tent, his face worried and unsure but his eyes determined, as if he could hold back the danger through pure will.

The lightning's frenzied dance, accompanied by the percussion of thunder, lasted only minutes, although it felt like hours. Then the flashes slowed, striking farther down the mountain, and the thunder receded into distant murmurs. Dana relaxed as the storm died down, but Alice was still shaking.

I need to calm her down somehow, Dana told herself, trying to think of some way to get Alice's mind off the storm. The only thing she could think of was *The Screwtape Letters*.

She picked up the book and set it in Alice's lap.

"So, how far have you gotten?" she asked.

Alice, still shaking, loosened her grip around Dana and put one hand on the book.

"I finished it," she said.

"But you're still reading it?"

"I think I missed something."

"What do you mean?"

Alice only shook her head, hugging the book to her chest and leaning into Dana. She was shaking less but still needed to calm down.

"Hey," Dana said, remembering that Alice hadn't seen her "animal" today. "So, that animal stopped following you. That's good, right?"

"Maybe," Alice said, not shaking any more, and Dana let the conversation drop.

The two of them sat there together in the tent, Simon still crouching in front, all of them gazing down at the road, the final echoes of thunder reaching them from far away on the mountain.

Eventually the rain stopped, the thunder and lightning long gone. Simon stood and removed his poncho. He started arranging the campsite as Dana came out of the tent. He found a large log between some trees and rolled it into the camp. Then he cleared an area between the tent and the log for a fire, moving all the twigs and leaves safely behind the log before making a circle of small stones on the newly cleared ground.

"So you're going to try for a fire after all?" Dana asked.

"Might as well," Simon told her. "But don't get your hopes up."

The day almost gone, Simon got out the lantern and turned it on, resting it on a rock by the tent. Then he gathered an armful of wood and dumped it beside the fire circle before getting out his paper and matches.

"See, it's all wet," he said as he arranged the wood for the fire. "I don't think this is going to work."

He attempted to light the fire the same way he had the night before, lightning a few matches and burning the paper. But the wood never caught for long. The night was cold.

"Sorry," Simon said. He put the matches away.

"That's okay," Dana told him. "Maybe we'll have better luck tomorrow night."

But she remembered that Simon had told her it'd take a miracle to find dry wood after all the rain. He's probably right, she said to herself, although a fire would sure feel nice right now.

She pulled the sleeping bag out of her backpack and set it in the tent beside Alice, who was once more reading her book. Then Simon got out their dinner and passed it around, the same meal as the night before. Already sick of the food, Dana thought of saying something sarcastic but decided against it. Tonight will be better than last night, she promised herself, determined to be kind to Simon. He was her friend and he deserved to be treated well, especially with everything he was doing for her and Alice.

Simon asked Dana if he could see her walking stick. She handed it to him.

"Is it okay if I work on it a little bit?" he asked.

"Of course," she said. "What are you going to do to it?"

"We'll see."

He pulled out a knife from his pack and flipped the blade from the handle, then sat down on his poncho in front of the log. Dana sat down beside him on the poncho and forced down her dinner as she leaned back against the log and watched him make the first cut.

And watching him, she wondered again about his resistance. What you're attracted to makes you what you are, doesn't it? she asked herself. Gay, straight, whatever? But what about Simon? If attraction truly makes people what they are, then I know what his attraction makes him—except, that doesn't seem to fit right. Could there be something that I'm missing? And how does he resist it? she thought. And when did he first know? I wonder how long he has been resisting.

The night had fallen, the only light the pale glow of the lantern, and looking out at the trees Dana thought again of the shadow that kept stalking Alice. It was some sort of animal surely, but what? She would ask Simon what it was later when Alice was asleep. The dark woods around them seemed creepy. Too quiet after the violent thunderstorm.

Simon was slowly carving a shape toward the bottom of the walking stick. What is that? Dana wondered. It was hard to tell. She glanced over at Alice, who was still reading inside the tent, squinting in the dull light, her dinner finished and the empty MRE package lying beside her.

I hope she doesn't hurt her eyes, Dana thought before turning her attention back to Simon. He cut slowly, whittling away at the walking stick, willing the design out of its form.

A short time later, Alice started to nod off. Dana asked her if she was ready for bed, but she held out at first, wanting to read a little longer. However, eventually she agreed. She put away her book as Dana packed up the remains of her dinner. She's probably too tired to concentrate, Dana thought, helping Alice roll out the sleeping bag and get situated.

"I'll be back in a little bit," Dana told her.

Alice looked worried at being alone, but Dana reassured her that she'd be just outside talking. Then she left the tent and sat by Simon, who was still cutting slowly, the shape not yet defined.

After waiting a few minutes, Dana leaned toward him and whispered: "So, what kind of animal do you think Alice could be seeing?"

Simon stopped carving.

"Maybe a deer, if anything," he said softly.

"But why would it have followed her then? It was like it was stalking her. Could it be something dangerous? Like a bear or a wolf? Maybe some kind of mountain lion?"

"I don't know," he said. "If it was a bear, then why didn't we see it? And there are no wolves here. I'm not sure about mountain lions, though."

Then he set down the knife and walking stick and looked at Dana.

"You know, it's possible that she's just imagining things," he told her. "You haven't read *The Screwtape Letters,* have you?"

"No, why?"

"Did you know it's about devils?"

"What?" Dana said. "I didn't think it was a horror book." That's probably what's making Alice see things, she thought. I should have paid more attention to what the book was about instead of just buying it out of spite.

"Oh, no, it's not like that," Simon told her. "It's not horror. It's fake letters between two devils, the older advising the younger on temptation. But it's not scary at all. That's not the point of the book. The point is to show how temptation works and how it can affect you."

This reminded Dana of what Simon had said about the landslide and about how there is always something trying to pull you down. He'd pointed at Alice's book then, hadn't he? But he said something else about her book, too, while we were walking this afternoon.

"So, what about the ending? You said it was a happy one, didn't you?"

"I said that depends on who you're rooting for."

"What do you mean by that?"

"The devils lose. The man dies before they can make him fall."

"He dies? How can that be a happy ending?"

Simon shrugged. "Everyone dies one day or another. But he lived well and he died well. What more can a man ask from life?"

Dana thought for a moment.

"But if it's not a scary book," she said, "then what does it have to do with what Alice is seeing?"

"I don't know," Simon said. "I was just wondering if maybe reading so much about devils might make her think about them a lot. And if she's thinking about them a lot, then maybe she'd start seeing things, you know?"

"I don't know about that. Maybe, I guess."

"Has she ever done anything like this before?"

"No."

Simon picked up the knife and walking stick again.

"You know," he said. "It could just be shock."

"I thought about that. She has been through a lot these past few days," Dana said. "You should have felt how much she was shaking during the lightning."

"Well," Simon said, beginning to carve again. "I wouldn't worry too much about anything following her. If something really were following her, then I doubt it'd bother her when there are two adults around. I don't think anything in these mountains is *that* dangerous."

They let the topic drop, and Dana watched Simon as he continued to carve. She still couldn't tell what he was making. But, whatever it was, Simon was giving it texture. It looked almost like a circle, except the edges weren't quite round and he wasn't making the inside smooth. Simon cut at small angles, the interior of the shape rising and falling.

And he was making it for her. But what about Simon? she repeated to herself. Then she thought of his attraction and wondered again when he first knew about it. She stood and walked to the tent, peeking in to make sure that Alice was sleeping. She didn't want to risk her hearing this conversation. Then she returned to her seat in front of the log.

"Simon, can I ask you a personal question?"

He stopped carving and looked up at her.

"Of course."

"But I don't want to make you mad."

He set down the knife and stick, and he raised his knees to rest his arms upon them, his hands clasped in front of him. He leaned back against the log, looking at her.

"I won't be mad."

Dana adjusted herself on the poncho, gathering her courage, and asked: "So, I just wondered how long you've known, you know, that you're a—"

"Don't call me that!" Simon leaned forward with a jerk.

The interruption confused her. I thought that's what he is, she said to herself. If being attracted to men makes a man gay, then Simon's attraction makes him a . . .

But concern about upsetting him overwhelmed her thinking. Putting her hand on his arm, she told him, "See, I didn't want to offend you, Simon. I thought that was the word for it."

He looked down at her hand on his arm, staring at it until she drew it back. Then he looked up at her.

"Dana, I don't care what the dictionary says. I don't care what psychologists say. I don't care what anyone says. Just, please, don't call me that. I am *not* my attraction. Attraction is something that you feel, not something that you are."

And her guilt was back, just like the night before. She offended him even when she didn't mean to. I'm tired of hurting him when he's only trying to do his best, she thought. But I didn't even know this would hurt him. She wished she understood him better. Then, maybe she could avoid offending him again.

"I'm sorry, Simon," she said. "I didn't mean—"

But Simon waved her off, picking up the walking stick again. "Don't worry about it," he said. "I told you I wouldn't be mad, and I get why you'd say it that way."

Then he looked at her again. "It's just these dumb labels we stick on people, you know? They're so pointless. We're so stupid about sexual desire. We use the same word for attraction as we do for action, mixing them together, making it seem like there is nothing separating the two, no thought, no choice, like we're just slaves to our desires, just machines, incapable of deciding whether to follow our attractions or reject them."

He flipped over the walking stick, returning to where he had stopped carving.

"And it's stupid," he said. "Completely stupid. I mean, some people claim that when you ignore your desires you're rejecting yourself. But seriously? I mean, come on, life doesn't revolve around sex."

"Actually, for a lot of guys, I think it kind of does," Dana told him.

Simon smiled, and Dana was happy to see that her lightness had worked and that he wasn't too offended. She set aside her question for later, telling herself to take the conversation slower next time and figure out a way to ask without upsetting him.

"Really, though, it's just lazy," Simon told her, going back to what he had been saying. "You feel same-sex attraction so people say you're gay. You feel normal attraction so people say you're straight. But what about me? What does that make me?"

Dana didn't want to answer him.

"Because if the other labels fit, then you know there's only one answer," he said. "If it's true that we have no choice or agency, then I'm just a monster. According to them, that's all I am and that's all I'll ever be—just a monster."

Yes, Dana, he is a monster. You know what he wants. You know what that makes him. You cannot expect anything good from him. He is nothing more than a monster.

Dana didn't know what to say. She remembered her earlier thoughts about men being gay if they liked other men. But what about Simon? If it's true that there is no choice in the matter, if our attractions are our core, if they are what matters most about us, then doesn't that mean that Simon really is a monster? And if he really is a monster, then what? Should we simply throw him in a cage?

No, she couldn't agree with that. No matter what it means, she said to herself, Simon isn't a monster. Something else must be wrong in the way I'm thinking about attraction—because if he ignores his attraction, then he isn't a monster. Except, Dana realized, wouldn't that mean that if a man ignores his same-sex attraction, then he isn't gay? That felt controversial to Dana. She decided she'd have to think about it more.

"But we're humans, Dana," Simon told her. "We're not machines. We don't have to accept what comes easiest. We don't have to just bow. We have the ability to choose—to choose which desires to indulge, to choose which desires to resist. Our attractions are there, yes, but we *choose* our actions. And it's our choices that matter, not our desires, because *that* is who we are, that is the deeper layer within us, that is the place where we decide what it is that we truly want to be."

The agitation had left his voice, replaced by the same enthusiasm he had shown while talking to her earlier that day.

"Call it your mind, your soul, your conscience, whatever," he said. "But that is what is in charge. And it's true for all attractions: normal attraction, same-sex attraction, everything. Whatever the attraction, the truth is the same: what we want is *not* who we are. We are who we choose to be."

Dana was silent as she considered what he had said. I shouldn't think of Simon as a monster, she thought, understanding that he did, in fact, have the ability to choose his own actions and that that was what really mattered. She imagined his attraction as a black slime, sticky and foul, covering part of him but only on the outside. And on the inside was Simon, not his attraction. He decided the course of his life. He chose what actions he would take. He chose whether he indulged or ignored his attraction.

But there was something he had said that made her uncomfortable. She thought about it and realized it was when he had used the word "normal."

"When you said 'normal,' were you talking about straight?" she asked. "Because I thought that wasn't supposed to be called 'normal.'"

Simon was working on the carving again.

"Supposed to?" he said. "What, are the Thought Police hiding in your pocket or something? And why wouldn't I call normal attraction normal?"

His eyes focused on the cut his knife was making.

"It's the only sexual desire that's actually needed, isn't it?" he asked her. "I mean, every other sexual attraction is pretty much pointless if you think about it. All other attractions could vanish from everyone tomorrow and we wouldn't miss a thing. But the attraction between man and woman? That one would be missed. That one is needed. That one matters. And if that doesn't make it normal, then what in the world is normal?"

Dana admitted to herself that he had a point, but hearing it still made her feel uncomfortable.

Then Simon laughed. "Besides, if it *isn't* normal, then the human race is pretty much screwed, aren't we?"

Dana smiled. It is where we all come from, she thought. He's right about that.

"Fine, okay," she said. "But people are so sensitive nowadays. It's easy to offend people when you say stuff like that. Not everyone looks at things like you do."

She didn't add that he himself had just been offended by something she had said. But he had been right about that, too, hadn't he? she thought.

Simon shrugged. "Some people get offended when you tell them that water is wet. What can you do? Life is too short to worry about it."

He returned to his carving, using his fingers to measure and then cutting a thin line around the stick before returning to the top of the line and carving deeper. While he worked, Dana got up to check on Alice again. Alice was still in the sleeping bag, sound asleep. The night had grown colder, and Dana hugged her coat tight against herself as she sat down beside Simon again. It'd be warmer to sit closer to him, she thought, but she didn't move. She was happy to let the prior topic drop. Right or not, it was taboo to talk like that. But Simon seems so sure about himself, she thought. And isn't it good that he separates his attraction from himself? Wouldn't it be good if all men did that?

You cannot trust men, Dana. Always led by their attractions, they follow their lust—every one of them: your father, Alice's father. Simon is no different. You know what that means.

But Dana didn't want to believe that Simon was as shallow as other men or that he would make the same mistakes.

"Okay, " she said, "so attraction isn't an excuse for our actions. But what about love? Does that justify anything and everything?"

"What do you mean?" Simon asked, concentrating on his cut.

Dana didn't know how to say it.

"Well, some people," she began, wanting to say "some men" but deciding it was safer to make it more general, "some people claim that love is more important than any commitment or promise they made in the past. So, what do you think about that?"

Simon looked up from his carving.

"That's kind of a weird question, Dana. Why are you asking me that?"

Dana sighed. She had hoped to avoid sharing the details.

"I was just thinking about my father," she told him. "He left my mom, chasing after some young co-worker of his. He claimed he was in love with her. Following his heart. You know, the usual crap," she said, and then she snorted. "And he was surprised that I got mad at him for it!"

Simon thought for a moment, glancing down at the walking stick before looking back at Dana.

"That's pretty much the same thing I was saying before," he told her. "People feel something and then they claim they must act on their feelings or else they'll be unhappy or unfulfilled or something dramatic and cheesy like that. They treat love like it's just an excuse, just a way to rationalize whatever it is they wanted to do anyway."

Simon shook his head.

"It's pathetic, though," he told her. "And I don't care what your dad said—it wasn't love that made him do what he did. Love doesn't make a man cheat on his wife. Lust might. But not love."

Dana nodded, happy that Simon was a better man than her father yet sad for the same reason.

"So what is he doing now?" Simon asked.

"Now?" she said. "I don't know. I don't talk to him much. The last I heard, he had left the other woman for a different other woman." She shook her head. "Which just proves that women really are idiots. Once a cheater, always a cheater, right? So, why do women so often think their cheater is different from the rest?"

Simon raised his eyebrows, smiling a little. "I wouldn't be the one to say," he told her.

Smart answer, Dana thought, glad that he didn't want to pile on. Besides, I shouldn't judge women so harshly when they do things like that, she told herself. Who knows what I would do in the same situation? Like, what if I found out that Simon was already married? What would I do then? But then she reminded herself that it wouldn't matter since the two of them were only going to be friends. Too bad, she thought. I doubt I'll ever meet another man like him. Too many men throw away their commitments nowadays as if they mean nothing.

"Simon, I wish more men were like you."

"I don't," he said softly.

"Oh." Busy thinking of his good points, she had forgotten his bad one. "That's not what I meant. I was talking about the good things."

He nodded and returned to his work.

"I guess there's a plus and a minus to everything," he told her.

"What do you mean by that?"

"I mean, maybe if there are good things about me, they are only there because I fight against the bad things. Maybe my weaknesses are the reason for my strengths. Does that make any sense at all?"

She thought about it. If something comes easily for someone, then they never have to put much effort into it; but when someone struggles, wouldn't that have an impact on them?

"Yes, I think so," she said. "With what you deal with every day, it makes sense that it would make you stronger and wiser about this."

"Wiser?" Simon laughed. "More annoyed, maybe."

"Why annoyed?"

"Because people take attraction too seriously," he said. "They pretend that denying their desires is the same as denying themselves."

He set down the knife and walking stick and leaned toward her as he spoke.

"You hear it all the time," he said, "and I'm not just talking about same-sex attraction either. Think about it. How many middle-aged men end up falling in love with their secretary or whatever? A woman who is—of course—half as old as their wife. It's the same story again and again, composed in the same fake, flowery language." He shook his head. "But the poetry they keep spewing isn't profound, not if you really listen. They're just talking about what turns them on—that's it. Just what turns them on."

Does the reason a man gives for betraying his wife make a difference? Dana asked herself. Whether he claims he's gay or he claims he's in love with another woman, either way he's putting his personal desire over his commitment and loyalty to his wife, isn't he?

Simon, meanwhile, had more to say. "It's ridiculous!" he told Dana. "They ramble on and on, pretending that their words are meaningful. Love this, love that. I mean, come on, strip away all the flowery mumbo jumbo and all they're really talking about is what makes them—"

He cut himself off, blushing.

"I can't believe I almost said that," he muttered under his breath.

Almost said what? Dana wondered, the confusion and blush on his face making her want to laugh.

Simon rubbed his nose and coughed.

"Yeah, sorry, I got a little carried away," he told her. "But just imagine if I agreed with what they said about attraction. Just think what that would do to me."

He glanced at the tent and then looked back at Dana.

"When people talk like that," he said, "they're telling me to surrender, not to resist. They might not realize they're telling me that, and they probably won't admit they're telling me that, but they are. And, frankly, it pisses me off. Because how could they be so blind?"

He looked down, searching for where he had laid the walking stick.

"Anyway, enough about that," he said. "Maybe we should talk about something else."

"Good idea," Dana said and laughed.

She was glad he didn't let his attraction define him. But what would that mean for him in a relationship? she wondered. Not that it matters for me, of course, she reminded herself, since we're just going to be friends.

Simon picked up the walking stick and knife, moving the stick around and staring at the uncompleted portion before looking up at Dana, who had been watching him.

"So what's the big secret, anyway?" he asked her. "What did Alice's father do that forced you two to hide up here?"

Dana got up and peeked inside the tent, making sure that Alice was still asleep. Then, returning to her seat, she told him: "The same thing we've been talking about."

"Cheated?"

"Yes," she said. "He's a good dad—he really is. But he's a crappy husband."

"A good dad cheats on his daughter's mother?"

"I know. I know. You're right," she said. "But he really does love Alice, and she completely adores him. They have a great relationship. Maybe it helps that she's young so she doesn't understand what's going on. Well, that and the fact that she doesn't like her mother anyways."

"What's wrong with her mom?"

"Let's just say the dislike is mutual," Dana said. "*Ms.* Miller is not exactly mother material. She treats Alice like a fashion accessory, not a daughter. I guess that's the way Ms. Miller looks at life: just a big show, just one never-ending dinner party. Going to the right social gatherings, giving to the right charities, being seen giving to the right charities, caring about the right causes, having everyone know that she cares about the right causes—that's it, that's her life."

Dana paused and glanced back at the tent before continuing more quietly. "I actually think Ms. Miller knows about the senator's affairs. I think she knows and she doesn't care as long as he's discreet. I bet she has her own as well. It's just a political marriage. That's what I think. All opportunity, no love."

"Wait. Senator?" Simon said. "As in Senator Miller? Alice is Senator Miller's daughter?"

Dana frowned. "Uh, yes, but I probably wasn't supposed to tell you that." She laughed nervously.

"I guess it's too late now," she said.

Then, the secret revealed, it didn't hurt for her to go on. "So, maybe you heard about the senator's recent escapade with his campaign aid? His *nineteen-year-old* campaign aid?" Dana shook her head. "Just like you said: half his wife's age." Then she reconsidered: "Actually, in this case, maybe less than half. Hard to say for certain. Ms. Miller lies about her age."

"I don't remember if I heard about it or not," Simon told her, "but what does that have to do with you?"

Dana smiled. "So, his advisers thought it wouldn't be the best idea to draw attention to me, his daughter's young, single, live-in nanny." She touched her hair. "He's always had a thing for blondes. That's why

Ms. Miller went blonde, I think. It's not natural—not that anything about her is natural anymore—but she knew how to trap him."

Then, letting go of her hair, Dana continued: "Anyways, they thought having me there might raise questions and make the scandal worse, so they sent us up here for a long 'vacation' until things blow over. Alice's family owns, or I guess now I should say 'owned,' a cabin here on the mountain. That's where we've been staying."

"But why did Alice come? Why not just send you away?"

"Then who would take care of Alice?" Dana said. "Ms. Miller? I don't think so." She looked back at the tent. "I've raised Alice since she was a toddler. I wouldn't leave her, not alone with that—"

"Since a toddler? You're not old enough to have raised her that long."

"They hired me right out of high school," she told him. "It was luck on my part. The senator—well, he wasn't a senator then but was running in the special election for the office—anyways, he discovered he had a 'nanny problem,' so he fired her and had to hire a new one that same day. I had submitted my name to some agencies and, well, like I said—he's always had a thing for blondes."

Simon returned to his work, curving the shape around the walking stick as he carved it. Then he quietly asked: "Did the senator ever try anything with you?"

Dana shook her head. "No. Oh, he flirts all the time," she said, "but that's because he's the kind of man that doesn't know how *not* to flirt. But, even with the man that he is, I don't think he would try anything with me. Like I said, he really does love Alice, and even he can see what that would do to her."

"An unprincipled man with some principles?"

"I guess so," Dana said. "The thing is, it's hard for me to dislike him when I see how well he treats Alice and how much she loves him. I know you're right. I know he doesn't understand loyalty—or even self-control—and I know that someday Alice is going to understand what he is like, and that won't be good for her. But, even knowing all that, it's still difficult to think badly of him. He's just so smooth and charismatic. And he's very romantic when he wants to be."

Simon grimaced. "Romantic? Seems to me that *romantic* men are always going from woman to woman to woman. Is that romance? I think women see romance when what is really there is just cheap seduction. That's why guys cringe when we see it—we know what *romantic* men are really like."

Dana turned to Simon, surprised at the bitterness in his voice; but he was looking down at his carving, not at her. She didn't like the implication of his words. They made it seem like women were fools.

I get to say that, not him, she thought.

The fact that he viewed Senator Miller as a threat was amusing. The senator might be charming, but she knew him too well and for too long to fall for his games. Besides, with Alice in the picture, that was never going to happen.

But what surprised her most about his tone was how jealous it made him sound. He's obviously still thinking about us as more than just friends, she thought. Why else would he sound like that? But, with what I know about him, he really thinks he still has a chance?

Then Dana asked herself the same question: *does* he still have a chance? She wasn't sure what the answer was. She was happy, though, to know he felt jealous.

Simon put his knife away and handed the walking stick back to Dana. "Is it finished?" she asked.

"For now," he said. "There's still a little room for later."

She ran her finger along the new carving—a tree, twisting around the walking stick from the top of its leaves to the bottom of its trunk. It was beautiful.

"Simon. Have you ever thought about doing something with this— custom woodworking, cabinetry, that sort of thing? You're really good."

He shrugged. "I guess that's an idea. I do enjoy it. But how much could I really make doing that? I mean, is that the kind of job I could support a family with?"

"I'm sure you could make it work," Dana said, surprising herself with how close she came to saying "we" instead of "you." With the way they had been talking, saying "we" almost seemed more natural.

She set down the walking stick beside the tent. "Thanks again, Simon. It really is beautiful."

"Well, uh, I wanted it to match you, you know—beautiful."

Dana laughed and Simon blushed bright red again, followed by a few seconds of awkward silence before the lantern, mercifully, shut off.

"I think that's a hint," Dana said, grateful for the darkness.

"Yeah, I guess it is." He sounded embarrassed.

"So, please tell me you brought more batteries," she said.

"Yeah, I'll replace them tomorrow."

They said their good-nights then, and as Dana got in her sleeping bag, she thought about Simon and his awkward compliment. Senator Miller might need lessons on loyalty from Simon, she said to herself, but Simon definitely needs lessons on flirting from Senator Miller. She smiled at the idea.

It was strange that Simon still thought of her that way. She had gotten the earlier hint, but this made it explicit. And now she didn't know what to think. She liked the way Simon thought about love, desire, and loyalty. It was exactly what she wanted in a husband. If only he didn't have that horrible attraction, she thought. Without it, he would be perfect.

But without it, Simon might not be Simon, she reminded herself. Maybe moving forward with him would mean accepting the bad along with the good? She wondered if she could do that.

Not before I know how he resists it, she thought. I need to know if I can trust his method. Unless there's some way for his attraction to just go away…

But people always said that gays can't change, so Dana assumed that would be the same for someone like Simon as well. Except, what if they're wrong? she thought. In that case, we could have a chance, couldn't we?

Simon was walking around the camp, muttering to himself. He sounded upset. I hope he's not mad at himself for blowing things tonight, Dana thought. He wasn't that bad. Not that good either, but not that bad. She heard him walk out of camp, and everything was quiet until he returned a few minutes later, no longer muttering. Dana listened as he unrolled his sleeping bag and got inside. Then the night was silent. She stared up at the darkness, wondering what to do about Simon, when Alice sat up.

"Do you need to go to the bathroom?" Dana asked her, leaning up on one elbow but unable to see anything in the dark.

She felt Alice leave the sleeping bag and crawl across the tent floor. The tent's zipper started to move.

"Oh, no, not this again," Dana said, grabbing Alice before she could leave the tent.

"They want him to forget. They want—" Alice mumbled.

But Dana hugged her tightly, shushing her and rocking her back and forth. Alice immediately quieted.

Is she dreaming about her father? Dana asked herself as she felt Alice relax in her arms. She lowered Alice back down into the sleeping bag and closed the tent flap. Then, shivering in the cold, Dana sat beside Alice and waited a few minutes to make sure Alice wouldn't try to get up again. Could this be something bad, Dana wondered, or is she just worried about her father? And how long will it take Senator Miller to realize that something has happened? He would come looking for us if he knew. But when will he know? Dana wasn't sure.

Then, lying down beside Alice, Dana laid an arm across her, hoping that nothing was wrong. I should ask Simon about the sleepwalking when I talk to him tomorrow, she thought. Maybe he'll have some ideas.

Dana cleared her mind, then, setting aside her worries until the morning; and, finally, she fell asleep.

Chapter Eight

WHEN DANA LEFT HER TENT THE FOLLOWING MORNING, she couldn't see Simon anywhere in the camp. It was cold, and she hugged herself to keep warm as she walked through the trees in search of him. Then she caught a glimpse behind a tree; and, seeing him there, she left him to his morning routine—because it wasn't for her to bring it up—and returned to the tent to wake Alice, who rose reluctantly. The temperature had dropped overnight. They could feel the brisk air in their nostrils and see it when they spoke, a white vanishing mist. Everything was covered with a thin layer of frost. Dana wiped off the log before they sat down and picked up the small breakfast that Simon had left for them, the same as the day before. Alice sat quietly, eating her food slowly as she read *The Screwtape Letters*, her coat sleeves pulled down to cover her cold hands.

"So, Alice, you sleepwalked again last night."

"I did?"

"Were you dreaming about your dad?"

"I don't remember."

Then Alice's eyes brightened as she looked up from her book to ask Dana: "Do you think he'll come get us?"

"I'm sure he'll come as soon as he knows what happened," Dana said. But when will that be? she asked herself before saying: "We'll just keep heading down the mountain in the meantime. Maybe we'll meet him halfway."

That last sentence had been as much for Dana herself as it had been for Alice. It really is cold this morning, Dana thought. I can't wait to get home.

Alice nodded and returned to her book, the brightness in her eyes already gone. She looked pale. I hope that's just the cold, Dana thought. But it isn't the cold that's giving her those circles underneath her eyes. The trip is wearing on her.

Simon walked past the camp, heading toward the road, and Dana got up to follow him, her mind full of questions from the night before. Could we have a chance? How does he resist it? Can he just get rid of it? Or, if not, could I be with him anyways? How?

Then he stopped and she stopped beside him, both looking down at the road below, where they would be walking again soon. They said their good mornings, Simon a little shy, Dana curious at her own feelings.

He's probably still embarrassed from last night, she said to herself. He just needs practice, that's all.

"How much longer do you think it will take?" she asked him.

"I don't know. Two more days, maybe, if we walk fast. We didn't get as far yesterday as I expected us to." Then he glanced up at the clouds, full and dark—looking like rain. "And if the weather lets us," he said.

"Maybe we'll run into someone on the road," Dana told him, cheered by the possibility.

"Yeah, maybe."

Dana turned around to check on Alice, who was still sitting on the log and concentrating on her book. She really does look pale this morning, Dana thought.

"So, Simon—Alice almost walked off again last night."

"She did? Like two nights ago?"

He turned and looked at Alice, and both of them watched her as she read, Dana ignoring the memory of that first night, not wanting to remember how she had treated him then.

"Yes, but I stopped her this time," she told him.

"Does she sleepwalk at home?"

"Not as far as I know. Just here. Just now."

"That's weird."

"And both times she's been saying the same thing: 'They want him to forget.' Over and over. It kind of freaks me out."

Simon thought for a moment.

"'They want him to forget'?" He raised his eyebrows. "Makes you wonder what she's dreaming about, doesn't it?"

"Probably her dad," Dana told him. "She asked me about him this morning."

Simon nodded, and they didn't speak for a few more minutes, both of them thinking their own thoughts. Then, still watching Alice, Simon touched Dana's elbow.

"How fast does Alice read?" he asked her.

Dana glanced at his hand on her arm before looking up at his face. Why were his eyes worried?

"I don't know," she said. "Why do you ask?"

"She isn't turning any pages."

"What?"

"This entire time. She's been reading the same page."

And Dana thought back to breakfast that morning. She remembered Alice sitting there and reading. But had she turned any pages? No, she hadn't, Dana realized. She's been reading the same page all morning.

"Let me talk to her," Dana said, and then she hurried back to Alice and sat down beside her.

But Alice only sat and read her book, not looking up, not noticing Dana next to her, not realizing she was being watched—and never turning a single page.

Dana put her arm around Alice's shoulders. "Listen," Dana said. "Are you okay?"

She felt neglectful. All that time worrying and thinking about Simon yesterday, she thought, when I should have been paying more attention to Alice.

Alice shook her head. "It's not here," she said.

"What's not here?"

Then Alice threw her book to the ground. "It's not here!" She buried her face in her hands, shoulders shaking.

Surprised at Alice's reaction, Dana tried to soothe her, asking her again what wasn't there. But Alice wouldn't answer, only crying and shaking her head. So Dana held her, rubbing her shoulders and patting her back. She glanced over at Simon, who was still standing where she had left him, although he'd turned and now faced the road. Something is obviously wrong with Alice, Dana thought. She's usually so happy, not like this. This isn't like her.

I think she just needs to get home, Dana said to herself. This is too much for her. We just need to get her home. And the sooner we get moving the better.

Dana picked up the book from the ground and set it in her lap, waiting for Alice to calm down before returning it to her. Then, thinking of something else, Dana leaned in toward Alice and told her: "At least that animal is gone. I'll bet it wandered off."

Although Dana had tried to sound cheerful, Alice only grunted. Then Alice looked up and, seeing the book in Dana's lap, took it and put it back in her pocket.

Dana couldn't decide if giving the book back was a good idea or not. Is it just messing with her head? she worried. But she was afraid to ask Alice to stop reading because that seemed like the only thing Alice was interested in doing. Would it be harder for Alice if she had nothing to do?

Then Dana thought of the phrase that Alice kept repeating in her sleep: "They want him to forget." Could that be something from the book? Simon told me that the book was about devils trying to tempt a man. So maybe that's what Alice is thinking about?

Probably not, Dana decided. Alice is probably just thinking about her father. Maybe she's worried that he'll forget her.

Simon entered the camp a few minutes later. "We'd better get going," he said. "I don't know how long before it'll start raining."

They packed up quickly and, once they had loaded their backpacks and picked up their walking sticks, they left the trees and returned to the road. Dana held Alice's hand tightly, and Simon walked ahead of the two of them, guiding them to the intersection, where they turned downhill, trading wet dirt for wet asphalt.

Alice was quiet, her cheeks red from crying or maybe from the cold. Dana glanced up at the clouds, which had grown darker. Simon's right:

it's going to rain soon, she thought. While the dirt road had been muddy at times, the water on the asphalt just pooled, leaving small puddles that they splashed through. They avoided the larger puddles, however, not wanting to let the cold water soak into their shoes.

Dana heard a low hum. She looked around to see what could be causing it, but it seemed to come from farther down the road, somewhere out of sight. Then she heard a bird call, up and to her left. And, looking, she found it: a small blue bird sitting alone in a large pine tree. She nudged Alice and pointed up at the lonely bird.

"We haven't heard that very much the last couple days," she told her.

Alice looked up at the bird and then nodded to Dana. But it didn't hold her attention for long, and she looked back down at the road almost immediately, gaze locked on her feet. Alice walked slowly, making Dana feel like she was dragging her along with each step. But the faster we go the sooner we'll get there, Dana thought, so she pulled Alice along, keeping her out of the deeper puddles.

The humming grew louder as they descended.

"What's that noise?" Dana finally asked Simon.

"The river."

"How close is it? I'm surprised we can hear it from here."

"With the storm, I'll bet it's pretty big right now," Simon told her. "Let's just hope it's not too big. This road turns soon to enter the canyon. We'll be walking by the river the rest of the way down the mountain."

Dana thought back to her drive here with Alice. She didn't remember the river, but they had been driving at night and she had been tired. She did remember a canyon, however. The steep drop-off to the side of the road had made her nervous, but she hadn't known then that a river lurked below out of sight. Could the river have washed out the road? she worried. What would we do then?

As they walked farther, the road bending through the forest, the hum became a roar, and then the road veered to the left into the canyon, a metal guardrail protecting unwary cars from plunging over its side. The rail was scuffed and dented, having served its purpose at least once. Dana didn't want to imagine what would have happened if it hadn't.

Then Dana caught her first glimpse of the river—swollen high, dark waters seeming to flow endlessly, white spray shooting up where it hit partially submerged rocks along the side, debris from upstream floating along the water's surface before sinking down, pulled by currents hidden beneath. Dana stopped walking and tightened her grip on Alice's hand, thinking of the terrible pull of the river and the threat it posed.

"Wow," Simon said, stopping to stare at the mass of moving water. "I thought it'd be big, but not this big."

"What about the road?" Dana asked.

The river churned only ten feet below them, its size and sound making it feel even closer.

"I guess we'll see," Simon said, peering down the road.

It started to drizzle.

"We better get moving," Simon told them. "Before the rain stops us."

They moved forward again, Dana in the middle, Alice's hand held tight in her own, Simon between the river and Dana.

"How much longer?" Alice asked.

"At least another day," Dana told her. "Unless we meet someone on the road."

But the road was empty, just wet pavement littered with rocks and dirt spilled from the hill to the left. The other side fell off steeply, nothing there but the swollen river.

The road curved following the river, each curve revealing more of the canyon, but still there was no sign of any cars. Dana had hoped they might see one. But maybe that hadn't been realistic given the late season.

"Do you think anyone will drive up here today?" she asked Simon.

"I don't know. I'm kind of worried that the road might be out farther down the mountain. I was hoping we'd run into someone. But if the road is out ... "

A tree lay in front of them, roots pulled from loose mud by its weight, now covering half of the road, forcing them to walk closer to the river. They returned to the opposite side of the road as soon as they could, the roar of the river seeming to be all around them.

Looking up at the hill, Dana noticed a small cave not far above the road. She pointed it out to Simon.

"Yeah, I saw a few of them on my hike up at the beginning of the summer," he said. "Some looked pretty deep, like they might go through to somewhere. I never checked though. You never know what might be inside, you know?"

But this cave looked small and not very deep, and soon it was far behind them. Then the drizzle turned into rain, and Simon pulled out their ponchos, which they threw on. But Dana could see that Alice needed a break, so they sat down off the side of the road and rested against the hill. Although a lone pine tree provided some cover, cold rain still dripped down the sides of their ponchos, and some dripped from Dana's hood onto her face. Then it began to pour, rain running down the side of the hill, forming a small stream beside them, then pooling into the shoulder of the road before spilling over and running across the pavement, pouring over the side and adding to the swell of the river. I'm so sick of the rain, Dana said to herself. I'd be happy to never see rain again.

Then they heard a noise above them, and turning around, they saw an avalanche of mud flowing down the hill. Simon jumped to his feet, pulling Dana, who grabbed Alice, and they all ran up the road a safe distance before looking back to watch the small landslide drift across the pavement, a large mass of mud pouring over the edge, rocks rolling into the river with large splashes, the tree that had covered them now leaning with the flow.

Rain fell all around them as Alice pointed at the hill above and yelled. "They did it! Just like at the cabin! They're trying to bury us!"

Dana grabbed Alice's arm, scared by the sudden outburst and the crazed look in her eyes. "Who, Alice?" she asked her. "Did you see someone?"

Alice shook her head, her eyes filling with tears. "No."

"Then what are you talking about?" Dana asked, facing Alice with her hands on both of Alice's arms. "Who did what?"

Simon, who had looked up at the hill after Alice yelled, now turned back to her. "Are you talking about your book, Alice?" he asked.

And Alice looked at him, hope in her face that someone might believe her. She nodded.

"That's not the way it works," Simon told her.

And, her brief hope gone, Alice covered her face with her hands. "You'll just say whatever Dana wants you to say!" she cried angrily, sinking down to her knees on the pavement in the middle of the rain.

Dana knelt beside her and put her arm around Alice's shoulder, adjusting the hood of Alice's poncho to keep the rain out of her face while she tried to calm Alice for the second time that day.

But Alice kept repeating that she didn't know what they wanted. She kept saying that she just wanted to go home.

Dana got Alice to her feet, telling her it would be okay, and walked her to the side of the road to sit beneath another tree, careful to avoid the pool of mud that was forming beneath it. Alice wiped tears from her face and stared down at the ground, Dana's arm around her and squeezing her shoulder.

Dana glanced up at the hill and looked for whatever had frightened Alice. But there was nothing there. Then she looked over at Simon, who had walked to the landslide and was testing it with his walking stick. He stepped up onto it, sinking a little into the soft soil but continuing forward. Suddenly he slipped and slid toward the water's edge, a rock hit by his foot rolling off the side into the river. Dana tensed, ready to yell; but Simon dug his walking stick deep into the earth and it held him in place, allowing him to stand and continue checking the slide before turning back. He didn't slip this time as he walked across the dirt toward them.

He stepped down off the slide and came back to talk to her, but Dana waved him off, needing more time for Alice. So Simon turned away and stood alone in the rain, the massive river flowing behind him as he looked up at the hill. Dana knew, however, that he would see no more than she had seen, which was nothing. There was nothing there. She patted Alice's back, telling her that they'd be home soon, that she'd see her dad soon, that everything would be okay.

Simon silently studied the hill, ignoring the rain running down his poncho. Could something really be up there, causing the slides? Dana wondered. No, stop it, she told herself. Stop being silly. That will only scare Alice more.

They sat for a while, Alice's tears slowing until, eventually, she raised her face. The rain, too, had lessened, no longer a downpour.

Dana took Alice's hand. "Are you ready to walk again?" she asked. "The faster we move, the sooner we'll be home."

Alice nodded and let Dana help her to her feet. Then they walked toward Simon, who led them to the edge of the landslide. Maybe a dozen feet long, the slide had left a wedge of dirt five feet deep that slanted into the river. They decided to walk down the middle of the slide because it wasn't as steep at that point and also wasn't too close to the edge. Dana glanced at the dark merciless waters of the river, currents waiting to drown any person trapped within their path. A branch stuck out as it floated along; then it turned down into the water, revealing the trunk it was attached to, the entire tree carried effortlessly by the powerful river. Dana shuddered, imagining again what it could do to a man. She forced herself to turn away.

"We'll steady ourselves with the walking sticks," Simon told them. He dug his in deep and stepped up onto the slide, sinking a few inches into the mud but not slipping. He pulled up the stick and dug it in again a few feet forward.

Dana followed, driving her walking stick into the mud and directing Alice to hold onto it. Then they both stepped up onto the slide. It felt unstable, and Dana glanced again at the river, only feet away from them. But they moved forward, Alice steadying herself between the two walking sticks, Simon's placed first, followed by Dana's, and then Simon's again, both walking sticks cold and slippery from the rain. The process worked, and they were near the end of the slide when Dana stumbled, her feet slipping in the mud. She fell to her knees as Alice panicked beside her. But Dana's fingers got a good grip on the carvings of her walking stick, and she pulled herself up. Then she told Alice, who was crying again, to move forward to the edge of the slide, where they stepped down, relieved, onto the pavement; and, safely there, Dana permitted herself to look again over at the river.

What if I hadn't been holding on so tightly? she thought. She shook her head and put her hand on Alice's shoulder again, trying to calm her down once more. Maybe we should have given her more time, Dana told herself, and they decided to rest again. The three of them moved to the side of the road and waited there, sitting on rocks, for the rain to stop. Dana's shoes and the bottom of her pants were coated in mud, as were Simon's, but Alice had escaped the worst of it, being lighter than the two of them and lucky enough not to slip.

Alice rested her head in her hands though she wasn't crying any longer, and Dana kept her arm around Alice's shoulder, wondering what she could do to help. Was it a mistake to hike down the mountain? We could have stayed in Simon's cabin, she reminded herself, if only I had trusted him more. We could be safe there, maybe even already found by the ranger and on our way home. Dana looked at the slide they had crossed and thought of how far they had hiked already. Well, we can't turn back now, she told herself.

When the rain stopped, they took off their ponchos, and Dana breathed easier. While her poncho kept out the rain, it seemed to keep out the air as well and made her feel stuffy while she wore it, almost trapped. Of course, that's better than getting soaked, she thought.

By then Alice was feeling better, and they decided to walk again, hoping to get farther before they stopped for lunch. Dana held tightly onto Alice's hand as they walked and puzzled over what she could do to help. Her backpack had become unsettled, the sleeping bag resting uncomfortably against one shoulder, but she ignored it right then, telling herself that she'd fix it at their next stop. Simon walked beside the two of them, looking out at the river, his interest reminding Dana of the carving he had worked into his bridge: "The river is always waiting." Surely, that means something to him, she thought. But what?

The dark waters didn't answer. They flowed onward, without remorse, destroying anything foolish enough to get in their way.

Then the three of them turned a corner and saw what they had hoped they wouldn't see: a washed out section of the road. The asphalt was cut in an abrupt half circle, the missing portion fallen and carried off by the river.

Simon walked forward to investigate, telling them to hold back.

Dana decided this would be a good time to adjust her backpack, so she let go of Alice's hand and knelt down on the wet pavement. She opened the pack and moved the sleeping bag around, trying to situate it in a way where it would stay in the center of her back. Then she stood and turned back to Alice, ready to hold her hand again—but Alice wasn't there. And, with the river beside her, Dana had a dark thought. She looked forward and saw Simon studying the fallen road; and there was Alice, still walking, staring at the river to her side as she headed straight for the drop-off, its jagged edge only steps away. Alice took another step forward.

"Simon! Stop her!"

He flipped around in time to see Alice's final step over the edge, and he grabbed her arm as she fell over the side, terror appearing on her face when she realized she was falling, the river waiting only feet below. But Simon pulled her back, twisting her around, and she fell onto her knees on the pavement. Then, looking up at Dana, who was already running toward her, Alice screamed, a finger pointing at the road behind them.

"It's walking like a man!"

Simon sprinted past Dana, who pulled Alice, face hidden in her hands, farther from the edge and hugged her tightly as Simon charged up the road, walking stick at the ready. But ready for what? Dana asked herself and turned to look. Walking like a man? What could it be? A grizzly bear? No, not in these mountains. But what could Simon do to a grizzly bear with just a walking stick? I wish I hadn't lost his hatchet.

She rested Alice's face on her shoulder and watched Simon, worried at what he might find. He ran to the corner and moved out of sight. Then he came back into view, walking now, a frustrated look on his face. He peered over the edge of the road before glancing back around the bend; then, kicking a rock into the water, he walked back, shaking his head.

"There's nothing there," he told Dana, the frustration clear in his voice as he stopped and stared down at the two of them.

"It went into the river," Alice told them.

Dana looked at the road's edge, imagining something sneaking along the side toward them.

"Could it have climbed down there?" she asked Simon.

"With the river like it is now?" He shook his head. "No way. Anything that did that would have drowned."

Alice pushed away from Dana.

"I'm not seeing things!"

Dana grabbed her arm. "It's okay, Alice, we don't think you're seeing things," she said, but a glance at Simon told her that he, for one, thought that Alice was.

"They want something!"

Alice broke free from Dana and sprang to her feet.

"What do they want?" Simon asked quietly.

Alice was almost weeping. "I don't know."

Dana stood and tried to calm her, but that only turned Alice's emotions into anger.

"They want something, Dana! I know they want something!"

She stormed away from them, skirting the drop-off too closely, Dana's breath catching as she ran after her, ready to spring if Alice fell; but Alice never slipped. She left the drop-off behind as she hurried down the road, Dana and Simon following behind.

Dana caught up to walk beside her, talking quietly in hopes of calming her, but Alice only grunted and shook her head. She was acting so strange, as if it wasn't even her, and Dana gave up trying to reach her, realizing that whatever was going on with her would just have to play itself out. But she kept close to her, matching her brisk pace, hoping that the walking would wear her down.

At first, Dana was filled with concern at what might be happening with Alice; but, as the minutes passed with no change in Alice's mood, Dana's patience grew thin and her concern was replaced by annoyance.

They walked like that for half an hour before, finally, Alice began to slow.

Simon, walking behind them, noticed the change. "We should stop and rest," he said. "We need some lunch."

Alice ignored him.

"Come on, Alice," he said, trying a different tone. "Let's stop and have some lunch. Aren't you hungry?"

She shook her head.

Then Simon stopped and leaned over his walking stick as he called to her: "Dana's tired, Alice. How about you let her rest?"

And she glanced at Dana, who really was starting to feel tired.

"Fine," Alice said. She stopped and walked back to Simon, but then she turned her back once she reached him, folding her arms and looking out at the river.

Dana mouthed a silent thank you to Simon, and they all walked to the side of the road and found rocks to sit on, Alice purposefully sitting a dozen feet away. She refused to take the offered food, but she did take the water, gulping it down quickly before throwing the empty bottle onto the ground beside her like an angry toddler. Dana shook her head. This is getting ridiculous, she thought. At least Simon was able to get through to her because I'm about to wring her neck.

Simon pulled a chocolate bar out of his backpack.

"I only had one left," he said quietly. "Here, give it to Alice. Maybe it'll cheer her up."

"No, I'm done with her for now," Dana said. "You go ahead."

"Um, that'd be pretty weird."

"Oh," Dana said, realizing that it would.

She took a deep breath. Getting upset doesn't help, she reminded herself. Alice is just having a hard time. And she took the candy bar and walked over to Alice. She offered it to her, but Alice refused, saying she wasn't hungry.

Dana picked up the empty water bottle. "Do you want to talk?" she asked.

"No," Alice said, her voice tired rather than angry.

"Want some alone time?"

Alice nodded, and Dana returned to Simon, putting away the water bottle and candy bar before sitting down and glancing back at Alice, who was looking down the road toward home. She hasn't read her book since this morning, Dana realized, not since she threw it down on the ground. But is that a good thing or a bad thing? Maybe bad, since she seems worse today. Of course, there had been the slide, and then she had almost fallen into the river . . .

And remembering what Alice had gone through made Dana feel petty for being upset with her. But can't I be stressed too? Dana thought. Then she answered herself: No. I'm the adult. I'm supposed to know better.

But it wasn't just Alice's attitude or even her stubbornness that had upset Dana. This whole jumping at shadows thing has got to stop, she thought. I might have believed that she'd seen an animal before, but now? No. What could it be, a man? But why would he hide from us?

Alice had pulled something out of her pocket, small and blue, like a piece of glass. Part of a wind chime? Dana wondered. She remembered how excited Alice had been each time they hung one of them up on the tree above the cabin. Where had that Alice gone? Dana asked herself. How can I get her back?

We just need to get her home and let her unwind, she decided. But in the meantime I'll keep her as calm as I can. As much as possible, anyways, she thought, the angry churn of the river ever present.

They returned to the road after lunch, and Dana walked the rest of the afternoon next to Alice, who was moving at a normal pace again. Dana talked to Alice about home and about the things they'd do once they got there. Dana talked about Alice's dad, telling Alice how she thought the election was going, exaggerating Senator Miller's strengths along with the weaknesses of his opponent. Dana even talked about Alice's mother, telling Alice she was sure her mother would be excited to see her. But saying that made Dana feel guilty—because she knew as she said it that it was almost certainly a lie.

And the whole time, Alice never responded beyond a simple yes or no, sometimes a grunt. However, she seemed more reasonable than she had before, more herself; and Dana eventually braved the topic of what Alice had seen, being careful not to make it sound like she didn't believe her but making it clear that Alice wasn't alone, that Dana was there with her and Simon was there to protect them as well.

The delays that day had cost them time, and Dana knew they would not make it off the mountain before dark. It had better be just one more day though, she told herself. And nothing else better happen, because otherwise I think Alice might crack.

Simon was quiet the whole afternoon, leaving Dana to reason with Alice. He walked a little behind, between them and the edge, his eyes frequently on the river, watching its flow, feeling its pull, never straying too close.

Chapter Nine

WHEN IT WAS ALMOST EVENING, THEY CAME TO A PART of the road where the shoulder lay beneath a stone overhang, leaving the area free of water and mud. They decided to camp there that night. Wood was scarce, and Dana doubted that Simon would even attempt to make a fire. Already she was dreading the cold that would come with the darkness. It had warmed during the day, but the temperature was dropping and she thought there might be frost again in the morning. She wondered if being by the river would make the temperature colder or not. We could be in a cabin right now, she reminded herself, if only I hadn't misjudged Simon.

Dana helped Simon set up the tent. But they didn't joke as they had before, mindful of Alice, who was sitting by herself and staring at the rock wall. Dana wasn't sure how to deal with her. While Alice's mood had improved that afternoon, she still seemed unreachable, like there was a shell around her that couldn't be pierced. Dana knew now that Alice was probably just seeing things, but Dana still glanced nervously up the road at times, wondering if something might really be out there. Simon's presence, however, calmed her, although she had had little chance to speak with him all day. Thinking of their conversation the night before—and where they had left it—she was excited to talk to him again once they were alone.

In the meantime, though, Dana needed to take care of Alice. She tried to speak with her as they ate their dinner, but Alice continued with her non-responses, just staring at the rock wall or out at the river, not even reading her book, a fact that made Dana nervous. Dana had been worried about Alice's excessive reading, but her not reading at all made Dana feel like Alice might be giving up—and that seemed worse.

A hundred yards back from their camp, they had passed a stream, which flowed down the hill into a drainage pipe beneath the road and dumped into the river. Wanting to clean up her clothes and prepare for bed, Dana went there with Alice and tried to scrape off some of the mud she had gotten on her pants and shoes. The water was frigid, almost freezing, and the air was not much warmer, but she scraped at the mud and got most of it off. They had brought the lantern with them; however, as the day's light faded, the lantern's pale glow couldn't push the darkness back very far, and suddenly Dana found Alice's stalker more realistic, making her constantly look over her shoulder and wish Simon wasn't so far away. Alice, however, didn't glance at the shadows or say much at all besides telling Dana that she was tired. *She probably is*, Dana thought. *Maybe she'll sleep it off and wake up normal. More normal, at least.*

After returning to their camp, Dana spread out the sleeping bag inside the tent, feeling the ground, cold and hard, through the tent's fabric. She laid the sleeping bag perpendicular to the door, planning to sleep between the door and Alice to make sure Alice couldn't get out of the tent by herself. *If she sleepwalks here, she'll end up in the river*, Dana thought, not expecting to sleep much that night given the cold, the hard ground, and the fear of Alice wandering off so close to the river.

Simon had laid his sleeping bag directly in front of the tent flap, one more precaution against Alice's sleepwalking. This gave Dana the passing thought—what if Alice hasn't just been seeing things? Simon will be out there, all alone . . . But she shook the thought away, lying on top of the sleeping bag while Alice fell asleep inside of it. *I hope she does sleep it off*, Dana thought. *I hope we get off the mountain tomorrow, too.*

Then, with Alice asleep, Dana crept out of the tent and found Simon sitting close by against the rock wall. She sat down beside him and together they looked out at the river, unable to see it but knowing where it lay by its sound. Simon handed her the candy bar from earlier.

"Since Alice didn't want it," he said.

Dana split it and gave half back to him.

After days of MREs and granola bars, the candy bar tasted fantastic. Dana had forgotten how good chocolate could be. Of course, we could be eating normal food right now, she reminded herself, if I hadn't decided to walk down the mountain, if I had chosen to stay at Simon's cabin instead.

The night was dark, the lantern's light not reaching very far, and the noise of the river was overwhelming. An eerie feeling—hearing the roar but being unable to see what caused it. Dana imagined the river rising unseen, higher and higher, reaching up onto the road, grasping Alice, sweeping her away. No, it couldn't rise that fast, could it? Dana asked herself. The darkness seemed to watch her, making her wonder again if Alice might actually be seeing something real.

"You don't think there is anything really following Alice, do you?" Dana asked.

"No. I think she's just seeing things."

Dana nodded and looked down at her feet. "It was stupid to have Alice hike down the mountain like this," she said. "I think it's just making it worse."

"I don't know what choice you had. She seemed pretty determined."

"Well, you sure didn't fight much about it."

Simon glanced at Dana and then looked back at the hidden river.

"Sorry, but I couldn't just leave things how they were after what I had said the night before. I wanted a chance to help you understand."

And hearing Simon's reason, Dana admitted to herself that she didn't really regret hiking down the mountain with him. It was different now between them. That night she had been so hurt, so angry, so afraid. But now she felt as if she was starting to understand him. And he wanted to be more than just friends—she understood that, too. Then she looked back up the road toward where Alice had last seen her stalker, wondering about the possibility. But Simon is right, she thought. Alice is just seeing things. What else could it be?

Simon asked to see her walking stick again, and Dana handed it to him. Getting his knife out, he turned the stick over to the uncarved portion and slowly made the first cut. Dana watched him, wondering if she could trust him as more than just a friend. People always talked about being gay or being straight. But what about Simon? She remembered what he had said about labels like that, and she knew he was right. *What we choose to do is more important than what attractions we feel,* she told herself, *because if that isn't true, then what's the point of being human?*

But how long has he been fighting it? she wondered, wanting more than anything to know if he could get rid of it. And, knowing what she wanted to talk about, she tried to think of the right way to start the conversation without upsetting him as she had the night before. But she couldn't think of a perfect way, giving her no better option than to take a deep breath and just jump right in.

"So, I don't think you ever did answer my question last night," Dana said.

"Which one?"

"When I asked you how long it's been since you . . . knew," she said, careful to avoid using the label that others might call him.

He doesn't have to be a monster, she reminded herself. *His attraction doesn't have to become action. He can still choose. But is that enough for me?*

Simon set down his knife and laid the walking stick across his lap, running his finger along the carvings.

"It's been a while," he said. "I guess I was fifteen or so."

"What happened?" Dana asked.

But Simon shook his head and picked up the knife as if ready to carve some more.

"Let's talk about something else," he said. "How about what Alice thinks is following her?"

"Why don't you want to talk about it?" Dana asked him, unwilling to let the topic go.

Simon paused before glancing at her.

"It wasn't exactly my finest hour," he said. "I like to think of myself as an honorable man, but at that time . . . well, at that time I wasn't."

"But you said you never hurt anyone, so it can't be that bad. Besides, you were just a teenager. Lots of teenage boys make mistakes."

"Not like this."

"Simon," Dana said to him, "please tell me."

"Why do you want to know so badly?"

"Because I want to understand you better."

He sighed and laid the knife back down.

"Okay, fine. Just remember that I've learned better since, okay?"

"I know," Dana told him.

"Well, like I said, I was fifteen or so, and my mom and I were living with my aunt and uncle," Simon began.

"Was it always like that?" Dana asked. "Just you and your mom? Your dad wasn't around?"

"Yeah, just me and my mom. My dad died before I was born."

"Sorry," Dana told him, although she wondered if it would have been easier for her to have never known her own father. Maybe I'd have less baggage that way, she thought.

Simon shrugged. "It's okay. I never knew him. But, yeah, just me and my mom. Anyway, that year money was tight, and we were living with my mom's sister and brother-in-law, my uncle."

"So, what happened?"

Simon was looking down at the carvings again.

"I think you can probably kind of guess, given that I avoid computers now."

Dana knew it had something to do with that, but she wanted to understand exactly what.

"Well," he continued, "I was alone most afternoons since everyone worked, so I had the house to myself and would usually pass the time playing computer games on my uncle's computer. He had lots of fun games and didn't care how much I played them while he was gone. But he'd lock himself in his office most nights, so afternoons were the only chance I had to play.

"What's wrong?" Simon asked, stopping his story and turning to Dana, who had picked up the lantern and was shining it up the road. She had heard something—or at least thought she had—but holding the light high, she saw nothing there. The only noise was the constant flow of the river. She felt silly to be giving in to childish fears.

"Sorry," she said, setting the lantern down. "I guess Alice must have creeped me out. Anyways, you were alone? So, what happened?"

Simon was looking up the road and did not answer for a moment, making Dana nervous that he might use her interruption as an excuse to change the subject, but then he turned back and continued.

"Yeah, well, one day the game I wanted to play wouldn't start. I tried the usual tricks: rebooting the computer—that kind of thing. But nothing worked."

Simon picked up the knife again and made a small cut to the walking stick before stopping to speak.

"Anyway, I decided to peek around in the computer's files to see if I could figure out what was wrong. Not that I knew what I was doing, but the game was fun and I wanted to fix it."

He paused, adding to the cut he had just started.

"I never did find what was wrong with the game, even after searching for a while—but I found something else."

And he stopped then to look out over the river.

"They were hidden," he told her, "but they weren't hidden well enough."

Dana felt the night's chill as he gave voice to the idea. She had known he must have done something like this given his hesitance to use computers, but hearing it—and guessing that worse was to come—she felt uncomfortable sitting so close to him. However, she held herself in place, refusing to scoot away, although she couldn't help but shift her shoulder a little, needing more space between them.

Attraction is what you are, Dana. It is all that you are. It is all that anyone is. It is useless to deny it. You cannot resist it.

But what about Simon? she responded. But what about Simon? He didn't have to be a monster, she reminded herself, although she doubted now that things could ever work out between the two of them. Because how could I overlook something like this? she thought. When I know that he's looked at those things?

Simon set the knife and walking stick aside and picked up a handful of rocks from the ground.

"I wasn't naive," he continued, throwing one of the rocks into the river. "I knew what I had found, and I knew it was wrong."

He threw another rock into the river.

"But, the thing is, I was at my aunt and uncle's house, you know? I mean, that kind of stuff wasn't supposed to be there. Does that make sense? I guess I was just shocked. It wasn't supposed to be there."

Shuffling the rocks around in his hand, he told her: "I turned the computer off and left the room right after I saw them. Then, sitting there in the living room, everything looking as it should, I thought that maybe I had just imagined it, you know? Maybe I had been mistaken. Maybe what I thought I had seen hadn't really been there."

He chose another rock and threw it hard into the river.

"But I knew better," he said.

Dana was glad it bothered him to tell the story. Wouldn't it be worse if he didn't feel guilty about it? she said to herself.

Then she asked: "Did you tell anyone?"

"No," he said, throwing the rest of the rocks into the darkness. "I should have. But, no, I didn't."

Simon picked up the knife and walking stick again. He spun the stick back to where he had last cut and set the knife into position, but then he spoke instead.

"I guess I was worried about getting into trouble. Like it would be my fault somehow. Like it would have been me that ruined their home by making what I saw real or something. Or maybe I was just scared I wouldn't get to play computer games anymore."

He shook his head. "Stupid, I know. But I didn't tell anyone. That first night, I just kind of pretended I hadn't seen anything."

But how did it get on the computer in the first place? Dana wondered.

Simon spun the walking stick a few times in his hand, as if looking for something to do. Dana could sense he was hesitating.

"So, what happened next?"

And then Simon scooted a little bit away from her, setting the walking stick down between them before folding up his knife and laying it down as well. Dana prepared herself for his story to get worse.

Simon looked at the ground as he spoke.

"This sounds horrible, knowing what it was—but I was curious, really curious. I had never seen something like that before. Heard about it, yeah, who hasn't? But actually seen it? No, of course not. And the computer had a folder full of it."

Then he glanced up at her, his eyes almost pleading.

"It's like this: I knew it was wrong, but part of me wanted to know *what* was wrong. Does that make any sense? I guess it was just stupid. Actually, I know it was just stupid. But still, I thought about it the entire time at school the next day, wondering what else was on there. Was it all the same? Was there something worse?"

He turned away from her, looking out at the unseen river.

"Then I was home again, and I was alone again, and I was curious—really, really curious. So I looked, pulling everything up, one after another. I looked at it all."

Dana wished that he hadn't.

"It's funny," Simon said, "the things you remember and the things you forget." His voice grew softer. "I still remember the feeling I felt once I was done—like the whole world had grown a little dimmer. That probably doesn't make sense. But everything seemed just a little less bright, a little less clear. Later, I didn't notice it anymore, but that first time, I noticed."

He probably got desensitized to it later, Dana thought. He must have grown used to how horrible it made him feel.

Simon leaned down, looked at the ground, and picked up a rock, which he held in his hand.

"But I kept looking at them every afternoon," he said. "And, over time, curiosity turned to desire and desire turned to excitement and excitement grew and grew until I couldn't hold back anymore—so I didn't."

He threw the rock into the river with a quick stroke of his hand.

Dana heard the splash over the noise of the river and felt disappointed at the thought of him doing that to himself. She knew that most men did it, maybe almost all—though she hoped not. But Simon was supposed to be different; and men doing that to themselves had always seemed so . . . pathetic, a judgment that didn't match what she thought of Simon.

"I told myself it would help," Simon continued, "but it only made it worse. And I couldn't stop. I tried but I couldn't, and I hated myself for it. I needed help but didn't dare tell anyone. I was alone. I couldn't stop."

Dana felt sympathy for his hopelessness. But he must have stopped somehow? she thought.

"So, what did you do?" she asked.

"Well, new files had been showing up on the computer every few days. And, well, I finally admitted to myself where everything was coming from."

"Your uncle?"

"Right."

"Wow."

"Yeah, and that's when it finally sank in," he said. "Even with how dim things had become for me. A man I knew, my own uncle, involved in that stuff—carrying that kind of secret, hiding it from everyone, even his wife. I mean, was that what I wanted my life to be like? And who knew what else he was doing, right? Which meant, who knew what I would be doing?—if I didn't stop."

Disgusted at Simon's uncle, Dana was glad that Simon wanted to be different from him.

"But I couldn't stop, not by myself. Trust me, I had tried—lots of times. Each night I'd promise myself I'd never do it again, but then each afternoon I'd break my promise. Every time. Day after day."

Such weakness didn't match Simon at all. Dana hated to even think of him like that. But somehow he had stopped, she reminded herself.

"So, what did it?" she asked. "Were you caught?"

"No. I wasn't caught," he said.

Then he paused, seeming to be searching for the right words, and the look in his eyes gave Dana a feeling for what was coming, the same look he got every time he strayed close to the subject they had never really spoken about.

"Some things don't click when you first learn them, do you know what I mean? You hear about them, you're taught them when you're little, but they just don't seem real until one day—they do. Anyway, I remembered a way that I could ask for help without anyone else knowing. Just me and . . ."

Dana nodded, catching his meaning.

"So I did it, every day—asked for help, asked to have the desire taken away. I didn't want to *want* to look anymore, so I asked to have it just gone. Then, each afternoon, I'd be back at the computer again. No change."

How could it not help? Dana wondered. It always helped in the stories—a miracle or whatever. And if it didn't help, then why did he still do it so often? she asked herself, remembering that she'd seen him more than once.

"So, it didn't help?" she asked.

"It wasn't working, no. But I kept trying because—what else could I do? Eventually, though, I gave up on asking for my attraction to disappear. I finally admitted that it was never going to go away. Instead, I just asked for the strength to deal with it—to resist it—and the ability to avoid it. And that's when something happened."

Is that what makes the difference? Dana wondered. Asking for help to deal with life as it is instead of asking for life itself to change?

"I'd already looked that day. I was done and just sitting there in front of the screen, pathetic, when the thought occurred to me that I should just delete them. Such a simple thing—and I did it. Two clicks of the computer's mouse and they were all gone, just like that."

Except, it hadn't only been Simon that was looking, Dana thought.

"But what about . . . "

"Yeah," Simon said. "I was so excited that I'd forgotten about him, and everything was already deleted by the time I remembered. And what would he do when he found out? He'd know then that I knew. And what then? If he was willing to look at things like that, what would he be capable of doing?"

But Simon had looked at them as well, Dana reminded herself. So, what is *he* capable of doing?

"But it was too late," he said. "They were already gone. I panicked and decided to hide what I had done by destroying everything. I just kept deleting things: files, folders, whatever—anything the computer would let me delete. Then eventually the computer just hung, so I turned if off."

Dana worried about his uncle's reaction. Surely he hadn't done anything violent to Simon, had he?

"My uncle was furious," Simon continued. "He cursed at me, demanding that I explain what I had done. But I wouldn't. I mean, what could I say? So, I was banned from the computer and grounded to my room. Still, even with all that, I was happy—because it was gone. And I promised myself, I mean, really promised myself this time that I wouldn't look again. *Ever* again."

Then Simon paused, making Dana feel like something was missing.

"So, that was it?" she asked.

He shook his head. "If I were a better man, maybe. But even then, even after everything, even after that promise I had made, even then—I didn't last through the next day."

Dana was surprised. He hadn't been able to make it just one day? That didn't seem like him. Had she misjudged him? No, there must be more, she told herself.

"Because the next afternoon when I was alone, I realized that my uncle had probably fixed his computer the night before—he had been up all night working on it—which meant that there was probably something new to see."

"And your promise?" Dana asked, as if she were there with him at the time and trying to convince him to do the right thing.

"It didn't matter," Simon said. "Just one day later and it didn't matter. See, I wanted to look—more than I ever had before—and wasn't that proof that I wasn't ready to stop looking? Didn't the fact that I wanted to look so badly mean that I needed to look, maybe just one more time?"

But that made no sense at all, Dana thought. How could Simon have fallen for that? Then she remembered the example he had made of the hill being torn down by the rain. Is that what he meant? she wondered. The little rationalizations that tear down our resolutions? It reminded her of what she had imagined the day before: Simon being overwhelmed, pulled down by ill-seeking hands. And the image gave her a creepy feeling, as if something were watching them. But she fought the urge to pick up the lantern and look, not wanting to give in to the creeps just because Alice was freaking her out. It's just the darkness playing tricks on me, she told herself, determined to ignore it.

"And those thoughts kept bouncing around in my head," Simon said, "until they started to make sense to me. I told myself that I needed more motivation if I really wanted to quit. And what would give me more motivation than shame? And what would give me more shame than to look again, to look that very day after all I went through the day before?"

Dana groaned inside of herself at Simon's lame reasoning. It was hard to imagine him being that weak and easily misled. He's so strong today, she thought. What changed him? What made him strong?

"So, I was going to look," he told her. "I walked to my uncle's office, and I was ready to go in, turn on the computer, and look. My decision was made. My promise already broken. The door, however, was locked."

Dana wanted to cheer.

"Funny, isn't it?" Simon told her. "All that time asking for help, and what was my response? A locked door."

He should give himself more credit, Dana said to herself. It wasn't only the locked door.

"But you deleted the files, Simon. That was you. You chose to do it."

"Sure, once," he said. "I was strong for *one* day. And the next?"

He glanced down at the walking stick, as if he were thinking about picking it up again but decided against it.

"Still, don't get me wrong," he said. "I'm grateful that the door was locked. Even at the time I was grateful. But I also felt pathetic because it wasn't me that kept my promise that day—it was a locked door."

He's being too hard on himself, Dana thought. The door was locked then, yes, but that was years ago, and he's still resisting today. That's him, not some locked door. But how does he do it? she wondered. First, though, she wanted to hear the end of the story.

"So, what happened to your uncle?" she asked.

"He got arrested a couple weeks later," Simon told her. "The police just showed up one day, confiscated his computer, and arrested him. He ended up spending two years in jail. My aunt divorced him right before his release. I don't know what happened to him after that."

Good, Dana thought, happy that his uncle got what was coming to him. Was that what had made Simon strong?

"And seeing that helped you never do it again?" she asked.

"A little, yeah. I mean, it was a pretty strong warning. But the want was still there, strong as ever. I kept asking for help in my own way, but I knew I needed something more. I just wasn't sure where to find it."

"What about your mother?"

"No. That just wasn't an option for me. But, luckily, she was really worried that something might have happened between my uncle and me. I mean, he had been looking at the stuff so she thought . . . you know. Anyway, I tried to convince her that nothing had happened, but she thought that maybe I was too embarrassed to talk to her about it. So, she sent me to talk to a local leader at our church."

Dana thought again of the Double Waterfall, but she quickly turned her attention back to what he was saying.

"When I spoke with him," Simon said, "it started out pretty much how my conversations with my mom had gone: the same questions, the same answers. Except, he dug more, somehow sensing that something was there; and, reaching deeper, he found it. I broke down, telling him everything: what I'd been looking at, what I'd done while looking, what I still wanted to do. I told him that I didn't know how to stop, that I wasn't sure if I could stop, not forever. I confessed that I thought I might be a monster."

Culture had burned the idea into Dana that attraction made people who they were, that men who liked women were straight, that men who liked men were gay. But what about Simon? Didn't that make him a monster? No, she reminded herself, he's not a monster. Attraction is something that you feel, not something that you are, she thought, repeating Simon's words from the day before.

"He listened to everything without saying a word," Simon told her. "And when I was done I wasn't sure what would happen next. Would he call the police? It wasn't my computer. I hadn't downloaded it. But I had known about it and I had looked at it. Or would he throw me out of his office? Maybe he'd kick me out of the church. Maybe he'd tell my mom that I was a monster and she should disown me. Any of those seemed likely at the time. Any of them would have been deserved, I thought. But that's not what he did. He just waited, sitting there looking at me until

I finally met his eyes, and then he leaned forward across his desk and he said to me: 'Simon, you know who it is that wants you to believe that you're only a monster. You know who it is that wants you to just give up. Now, don't you fall for that nonsense—you're smarter than that, you're better than that. Always remember this: What you want is not who you are. You are who you choose to be.'"

Dana repeated the words to herself: "What you want is not who you are. You are who you choose to be." The phrase confused her at first. Wouldn't Simon have to want something before he would choose it? But, after thinking about it, she realized that the second sentence wasn't talking about shallow physical wants like the first sentence. It was talking about something deeper.

"I didn't believe that at first," Simon said, "but I kept meeting with him and talking about it. He counseled me for years; without that help I don't know if I would be here today. But thanks to him, I think I've learned better. He was the one who helped me learn it."

Dana wondered again if Simon was giving himself enough credit. But he had been so weak back then, she thought. Whatever it was that had done it, he was stronger now.

"I think just having someone know helped a lot," he told her. "I mean, things like this—keeping them a secret lets them eat away at you. It's like they trick you, seeming too big to fight one minute and then seeming too small to bother with the next, the lies contradicting each other but working together to keep you stuck in the same place: unable or unwilling to resist."

This reminded Dana of how darkness could play tricks on you, like her current nervousness about Alice's stalker. During the day, Dana knew it was just Alice's imagination, but at night it suddenly seemed possible. Light really does help us see things as they really are, she thought.

"But it wasn't only that," Simon continued. "He also helped me understand what things I should and shouldn't do if I wanted to keep myself from falling—staying away from computers, that sort of thing. And that's really what did it. I had the help I needed and I finally started to believe that I really could be who I chose to be. Because, so what if I had this desire—what did that matter? Why should I let *that* dictate my life? Didn't I have my agency? Didn't I have the ability to choose? And couldn't I choose to resist?"

Dana thought again about the words Simon had been told: "What you want is not who you are. You are who you choose to be." The saying really does fit him, she thought. After all, why should his attraction define him? If his core is strong, and he has the help he needs to keep it strong, then can't he ignore his unwanted wants and live the life that he—not his attraction—wants himself to live? She wanted to believe it was true, but what she wanted even more was to know if he could get rid of it and be normal. Yes, he can choose to be a good man, she said to herself, but that doesn't mean I'd feel comfortable being with him like he is now. Still, Simon had obviously gotten the exact help he had needed at that time of his life. Dana was grateful for that.

"Are you still close?" she asked.

Simon paused. "We were—he died last year."

That must have been like losing a father, Dana thought, putting her fingertips on his arm. "I'm sorry, Simon," she told him, realizing that it wasn't only a father he had lost. Simon needed someone to know, and he had lost that. But then she realized—now I'm the one who knows.

Simon nodded, gesturing with his head back up the road. "The cabin I've been staying in was actually his. I stayed there a lot over the years with him and his sons. He could tell it helped me to get away from everything for a while. I guess that's why he left me the cabin when he died. This summer is the first time I've been back since he passed away."

Dana considered the difference those two men had made in Simon's life: his uncle, who unknowingly introduced Simon to the desire he now had to fight every day; and this other man, who helped Simon overcome it. But what a scumbag his uncle was, she thought, and then she wondered—what if Simon had never been given a chance to look? Would he not have his attraction then? Or was he born the way he is? People always said that gays were born that way. But what about Simon?

"So, what if you had never lived with your uncle?" Dana asked. "Would you not be dealing with this, or do you think it's always been there?"

Simon shrugged and picked up the knife and walking stick, starting to cut along the bottom again.

"I don't know. I can't remember it being a problem before, but maybe I was just too young to notice. Either way though—does it matter? It's here. I deal with it. Who cares where it came from?"

Dana admitted to herself that it really didn't matter, but she still wanted to know if it was something within him that would have to be ripped out or if it was something outside of him like a slime that he could just scrape off.

"I'm just wondering," she said. "You know how people talk about being born one way or another."

"Ah, that. Well, that's just politics is all. I mean, if you want to hijack the civil rights bandwagon, then you have to pretend that sexuality is as permanent as skin color, right?"

He spun the walking stick a little, carving at a different point from the tree than he had carved the night before.

"But that's just nonsense," he said. "I mean, we're a whole lot more flexible than most are willing to admit—there's nothing permanent about that. Sure, maybe some are more susceptible to one thing or another; but if you pay attention to what's going on around you, then I think it's pretty obvious that society plays a large role in what attractions we end up with."

One more way that Simon ignores the conventional wisdom, Dana thought. Of course, what would the conventional wisdom say about a man like him? Given how little it has to offer him, why should he follow it? Shouldn't I want him to keep doing what he's doing, believing what he's believing, and ignoring everybody else?

"You know, though, it's not just politics that makes the 'born this way' story so attractive," he said. "It's also fear."

"Why fear?" she asked.

"Because possibility is scary. Think about it. What straight guy wants to admit he gets a weird feeling around some men? *Of course* he doesn't want to face that or what it might mean. He'd rather just shrug it off, remind himself he was born straight, and forget about it. And it goes the other way, too."

Simon continued to cut, turning the stick as he did so, the carving wrapping around the base.

"It just feels safer, you know?" he said. "Look at it like this: if everyone like me were born this way, and you aren't like me today—then you wouldn't have to worry that you might be like me tomorrow. See? It's more comfortable if we arrive premolded instead of having to worry about changing for the worse later in life."

"Besides," Simon told her. "What mother wants to deal with the fear that every person—every single person—could become a danger to her kids? That's too scary to handle. It's easier to group everyone as either good people or bad people, all determined at birth. It's a lie, but it's a comfortable lie."

Dana looked over at the tent. Could anyone really become a danger to Alice? she asked herself. Well, why couldn't they? she answered. The possibility scared her.

"Still, the whole 'born this way' story is pretty weird if you think about it," Simon said. "It's like people imagine there's a giant toggle switch inside of our heads, with one side marked 'gay' and one side marked 'straight.' And I guess the switch is supposed to be flipped one way or the other right at birth.

"But come on," he said. "That can't really be the way things work, because it simply wouldn't make any sense, not when you take in the whole picture. I mean, what about the people who bounce back and forth? Is their switch flipping from one setting to the other? And what about me? How do I even fit into that picture? Is my switch just defective? And don't think there are only three possibilities either. The rabbit hole goes far, far deeper."

His analogy excited Dana because he had hinted at change: people flipping back and forth. But what about Simon? she asked herself. Does that mean he could change? Is his attraction just a dark filth that could be scraped off, leaving him normal? But, worried about offending him, she didn't want to ask directly. Instead, she decided to stick with the topic of same-sex attraction, knowing that whatever he said about that attraction would apply to his attraction as well.

"So, you say people bounce back and forth," she said. "Does that mean they can change?"

Simon looked up from his carving. "Well, you know people who once said they were straight and later said they were gay, don't you?"

Dana could think of lots of examples. It was becoming more and more common every day, and the media loved to make it headline news whenever it happened. But she also remembered the explanation that went along with it.

"Sure," she said, "but that just means they were always gay and were hiding it before, right?"

Simon smiled as if he knew an inside joke. Then he set down the walking stick and knife again and turned toward Dana.

"Okay, and the reverse? People who once claimed to be gay but later decided they were straight?"

Again, Dana could think of examples, but she knew the explanation for that change as well.

"Sure, but I thought that meant they were never really gay," she said. "Either that or they're actually bisexual. So that's not really bouncing back and forth, right?"

Simon laughed. "In other words, we prove that no one can change their sexual orientation by disqualifying all of those who have?"

Dana thought about it and then laughed as well, realizing he was right: the conclusion that people can't change is predecided; any evidence to the contrary is ignored using one excuse or another.

Simon went on. "I mean, we've got these crazy rules about sexual orientation and change, but if you dig into them, they really make no sense. Look at it like this: so someone changes from straight to gay. That's supposed to mean they were always gay, right?"

"So people say," Dana told him.

"Yeah, so the *rules* say. And if they change from gay to straight, then they were always bisexual?"

"I guess, according to the rules, like you said."

"Okay, fine. So a guy tells you that he's straight. Now, what is he?"

Dana stared at Simon, unsure if she had heard him correctly. "Is this a trick question?" she asked.

"No. I'm just making a point. He told you that he's straight. So what is he?"

"Straight, I guess. That's what he said he is."

"Okay, and ten years, one wife, three kids later, he tells you that he's gay. So, now, what is he?"

"Whatever he said he is. Gay, I guess."

"Well, did he change?"

"He'd probably say he'd been gay all along."

"The entire time?"

"Yes."

"Even when he told you he was straight? Even then—he was actually gay?"

Dana paused before answering. "I guess so," she said, but then she thought about it more. What else would someone say in that situation? she asked herself. "But he might say he found himself later in life or something like that," she told Simon.

"Okay, but obviously *something* changed, didn't it? Maybe the *rules* won't let it be his sexuality, but come on, he's been calling himself straight for years, he's married a wife, he's had kids, he's done all of that— for years."

"He'd probably say it was all just a lie."

"Okay, but *when* did it become a lie? Was it a lie when he told us he was straight? What if he thought he was telling the truth at the time? What about when he fell in love with his wife and married her? Was it a lie then? Was their sex a lie? Were their children? Or did it not become a lie until the day he decided he was gay? Was it at that moment—that exact minute when he made the decision—that everything in his past switched from truth to a lie?"

"I don't know," Dana said. "He'd probably claim he knew he was lying the whole time or something."

"Maybe, but what are we, mind-readers? I mean, what if he had died before he decided he was gay? Before he *found himself* or whatever—what if he had died the day before he did that? Then would his past have been a lie or would it have been the truth? And, either way, how would we ever know?"

Surprised by Simon's reasoning, Dana wasn't sure what to say. "I don't know," she told him.

"Exactly," Simon said. "No one knows. That's exactly what I'm saying. We don't know because we can't know—the *rules* won't let us. We're bullied into believing this nonsense—these *rules*—and they don't even work. Instead, they leave us forever unsure what someone really is—gay or straight—because it doesn't matter what someone tells us today; if they say something different tomorrow, then the *rules* turn today's truth into yesterday's lie."

Simon's words confused Dana. What he said made some sense, but she was unsure because she hadn't thought of it before. It had always been easier to just go with the flow, not thinking too deeply about it.

"But couldn't we just take their word for it?" she asked Simon.

"Why should we?" he said. "Why should we waste our time believing what people tell us today when what they say tomorrow is what really matters? I mean, according to these pointless rules, I guess no one is actually straight—no matter what they say today. So, as far as I'm concerned, everyone is just potentially gay."

Dana laughed. That's one way to put it, she thought.

"Okay, potentially gay, huh? How about *maybe-gay* instead?" she told him. "That sounds better. It rhymes!"

"I like it," Simon said. "Now, remember, whenever someone claims to be straight, what they're really saying is they're *maybe-gay*."

Dana laughed again, louder this time. And what about the opposite direction? she said to herself. If a gay becomes straight, then don't we often claim they were always bisexual? So, that means we should call them, what, *could-be-bi*? She covered her mouth, feeling guilty about laughing at something so taboo. Then she asked herself—why shouldn't I laugh about these silly rules? Simon is right: they really don't make much sense. But, if no one is actually straight, she thought, then wouldn't that also mean . . .

"Wait," she said to Simon. "Are you saying that no one is gay?"

He shook his head. "No, Dana, you have it backwards. I'm not saying that no one is gay—I'm saying that *everyone* is. And everyone is straight too. That's my point: the labels are meaningless—they don't define us; they only confine us. Nature makes us men or women, not gay or straight. We're the ones who created this extra baggage. It's us who made up the labels, and it's us who pretend they mean something. Nature, however, knows better."

Dana understood what Simon was getting at, but it was hard to relate it to herself. She liked men—that was the way it'd always been for her. She could understand why some women might like women, but she'd always liked men. Besides, all this talk about gays and straights is beside the point, she thought, because that isn't Simon's problem. I want to know if he thinks people can change. I want to know if *he* can change.

"Okay," Dana said, "but you still haven't answered my question."

"Which one?"

"Can people change?" Dana began, deciding it was safer to still stick with the topic of same-sex attraction. "You say that everyone is both—gay and straight—or, I guess that the labels don't mean anything. Okay, but not everyone agrees with you. So, do you really think that someone who considers themself gay could become straight?"

"See, Dana, by the way you ask that question I can tell you're still thinking of sexual attraction like it's some magic toggle switch inside our brain where changing means to flip from one setting to another—gay to straight, straight to gay, that sort of thing. But that's not the way it works."

Dana wished he'd just answer her question. "Fine, it's not a switch," she said. "So what is it?"

Simon looked out at where the lantern's light ended, the darkness full of the roar of flowing water. "I think of attraction as a river," he said. "Actually, a set of rivers—one for each attraction—with each river flowing through all of us; or, at least, each *could* flow through all of us."

"Every attraction? Everyone could feel every attraction?" Dana asked, skeptical. What would that mean? she said to herself. Then she remembered what Simon had said about a mother fearing that anyone could become a threat to her child. She glanced at the tent again. Could Simon be right? she wondered. Could he actually be the least of my worries?

"Sure," Simon said. "They could learn to. I mean, yeah, some ground is rockier than other ground, but with enough effort a river could still be dug—though the potential depth might vary, I suppose."

The imagery of the rivers fascinated Dana. She imagined Simon with his normal river—which she hoped included her—but beside it flowed a murky river full of filth. She wished she could just dump dirt into it and make a dam so it wouldn't bother him anymore. Surely there must be some way?

"Okay, Simon," she said. "It's easy to say 'could' or things like that—but can people really change?"

"That depends on what you mean when you say 'change.' If you just mean 'learn something new,' then yes: any river can be dug. I have no doubt about that."

But Simon didn't need to learn anything new—Dana could tell he already liked her in that way—still, she was curious about what he had said.

"Really?" she asked. "Because people would disagree. Think about it. How many straight men would believe they could be attracted to other men?"

Simon just shrugged. "I don't know, but if they think they couldn't, then I think they're wrong. Look, it's impossible to read minds, and I don't doubt that many really believe they couldn't feel differently from the way they do now, but"—he shrugged again—"perhaps they just can't see it."

"And you can?" Dana asked, once again skeptical at what he was saying. Why should Simon know better than so many who claim otherwise? she thought. Of course, he does have a reason to search deeper than others, doesn't he? she said to herself. Doesn't he have a greater need to understand?

"Look," he told her, "most people tend to follow the well-traveled grooves of life. Do you know what I mean? Never really questioning, just doing what comes naturally, that sort of thing. And if following the common grooves leads a man to marry a wife, raise a family, and be a good husband and father, then what's the problem with that? He has a decent, useful life, and I say, let him have it! Leave the questions, the struggles, and the headaches to those of us who don't fit within the grooves. I mean, why create problems where none exist today?"

This made more sense to Dana. Her talks with Simon had convinced her that many people believed things simply because society expected them to. And she remembered what he had said about how politics and fear were involved as well. Maybe there is something to what he's saying, she thought, but that doesn't mean that others would accept it. And she still had a hard time imagining herself liking women.

"Still, the idea that anyone could feel both normal and same-sex attraction—that's quite a leap for most to believe," she told him.

"Well, what's the alternative? Is it less of a leap to believe that a little elf crawled into your ear at birth and flipped a magic switch inside your brain, making you permanently, unalterably gay or straight? How does that make any more sense? People can change in countless ways, but not that way? Why not? Because the imaginary switch is magically locked in place or something? And *that* isn't quite a leap for people to believe? Besides, how exactly would someone like me even fit into that fairy tale? Was the elf drunk on the job? Because he sure did mess up in here," Simon said, pointing at his head.

"What?"

Simon grunted, seeing Dana's confusion. "Sorry," he told her. "It's just annoying how clueless everyone is about something that should be so obvious. So, no, I really don't care what others think because, to be honest, I don't think that they think—not about this. They feel an attraction, everything clicks as it should, and that's that. There's no need to question where it comes from or how it got there. The elf did his job. Why bother with complications?"

"So, where do you think it comes from?" Dana asked.

Simon was quiet for a moment. Dana wondered if he was trying to calm down. Then he spoke.

"I don't know, probably lots of places," he said, "but a big one, I think, is society—both the messages it tells us as well as the way we fit within it."

The idea made Dana curious. Could people really have that much influence on others? she asked herself. Could they have that much influence on me?

"Here's how I look at it," Simon continued. "Society is like a giant plow, its many blades digging through our soil, creating the rivers that then flow within us. Sometimes the blades cut deep and sometimes the blades cut shallow. If the ground is loose to begin with, then it doesn't really matter either way because chances are that river will form no matter what. But even rocky ground can be cleared for a river if the blade cuts deep and strong enough."

Dana thought of past societies, both recent and ancient. Things had been quite different at times, she realized. Could people really be influenced so much by culture? Maybe Simon was right, she thought. But what would that mean?

"And everything factors in," Simon continued. "What we watch on TV, what we encourage in relationships, what we call marriage—it all has an effect. All of it influences the depth of the blades and how many rocks they remove.

"I mean, all these arguments we have—all this controversy swirling around same-sex attraction—all of it boils down to just one truth and one question," he said, holding up a finger to emphasize his point: "There are teenagers today who will decide they are gay who would never have decided that in an earlier generation—that is the truth, the one truth behind all the arguments. And I'm not saying they would have lied to themselves or been miserable or anything like that. No, I'm saying it wouldn't have even occurred to them. I'm saying they would have lived normal lives, completely unaware of the possibility that lay unearthed by their generation. But that blade digs deeper today, dredging up desires that so many now are forced to face. And here is the question, the one question we should ask ourselves as we finally open our eyes and see it happening all around us: Do we care?

"Do we care that their lives will be so different than they might have been?" he said. "Does that matter to us? Some pretend that life's paths are the same no matter which attraction we follow, but that isn't true—each attraction leads to a very different path. But—do we care? Perhaps some are naive enough or blind enough to expect that the elf's toggle switch will magically block all outside interference, but the rest of us see the impact we have on each other. We are the plow. We're digging deeper. Do we care?"

Simon's words struck Dana and his passion infected her, sending her thoughts inward to consider the effect people have on the lives of those around them. Could I think I was gay, were I growing up today? Dana didn't know the answer. But why not? she asked herself. So many things about us are flexible—why not that? And this gave her an odd thought: could there be a girl growing up today who is just like me except, growing up in a different generation, she'll decide she is gay? And were we to trade places, to swap generations, then would it be me calling myself gay and her calling herself straight? The image made Dana think of a TV show she had seen where a father was talking to his newborn son, telling his son how happy the father will be to see his son grow up and find a girl, but then he quickly added "or a boy" and the laugh track kicked in approvingly. Dana remembered how odd that scene had seemed, how sterile, how fake. Yes, parents should love their children no matter what, but shouldn't they also have a preference for their children's lives? Shouldn't they guide their children toward what they expect them to do and how they expect them to live?

And yet, Dana realized, it's not that we don't guide our children and give them direction in the way we expect them to live. No, we're only scared to give them direction about *that,* frightened to even admit that something could influence our children in that way. But we worry when games glorify gore, we worry when movies are full of violence, we worry when models are too thin, we worry when music celebrates drugs, we worry when role models fall, we worry when dolls are dressed like sluts, we worry when commercials sell junk food. We worry about all these things and so much more, recognizing the influence the world can have on a child—on every part of them: their honesty, their kindness, their responsibility, their wisdom, their compassion, everything about them. Everything, that is, except that unchangeable magic switch. That, alone, we claim is unmovable. That, alone, we claim is untouchable. And that's why we close our eyes, cover our ears, and shut our mouths, letting our children blow around in the wind, bowing to the guidance of an imaginary toggle switch as we raise them through fashionable negligence. Elf and the magic switch indeed! We're telling kids as young as toddlers that they can marry either a man or a woman, refusing to guide them one way or another, refusing to even *see* more value in one way over the other, and we foolishly expect our behavior to have no impact on them at all; we pretend it makes no difference. What fools we are! Blinded by the hands we hold in front of our eyes, not wanting to see—what cowards we are!—knowing that it's easier to be blind than to stand against the relentless push of something so obviously incorrect.

Then the words Simon had spoken the night before returned to her: "Besides, if it *isn't* normal, then the human race is pretty much screwed, aren't we?" Yes, she thought, and maybe we deserve to be.

But she pushed the frustration aside. That wasn't something she had to worry about tonight. The world might go mad, but she didn't have to follow. When I'm a mother, I won't just close my eyes and hope for the best, she told herself. I'll actually teach my children which path I expect them to take, but right now what I want to know about is Simon. If people are so flexible and change is so possible, then surely Simon can change, can't he? Not change by digging a new river—he doesn't need that—but change by damming his old one. Surely there must be some way to stop it from flowing. That's what I need to know, she said to herself. Because if not . . .

"So, you're just talking about what people stumble into without really thinking about it," Dana said. "But what about if they want to change? I don't see how that helps people to change."

"Again, what do you mean by 'change'?" he said. "Digging new rivers is only half of the problem. The other half is dealing with your old attractions, and those, unfortunately, never go away."

That was not what Dana wanted to hear.

"Never? They never go away?" she asked.

Simon shook his head. "No, they don't," he said. "That's not the way it works. Once a river has flowed inside of you, once you've acquired its taste, it'll always be a part of you—you'll always have to deal with it. Remember, we're humans, and humans never forget what brought pleasure in the past. Why would you expect us to? Sure, the river might lower at times, perhaps even go dry for a while. But that's just a trick to make you complacent. You start to think that the river is gone and it's safe to wander in the dry riverbed. And, then, once you're down there—that's when the floods come, that's when you drown."

Dana imagined Simon down in his river, drowning in a flood of dark filth.

"It might be hard to face," he said, "but it's true. No matter what you think, no matter how you feel, the river is always there. The river is always waiting."

If Simon will always have to deal with this, Dana thought, then how could I ever trust him? If it's always going to be there, how could I be in a relationship with him? Having to always worry about it . . .

"That's why, to me at least," Simon said, "change doesn't mean that the river goes away, because that will never happen, not forever at least."

The whole conversation frustrated Dana. "Then what's the point?" she said.

"What do you mean, 'what's the point'? Dana, just because the river is there doesn't mean I can't rise above it. Don't you see that? And that's what change means to me: rising above the river."

"I don't see how that helps," she told him.

"What other choice do I have? I'm okay alone here in the mountains, but I can't stay here forever."

"Yes, so you can't avoid it, and you can't get rid of it, so what's the point of change?"

"What I just said: you rise above it. You choose to resist it and then you build a bridge over the river. That's what I mean by rise above it. You need a way to be out in the world without risking that you'll drown in your river. A bridge gives you that."

Dana thought of the bridge Simon had built near his cabin and remembered the words he had carved into it, the same words he had just said: The river is always waiting.

"Is that why you built that bridge back at your cabin?" she asked him.

"Well, it was mainly to keep myself from getting wet in the creek; but, yeah, it serves as a reminder for me as well."

"How?"

"Even a small bridge like that needs a foundation, a base that everything can be stable upon; otherwise the bridge would just collapse."

Dana thought she knew what Simon's foundation was, but what about the rest?

"And the bridge is what?" she asked.

"Well, the bridge back at my cabin was built using wooden planks, so if you want to stay out of the creek you need to walk along those planks. And it's the same way with the bridge I built inside of me; except instead of planks, the bridge is built with rules, laid one by one across the river. Those rules are the things I need to do, along with the things I need to not do. I know what they are because I know my own strengths and weaknesses—I know what could lead me into trouble—so I set rules for myself. And following those rules is like walking across the planks. It keeps me above the river."

"And that's it?" Dana asked. "That's all it takes?"

"No, if you just laid the planks on a bridge with nothing to hold them in place, then sooner or later they'd come loose and the bridge would fall apart. And it's the same with this type of bridge as well: if you only focus on your rules, then eventually you'll forget why you needed those rules in the first place and you'll neglect your bridge, allowing it to collapse. So you need to fasten your planks tightly in place, and you do that using memories—memories of what it was like being in the river, memories of times you never want to happen again. You need those memories to remind yourself of why you built your bridge, why you follow your rules, why you need your foundation. Because, more than anything else, you need to remember that without your foundation you will fall."

Dana imagined the bridge Simon had assembled. She saw it reaching out over the dark flow of his river. She wondered if it would be enough.

"So, to me," he said, "change isn't flipping a switch—it's building a bridge. But that's a hard thing to do. Hardest of all, though, is the fact that you need to care for your bridge every day. Because if you don't—if you forget why you built it or forget to tend to your foundation—then eventually your bridge will collapse, and you'll find yourself once again drowning in your river."

This made sense to Dana; however, the lifelong commitment overwhelmed her. "But that seems impossible. Being strong every day for the rest of your life . . . How could you do that?" she said, thinking to herself: how could I trust him to do that?

"Well, yeah, if you look at it like that, then it is impossible," Simon said. "A life is a long time."

"So, how do you look at it then?"

"One day at a time," he told her. "'Sufficient unto the day is the evil thereof.' Being strong forever is impossible to imagine, but just one day?—that's doable. And it's not like this is something that I just made up by myself. It's a common way for people to deal with lifelong challenges they must stay above day after day. Because being strong for just today isn't impossible, right? And here's the thing: every day is today. That's why it works."

"So, you trick yourself?"

"I wouldn't put it like that. It's just keeping the right perspective. I can handle today. A lifetime?—maybe not. But I can handle today, and then the next day comes and once again it's today—because every day is today."

They fell silent, then, and Simon resumed his carving. Every day is today, Dana repeated to herself, knowing now that Simon would always be fighting against this—every day. He had his bridge, yes, but would that be enough? It scared her to think of what could happen if he fell. Then again, every woman faces betrayal from her husband, doesn't she? Dana thought. Every wife, lying in bed next to her husband, is lying next to a man who is maybe-gay. At any point, even years later, he could roll over after sex and claim to have liked men the whole time. Or he could leave her for another woman, claiming to do it because he's driven by his love rather than because he's disturbed by her stretch marks—scars that she earned bearing *his* children. Life is full of uncertainty; eventually you have to either trust or not trust. Yes, Simon has a further way to fall than most men, but he also seems more aware of the danger. And why should it matter what lies beneath him if his bridge always keeps him safely above it? What he does seems to work for him, Dana thought, as long as he never forgets. And he seems so strong—surely, I could trust him to always remember?

She watched Simon as he finished carving, newly added roots twisting around the walking stick, descending from the tree down to the stick's base. Then, his work completed, he handed the walking stick to her, allowing the new carvings to be admired. But the night was cold and they both were tired, so they said their good-nights and Dana entered the tent, realizing that she had stopped worrying about Alice's shadows a while ago. Maybe hearing and thinking about real problems drives imaginary ones away? she thought.

Part of her wanted to stay outside and talk to Simon longer—to talk all night—but it was cold, and Dana told herself they'd have plenty of time to talk tomorrow as they walked—and after that, too. Unless someone shows up tomorrow who can drive us back, she told herself, surprised to realize that part of her would be disappointed if someone actually did.

Chapter Ten

DANA DIDN'T REALIZE HOW COLD THE NIGHT HAD become until she got in the sleeping bag and felt the warmth inside. The bag was thick, made for low-temperature use, and it worked well, quickly warming her body as she lay next to Alice on the hard ground. But even in the warm sleeping bag, Dana was too excited to sleep, distracted by the heavy noise of the river.

She heard footsteps coming toward the tent, followed by a sleeping bag's zipper. Simon was returning from somewhere. Did he go up the road to make sure nothing was there? Dana wondered, thinking again of what Alice had seen that day.

But she was too tired to worry about that now, so she ignored the thought and turned in the sleeping bag from one side to the other, trying to get comfortable. She couldn't find a good position. The ground was hard and the river was loud and her conversation with Simon kept running through her head—everything working together to keep her awake.

She was disappointed at what he had said, that attractions never go away completely. But she knew it was true because it explained the behavior of others so well: one minute claiming to have beaten something and the next being right back in it, proving that Simon was right— it had been there all along.

She thought, then, of Simon's idea of building a bridge. Could it work? she asked herself. It seems like it should. After all, it's kept him strong for this long. But he'll have to stay strong every day for the rest of his life. Is that possible?

Only if he doesn't forget, Dana thought. So, could I help him remember? Every day is today. She liked saying that. Every day is today. What would it be like, she wondered, being with him, taking life one day at a time with him?

But isn't that what everyone does? she said to herself. We all have weaknesses. So many of us fall. Is it bad that Simon's weakness is so much worse than most?

Not as long as he doesn't fall, she told herself. Not as long as he always remembers.

Then Alice stirred, beginning to sit up as she had done the night before, and Dana could already picture her creeping out of the tent and heading straight into the river. She shook Alice's shoulders, whispering for her to wake up. Thankfully, it worked, and Alice lay back down, mumbling an incoherent question to Dana before sleeping silently again.

Would she have repeated the same thing as she had the last couple of nights? Dana wondered. She thought it was strange that Alice would have the same dream every night. It's got to be about her father, Dana told herself. She wants him to come find us. That must be what she keeps thinking about.

Then Dana was lying in the noisy darkness again. But the more time passed, the more obvious it became that she was not going to fall asleep any time soon. She wondered if Simon was awake. She'd rather talk to him some more than just lie there doing nothing. But she hadn't heard anything from outside for a while, not even his quiet muttering to himself.

"Simon," she whispered through the tent, "are you awake?"

Something rustled outside, Simon turning in his sleeping bag toward her.

"Yes," he said.

"Can you sleep?"

"No, not really."

Dana unzipped the tent flap, and Simon sat up. He moved the sleeping bag a little out of the way, giving Dana room to come out and sit down next to him in front of the tent with the sleeping bag laid across their laps. They put their coats on as well and then huddled together, the lantern still turned off, leaving them in the dark, no sound but the roar of the river.

It was cold again. Dana already missed the warmth of her sleeping bag, but she was comfortable sitting there beside Simon, even in the dark. For a moment she considered asking him to share his sleeping bag with her instead of just sitting underneath it together. It would certainly be warmer, and of course Simon wouldn't try anything, she told herself. But she doubted he'd be okay with that. It'd probably break one of his rules, she thought. Except his rules aren't meant for me, are they? Or does he have a whole set of rules for his normal attraction as well? Would that even work?

"So, this bridge idea of yours," she said. "Can it be used for any attraction?"

"Sure, why not?" Simon told her. "Attraction is attraction, after all. Normal attraction, same-sex attraction, whatever. You resist or you surrender. You change or you don't change. They all work the same."

That belief is certainly different from the rest of the world, Dana thought. How many others would believe that people could change? Especially not with same-sex attraction. It seems like everyone claims it's impossible for gays to change. Well, almost everyone.

"So, if gays can change, then the ex-gays are right, I guess?" she said.

Simon paused a moment before answering. "They're right to say they can change, but they're wrong if they think their attraction is gone, and they're foolish to base their life on what they aren't anymore."

"What do you mean, 'base their life on what they aren't anymore'?" she asked him.

"Well, imagine a man who's been divorced," Simon said. "Do you think he should go around and call himself an ex-husband for the rest of his life? I mean, why call yourself something you aren't anymore? How is that helpful? Be what you are today. That makes more sense to me."

"So, if they're not ex-gays, then what are they?"

"What do you mean, 'what are they'?" Simon replied. "Why do they have to *be* anything? They're just men and women who have chosen to resist. I don't think they need a label, and I don't think they should dwell on their mistakes. I mean, the number of people who call themselves straight despite experiences to the contrary is a whole lot larger than the number who call themselves ex-gay, and that seems like the way to do it. Hold your head high, leave the past in the past, and move on with your life—that's what I think."

Dana nodded, although Simon couldn't see her in the darkness. She knew that much of their conversation this night had been taboo, maybe most of it—but she no longer cared. Simon had shared a secret with her that he hadn't shared with any other living person. And that meant that he trusted her. That's what mattered to her right then, not what might offend the world. She did wonder, however, if he had ever told his opinions to others.

"Have you told anyone else what you think about same-sex attraction?" she asked him.

"I haven't had a reason to. Why?"

"I don't know, but I doubt that many would be happy with your opinion. I just imagine someone like Ms. Miller—it would completely freak her out. She wouldn't even try to understand what you're saying. She'd just start calling you anti-gay or homophobic or something ugly like that."

"Anti-gay? Calling me that is just lazy," Simon said, and Dana imagined him shrugging in the dark as he went on. "Still, why waste time paying attention to people who bully you around with insults like that? I mean, I'm not a huge fan of labels anyway, but if someone is just dying to call me pro- or anti- something, then I think the best name would be pro-resistance."

"I think that's a type of shoe."

"Oh, crap, really? So much for my idea then."

"I like it, though," Dana said. "Resistance!"

"Well, hey, that's what it's all about, right? I mean, attraction—who cares? Actions are what matters. And what I think is that everyone should resist—me, you, everyone. My attraction, same-sex attraction, they all should be resisted and ignored by everyone. In fact, even normal attraction should be kept under control; it's not meant to be fully shared with just a date—or even with just a girlfriend—and it's definitely not meant to be wasted on porn. That should all be resisted as well."

Dana wasn't surprised to hear him say this. He was the kind of guy who would think that way.

"And the other point of view?" she asked. "What's the right name for them?"

"The ones who believe the fairy tale of the elf and the magic switch?" he said, pausing to think for a moment before answering. "How about pro-surrender?"

"Um, I think they'd probably prefer something else."

"Why, is that a shoe too?"

"No, it just sounds too negative."

"Fine, fine," Simon said. "Let them choose then."

But Dana wondered what those who disagreed with Simon would say about his opinions. Trying to force his religion onto others, that's what many would probably claim, she thought. Except that accusation seemed strange now, unfair, unbalanced. Because it's not the presence of same-sex attraction that's in question, Dana realized. It's whether we should accept it or resist it. And how do we answer that question? How do we decide 'should'?

Then she remembered what Simon had said about values. Should we resist? People answer that question based on their values, she thought, and those values are not all the same. But isn't the source of our values always religion in one way or another? Not necessarily a formal religion—complete with churches, rites, and scripture—but often an informal one instead, an informal religion whose core can never be proven through science or reason, an informal religion whose beliefs are no less subjective than anything taught from a pulpit.

Which means there are two competing religious beliefs, she thought: the one preaching acceptance of our attractions being imposed now over the one recommending resistance. And why? Is it because the idea that we should accept our same-sex attraction is any more objective than the idea that we should resist it? No, that isn't why, she said to herself, remembering more of Simon's words from the day before. No, it's just more fashionable, that's all. It's conquering the other point of view because it's more popular, because it's being pushed by prettier people, more powerful people. And the impact is everywhere. Who would agree with Simon today? Who would dare? Dana didn't know.

Do you want to be on the losing side, Dana? All of the world's knowledge—all of its wisdom—all of it is moving in one direction. How can you claim to know better?

And Dana thought of all the smart people who would line up to tell Simon he was wrong.

"But even those who wouldn't label you unfairly would probably still disagree with you," she told him. "Just look at what psychologists say. How many of them would agree that people should resist their attraction?"

Simon shifted a little beside her, adjusting his weight on the hard ground. "You know, the psychologist view is easy to understand if you stop and think about it," he said. "Keep in mind that they used to call same-sex attraction a mental disorder, something like schizophrenia or multiple personalities, that sort of thing. A pretty extreme position, don't you think? Well, if the pendulum used to be so high in one direction, isn't it natural for gravity to pull it almost as high the opposite way? Still, give it time. Eventually it'll settle down in the center, where it should be."

"Meaning what?" Dana asked.

"Meaning they'll admit that people are flexible and that attraction is learnable," he said. "They'll admit that the choice to resist is at least as valid as the choice to not. And, more importantly, they'll start to truly support those who choose to rise above."

"They don't do that today?"

"I don't think so, no. Most of them just want you to climb into the box and close the lid on yourself."

"The box?"

"Yeah, the box. Some people like to use the term 'coming out of the closet,' but I think 'climbing into the box' is more accurate—a box too small for your potential, a box that's sealed only from the inside. And it seems to me like that's all psychologists focus on nowadays when it comes to same-sex attraction. They just want to keep you comfortable inside the box, not help you climb out of it. That's the way I see it, anyway."

Dana considered his analogy of the box. Gays aren't allowed to ever leave, are they? To ever change? That goes back to society's *rules* that Simon talked about earlier. Our sexuality isn't supposed to ever change because if it did change then it could change and if it could change then maybe it should change—and that conclusion angers those who like things as they are.

"It's not just attraction that's gone screwy either," Simon said. "It's gender: male, female—everything's been turned upside down. I mean, if a woman, who is not Joan of Arc, decides that she is Joan of Arc, we give her the counseling she needs to come to grips with reality; but if a woman, who is not a man, decides that she is a man, we cheer her on all the way to the operating table. It's all a little bizarre if you think about it.

"Don't get me wrong," he continued. "I know that some physical deformities can cause actual ambiguity; and in rare cases like that, all we can do is be compassionate and let those affected do their best—but too many people today are introducing confusion where no confusion needs to exist."

That's true, Dana thought. When Girl Scouts aren't required to actually be, well, actually girls anymore, it does seem like maybe modern life has become so simple that some have felt it necessary to add extra complications.

"Anyway," Simon said, "when it comes to psychologists, I really don't mean to trash the profession. In fact, I think we should cut them a lot of slack. Seriously, just look at the mess our society is in right now—with depression and stress everywhere. Psychologists have their hands full already. Besides, no one can be right about everything, and it's not like you can figure this stuff out by looking through a microscope. Plus, the politics are completely toxic today—even a hint of opinion in the unorthodox direction and a psychologist would be eaten alive. Anyway, enough about that. Just give them time and I think they'll come around. Meanwhile, yeah, people who struggle with this are pretty much on their own.

"But, Dana, you said that many would disagree with me; well, I really don't pay much attention to that. I mean, look, what can I do? When you keep your eyes open and you notice things around you—about life, about sex, about attraction—all those things are like individual pieces to a giant puzzle. And different people shuffle the pieces around in different ways, getting part of the picture right while leaving gaps in other areas. But when I line up the pieces my way—they fit. So, why would I trade the complete picture I have for the disjointed one that others offer me? Sure, theirs might be the socially acceptable version, but I'd rather have people disagree with me than have myself accept an interpretation that obviously doesn't fit no matter how hard you smash the pieces together."

Then Simon stopped talking, and the two of them silently listened to the river. Dana thought about what Simon had shared, both what he had said as well as the fact that she was now the only living person he had shared it with. His openness made her feel close to him.

But she still wondered if she really could trust his bridge. Can I trust him to always keep it strong? Because if he lets it fall . . . Then again, all relationships have risks, don't they? And isn't it better to be with a man who is responsible enough to face his risks head on?

But can I really trust that he'll remain strong even in the worst possible situation? Dana asked herself. She needed more time to think. She did like his focus on resistance, though. Because it's not lack of bad desires that makes good people good, is it? she asked herself. Isn't what makes them good the fact that they choose to resist the bad? And isn't that the case with all virtues? It's not lack of fear that makes someone brave. No, it's their choices. They choose to resist their fear, and that's what makes them brave. So it's not lack of vice that makes someone virtuous, it's resistance of vice. It all comes down to resistance, and Simon understands that—that's what his bridge is for. So, why do I feel so nervous now that a future with him seems so realistic?

The night continued to grow colder. Dana tried to pull the sleeping bag higher to cover herself more, but that only exposed her feet, so she left the bag where it was and sat shivering next to Simon until she felt like she was tired enough to fall asleep. Then, both yawning, they agreed it was time for bed. The day ahead promised another long hike, and they would need their energy.

Dana returned to the tent and zipped it shut behind her. Sitting there in the dark, she worried again for a moment about leaving Simon outside alone, but then she reminded herself that there was nothing to fear out there—the only fear was coming from her imagination.

She lay down in the sleeping bag and looked over at the unseen tent flap that separated her from Simon. It felt good to be lying so close to him, even if they were separated by the tent's thin fabric. She imagined Simon in his sleeping bag as he drifted off to sleep. And, eventually, she fell asleep herself, thinking of Simon, wondering about his bridge, the sound of the river always flowing beneath her dreams.

Chapter Eleven

IN THE MORNING, FOG COVERED THE CAMP, PRESSING down with a sense of foreboding, the unseen river strangely muted though its noise was still unnerving. They ate quietly as they shivered in the cold, Dana sitting between Simon and Alice, her thoughts switching back and forth between last night's conversation and the worry she felt for Alice, who once again was not reading, a look of hopelessness and failure on her face.

We just need to get off the mountain today, Dana thought. Just getting closer to home will probably help her. I'm sure all her stress will melt away at the first sight of her father. Just one more day, Dana reminded herself—as long as nothing else goes wrong.

The fog had weakened by the time they finished their breakfast, although it still lingered in thin trails of mist that lay across the road. Simon left, then, telling Dana he was going to scout out the road ahead. "Among other things," she said to herself, but not out loud. It was for him to bring up, not her.

While Simon was gone, Dana took the opportunity to return to the stream with Alice. She washed off her face this time rather than only her pants and shoes. She felt strangely self-conscious around Simon this morning, the dirt on her face from three days of hiking suddenly an emergency that needed to be fixed. But the cold water stung her face and froze her hands, so she only washed lightly while Alice sat by the stream beside her, saying nothing.

Dana missed her makeup. She considered herself almost pretty with it on but only plain without it. Sure, Simon might seem to like me now, she thought, but maybe that's just a lack of options. He's been up here for months, after all. Once he's back around other women, prettier women, will he like me as much? Of course, then I could make myself up better, but ...

Dana sighed, drying off her hands on her pants before burying them in her pockets in an attempt to warm them. She wished Alice wasn't so quiet. The dark clouds, the earlier fog, the river still loud beside them—everything seemed to be working together in an effort to make her uneasy. It felt as if something was coming, something that she wouldn't like. She stood and took Alice's hand to walk back to the camp.

What should we do when we reach the town today? she asked herself. We'll call Alice's father immediately, of course, but where should we call from? Finding a store might take hours longer. Should we just knock on the door of the first house we find and ask to use their phone? I'll have to see what Simon thinks, Dana decided, wondering if he had planned what to do when they made it to the bottom of the mountain today. And what if we don't make it today? she asked herself.

Simon was back at the camp already taking down the tent, and Dana started to help as soon as she returned. They stuffed a sleeping bag and flashlight into her backpack and then attached the other sleeping bag and tent to his pack before loading everything else inside of it. But the unequal weight of the two packs made Dana feel unsettled.

"Why don't you put some of the food and water into my pack and give yourself a break today?" she told Simon.

"No, that's fine," he said. "We only have a little left anyway. It's not a big deal."

But Dana insisted, feeling it was important, and Simon finally agreed, giving her a couple of the water bottles and a handful of granola bars to put in her backpack. It didn't add much weight to her pack, or remove much from Simon's, but it did made her feel better to be carrying more of her share.

They stood, then, and started to walk down the road, Dana looking one last time at the rock wall where she and Simon had sat and talked the night before. The river was as strong and as loud as it had been then, but it was below them and not a danger to those who kept their distance. I guess I might have to get used to it, she thought, walking next to Alice, holding her hand again as they continued down the road. The sky above was thick and swirling slowly, the storm not done, maybe only beginning, and a nagging worry festered in Dana's mind.

"We should get off the mountain today," Dana said to Alice, her voice more optimistic than she felt.

"That's good," Alice said, sounding better than before but still deflated somehow.

Dana wondered if Alice might have slept off her weird mood from the day before. Will I be able to talk some sense into her now? Dana asked herself. She decided to try.

Lowering her voice so that Simon, who was walking a little bit ahead—between them and the river—could not hear, she began: "Alice," she said, choosing her words carefully, "do you think it's possible that you might just be seeing things?"

Alice shrugged. "Maybe," she said.

"Do you think it might be ideas that you're getting from your book instead of something that's actually out there?" Dana asked.

"I don't know," Alice said. "I guess it might be." She didn't become angry as she had before.

Maybe she's finally realizing that it's only been her imagination, Dana thought. She still seems so frustrated though. And Dana wondered again if it was a good thing or a bad thing that Alice had stopped reading her book. Has she just given up?

Heaviness hung above them with a sense of inevitability. Rain would come today, the only questions being when it would start and when it would end.

Simon didn't talk much as they walked, only commenting on the hike itself: the cold of the air, the condition of the road, the continued surge of the river. Dana longed for the closeness she had felt with him the night before but knew they could only have it again when they were alone, and she wasn't sure when they'd have another chance to speak like that again.

Then the rain started, a small trickle building quickly to a downpour. They retreated to the shoulder of the road, seeking shelter beneath the trees that grew along the base of the hill; they rested there, sitting on rocks, and watched the rain come down, Dana wondering when the storm would end or if it ever would.

It was only mid-morning, and they had hoped to go farther before lunch, but none of them wanted to deal with the ponchos that day if they didn't have to, so they waited for the rain to stop, hoping it wouldn't last long.

"It's crazy that there haven't been any cars," Dana said to Simon.

"Yeah," he said. "Makes me think that the road probably is out somewhere down there. Unless no one has a reason to drive up this time of year, I guess."

"What if it is?" Dana asked, looking down at the river, its water loud and too close. "What do we do then?"

"I guess we'd have to go up and around," Simon told her. "Hopefully it'd be someplace that's easy to climb."

Then Alice spoke: "Do you think my dad knows that something happened?" she asked Dana.

"I don't know," Dana said. "He wasn't supposed to call us for a few days. But I guess it's been a few days now. Either way, we'll be calling him tonight, right?"

This seemed to cheer Alice a little, and she let the subject drop, her hands hidden in her coat pockets to keep warm. But Dana's words made Dana herself feel apprehensive. However, she pushed the nervousness aside, sitting there beside Simon and wondering again at how comfortable it felt to sit next to him despite the ever-present danger. Is it because of the bridge he has built? she asked herself. Is it because I trust him to maintain it and to always do the right thing?

Then she wondered what the world would be like if every man were like that: if every one of them identified his weaknesses and did what was necessary to resist them. It hadn't occurred to her before, but it seemed so obvious now: if you know you'll be weak in the future, then you should set rules now and make habits that will allow your current strength to carry you through your future weakness.

So, why don't people understand that? she asked herself. Why doesn't everyone do it? Maybe, she thought, it's because no one has showed them how.

"Simon," she said, "about our conversation last night—have you ever thought about sharing your ideas with others? Maybe convincing them to see things your way?"

"We talked about lots of things last night," he said.

"The bridge stuff."

"But it all ties together, though, and that's the problem with sharing it," Simon told her. "Even the very suggestion of resistance would cause trouble—I mean, the politics of same-sex attraction are just too stubborn and unthinking right now. I don't know how I could say anything useful that would get around that. It's like you're trying to teach someone math when all their life they've been taught that two plus two equals five. How can you even have a conversation? It's just a waste of time. All you get are shouting matches."

"Well, couldn't something be done?" Dana asked.

Simon thought for a moment.

"I don't know," he said. "I guess you could show people rather than tell them. People just need to think, really think, about what they're being fed. I mean, the background music might be playing and the lighting might be subtle and the Hollywood stars might be performing their lines with scripted perfection—but what's underneath? What's there when the music stops? What's there when the lights turn off and the celebrities remove their makeup? What's there then? I mean, the truth is right in front of everyone if they'd only turn their eyes away from their screens long enough to see it."

"So, why don't you show them?"

"Me?" Simon shook his head. "No, I don't think so. That's somebody else's problem. Look, everyone has their challenges, but I think mine is worse than most; for me to just keep myself in check is difficult enough.

I can't take on another headache. Let those with weaker demons deal with it instead. Oh, I guess they'd have to be haunted by something—because why else would they bother?—but not by *this*."

Simon paused, Alice's close presence weighing on the conversation even though she wasn't paying attention. Then he went on: "So, no, that's for others, not for me. Let me just concentrate on staying strong and keeping myself out of trouble. That's enough for me."

But what a perfect example Simon would be, Dana thought. A good man struggling against an attraction that *everyone* would want him to resist. Who wouldn't cheer for him to succeed? Who wouldn't groan when he made a mistake? Such complete support wouldn't be possible for someone who struggles against something more socially acceptable like same-sex attraction because its morality has become too muddled, causing more and more people now to see nothing wrong with simply giving in. But there's no confusion about what Simon fights against. With Simon, anyone could see the virtue of resistance; with Simon, anyone could see the line between right and wrong; with Simon, anyone could see what helps him—and what threatens to tear him down. And, while seeing it might make us feel uncomfortable, maybe that's what we need to feel in order to finally wake up—to finally wake up and apply Simon's example to ourselves, feeling grateful that our challenges are so much easier than the one he faces every day because, compared to Simon's attraction, how difficult is same-sex attraction or anything else we each might have to face?

And society obviously needs examples like his, Dana said to herself. Just think of pornography—what an awful waste; yet, most men today look at it—on their computers, even on their mobile devices—and women do, too, especially now that it's sold at the supermarket, hiding under the fancy-sounding name of "erotica."

But Simon could show them that not everyone simply gives in, Dana thought. He could show them that some choose to resist, and that they can make that choice also. Because it's our choices that determine our virtue, not our lack of desire to do wrong. The brave are not brave because they never fight fear. No, their resistance of cowardice is what makes them brave, and others can resist their challenges too, in the exact same way.

Yes, Dana thought, it's too bad Simon, who understands resistance better than anyone I know, doesn't feel like he could handle sharing his example with others. But I do see his reason to want to stay out of it. He does have further to fall than most men. Besides, no one should be expected to solve all the world's problems by himself, right? Still, Dana felt like Simon was selling himself short when he talked so much about having to keep himself strong, sounding as if he were at risk of stumbling even today.

"You seem plenty strong to me," she told him.

Simon grunted before responding.

"Maybe I seem that way now," he said, "but we never know what's coming just around the corner. I mean, one minute you feel strong enough to take on the world, and the next you find all your strength is gone for a reason you never imagined. That's when you learn the truth about yourself, I guess, isn't it?"

But Dana couldn't believe that Simon would ever fall. He was just too strong—him against the world, him ignoring everyone else as they told him to give in to his attraction. They don't say that about his attraction specifically, she clarified to herself, but attraction is attraction, just like Simon told me. Still, he ignores them. And if he can stand against that—against everyone else—then surely he will never fall. Surely, his foundation will never fail him—as long as he doesn't let himself forget.

After the rain ended, they continued down the road, turning a corner to see the hill sloping to the left up into the dark sky, the hill full of trees—evergreens, oaks, maples—and dotted by large boulders, streaks of brown mud mixed with the green of brush, a rock ledge jutting out of the side farther down the mountain, maybe ten feet above the road. And the road itself was washed out beneath the ledge, fallen into the river for dozens of yards, a steady flow of water from the hill crossing the road before the drop-off, the river smashing against the collapsed road, white spray shooting up as it hit the rock wall of the canyon, the entire scene giving Dana a sense of instability.

No wonder there have been no cars, Dana thought. She watched a small section of mud slide down the hill before stopping, caught among bushes and trees. But Simon's gaze was forward as he walked toward the broken road, Dana and Alice following after. Halfway there, Dana noticed a small cave in the hillside only a few feet from the shoulder, bigger than the other one she had seen but barely large enough for her to enter crouching down. Curious about the cave, she wanted to point it out to Simon, but he had already walked past, still studying the upcoming ledge, probably planning a way for them to climb up onto it and pass over the missing road.

The water that ran across the road was clear, a few feet wide, and only an inch or two deep; but they hurried over it, not wanting to slip on the slick asphalt or be tripped by the moving water. Then they came to the ledge, which began a few feet before the road fell away, the rock face offering plenty of handholds and not looking difficult to climb even though the rain had made it slippery.

"I'll go up first; then I can help pull Alice up," Simon told Dana. He handed her his walking stick, grabbed hold of the rock wall, and climbed to the top, pulling himself easily up onto the ledge.

Dana passed him his walking stick, which he set down beside him. Then she showed Alice where to put her hands and her feet, guiding her as she climbed, Simon crouching above, ready to reach down and grab her should she slip.

But Alice never lost hold and she reached the top, Simon helping her up onto the ledge before taking a wary step backward as she stood and looked back at the road they had just walked down.

Dana handed her walking stick up to Simon. She thought of taking off her backpack as well but decided against it, feeling better with it on. Then she found the same spots she had shown to Alice and was about to start climbing when she noticed Alice looking down at the ground, her face pale. Dana knew what that probably meant.

"Did you see something?" she asked Alice.

Alice only nodded, barely moving her hand to point back up the road.

Dana looked back but saw nothing. Of course, the trees are thick along the base of the hill, so something could have crawled up there, she thought. And there's the cave, too. Who knows what might be hiding in there? She looked at Simon, the two of them sharing a glance before she told Alice she'd go check it out really quick. Dana felt silly doing so, knowing it was nothing. But maybe having me take her seriously will make Alice feel better, she thought. And if humoring Alice this one time will keep her calm for the rest of the walk down the mountain today, then it's worth it, she decided, ignoring her misgivings as she started to walk toward where Alice had pointed.

"Wait," Simon called.

Dana turned and caught the walking stick he tossed down to her.

"Just in case," he told her, the concern on his face genuine yet unsure, as if something unknown were troubling him.

Dana smiled up at him, telling herself there was nothing to be worried about. Then, her walking stick in hand, she turned back up the road to search for Alice's imaginary stalker.

She hurried through the runoff, which was now higher, its flow stronger and no longer clear—now mixed with dirt and mud. It might have given her warning had she been paying attention, but she was watching the trees along the road instead, looking for any sign of life though she knew there would be none.

Dana passed the cave, finding nothing along the way, just as she had expected. Then she returned back to the cave's opening and peered inside. Could something be hiding in there? she wondered. She looked back at Simon, who was standing on the ledge and staring at her, a concerned look still on his face. Alice was sitting down and watching her as well. She looks upset, Dana thought. Probably because there's nothing here and she has to admit to herself that it's just her imagination.

But Dana wanted to check the cave, just in case. And so, dark clouds above her, the river loud behind, she stared into the cave's blackness. Noticing a pale light far within, Dana reached for her backpack to pull out the flashlight and take a quick look. That's when she heard the first shout.

Startled, she looked back at Simon, who was waving his arms and yelling at her, Alice now standing and pointing at the hill above Dana. Then a large boulder flew across the road between them, the asphalt breaking and cracking with each bounce until the boulder reached the river, tearing a chunk off the edge of road as it fell and hit the water with a huge splash.

The runoff that separated her from the others was now a steady flow of thick mud. She heard a rumbling from above. Looking up, she saw the mountain rushing downward, a wave of green and brown, trees bouncing up as they were ripped from their soil, everything joining the flow that thundered down toward her. She looked back at Simon, but trees now flowed down the mountain between them, blocking her view as they slid downward, still clumped together, their branches and leaves waving, the sound of cracking wood and moving earth overpowering even the noise of the massive river the trees raced toward.

Dana looked up the road in the opposite direction, but the slide had spread too far—she couldn't get clear either way. Rocks and trees poured over the road on both sides, and a mass of mud and destruction bore down upon her. The cave was just ahead; the landslide was too near.

She turned her head to look for Simon and Alice again, and a break in the falling trees gave her one final glimpse—Simon standing on the ledge, Simon standing all alone, Alice there beside him.

Then Dana jumped.

End of Part Two

At the Double Waterfall

*S*UNLIGHT TRICKLED THROUGH OVERHANGING BRANCHES AS
Simon hiked up the mountain, the sun's warm light on his skin, a newly
finished walking stick in his hand, Simon feeling excited but nervous—
unsure how he should think of the way things were going.

For years he had expected to live his life alone, a life of solitary strength,
a noble life though one with a large gap inside. But now, could it be possible
for that gap to be filled? He shook his head, unwilling to let himself go too
far, feeling sure that his chances were small.

"Someone like her with someone like me?" he said. "It doesn't seem
possible."

But he continued his search, determined to find the perfect branch to use
for Dana's walking stick. He had finished the last carving on his own this
morning and then added the long black scar as an afterthought, burning it
into the wood slowly, the walking stick not truly his without it—a reflection
of his own soul. But not Dana's, no, there will be no dark streak in hers, he
thought.

"She's beautiful inside and out."

Any woman can appear alluring in the dim lights of a bar or trendy
restaurant, he told himself, with the music blaring so loud you have to yell
to speak to someone standing right in front of you. But true beauty is visible
in the clear light of day, and Dana looks just as good with the midday sun
shining down on her, the kind of woman who doesn't even need makeup to
look beautiful.

Simon bent down from time to time as he walked, examining each stick
that looked the right length, but none of them matched her, none of them

seemed to fit. He continued up the hill, a soft breeze blowing through the leaves, the sound of birds all around, everything filling him with a gratitude for life, even a life such as his own, a life that included the challenge he faced each day, the challenge of knowing that the desire he felt for Dana was not as powerful as his other, unwanted, desire; but he felt grateful that he was able to feel what desire he did for her, and that was enough—for he knew what he truly wanted.

"But can I have it?" he asked himself, "or should I just end things before I let my hopes go too far?"

Because how could any woman accept someone as flawed as I am? he thought.

Still, he searched, picking up each possible branch, hoping to express something to her through this gift.

"But will she understand what it means?" he said, "or will she get the wrong idea, focusing on the shape or something foolish like that?"

No, of course not, he told himself. But what do I want it to mean?

"Time," he answered.

And when she sees it and knows the effort it took me to make it, he thought, then she'll know that I really care for her, and maybe she'll care for me too, and maybe I'll be able to tell her everything, and maybe she'll be able to handle it.

"But can I be strong enough?"

That's true, he said to himself. I need to know that first. Can I be strong? Because if I can't, then I don't deserve her or anyone else. But if I know that I can be strong, then maybe . . .

He heard the sound, then, of falling water and realized where he was. Turning to the side, he hurried over a hill and walked down to where it fell—the Double Waterfall. Here the stream dropped a few feet before dropping even more, both falls combined descending perhaps ten feet, the lower fall providing enough space to sit behind and look out through the falling water. It was Dana's favorite place to visit.

Which makes it the perfect place for it, he thought; and he started, going through all his concerns and doubts, admitting his faults, asking for the strength to stand in spite of them, and more than anything, asking for the *knowledge, the assurance, that he could be a safe man for Dana, a safe husband, a safe father. Because all fathers must adapt to life's changes as their cute daughters grow into beautiful women—fathers learning, as if by instinct, to kill the unformed thoughts that would appear unbidden were the attractive woman before them not their own daughter—but for Simon it would come sooner, and the risk would be greater. He had to know, because without that assurance he didn't feel right continuing the relationship. He simply had to know.*

And, as he finished, he felt strength flowing into him, the same strength he always received when he asked for it—not the lessening of his trials, but the ability to meet them, to endure them.

Then, looking up, he saw a branch lying before him on the streambed, wet, carried down from farther up the mountain. He picked it up and stripped off a small piece of bark, revealing pure white within, the exact opposite of the mark he had burned into his own walking stick. Excited, he mentally measured the height.

"It's perfect!" he told himself, scraping off the mud that clung to it and getting out his knife, already eager to begin preparing his gift, imagining what designs he would carve into it once he had removed all the bark and polished the surface.

He crawled behind the lower fall on his hands and knees, dragging the branch with him. And then he sat there, the branch in his lap, cutting off more of the bark, when the thought came to him—ask, and ye shall receive; yet doesn't the answer often come in an unexpected way?

But he brushed the thought aside as he looked at the branch, dreaming of the expression on Dana's face when he gave it to her, hoping his impossible hope.

"This is going to take some time," he said. "But she's worth it."

Part Three
Nothing Stands Forever

Chapter Twelve

STANDING THERE ON THE LEDGE, SIMON SAW DANA JUMP toward the hill before the landslide struck and covered her with tons of rock, soil, and trees as the merciless mass flowed into the river, the impact sending a surge of water down the canyon almost high enough to claim Simon, who had fallen to his knees and was staring in disbelief at the destruction before him, his arms still in the air though no longer waving.

All sound was gone though the mountain continued to pour like water, dust rising despite the wet earth, covering everything like the hill's dying breath. Then the movement spread farther, reaching above Simon, the rock beneath him trembling as the entire mountain started to shift. Soon he would be covered, just like Dana. That's how it should be—this is how I should end.

A scream broke through the silence. Simon looked to his side and noticed Alice there, Dana's Alice.

The thought brought him to his feet—strength to grab her arm—pull her to safety—hysterical—screaming—all he heard was the mountain— all he thought of was what it had buried—running—dragging her—still screaming—"We need to go back for Dana!"—No, no vain hope— river's surge rising higher—Dana's Alice—a ledge above—almost there—run faster—must get higher—Dana's Alice—there—throw her higher—jump up—just in time—he collapsed—Alice there some- where—still hysterical—he didn't care—staring up at dark clouds—see- ing faces—laughing faces—mocking faces—what a fool!—Alice's head on her knees—rocking back and forth—"Dana isn't dead!"—"It's all my fault!"—she won't stop crying—she won't stop crying.

Simon sat and stared—the entire canyon changed, the majority of the mountainside collapsed, the river completely dammed, the water below draining away. All of that water from all of that rain and soon it'll be like it was never there at all. Has this really happened? Could it just be a dream, a nightmare?

But Simon didn't wake up, and Dana's thousand-ton tomb stared silently back at him. He wiped tears off his cheeks, turning the dust on his face into mud. Pointless. Who cares? Dropping his face to his knees, he let them all out.

Darker now, later, Simon staring at the mountain, imagining a hand breaking through the dirt clutching a white walking stick, Dana climbing out safe and unharmed. But something stirred inside him then, a feeling that they needed to move. His hiking pack lay beside him. He put it on and looked at Alice, Dana's Alice, who sat asleep, her head still on her knees, her book, *The Screwtape Letters,* fallen from her pocket, the gargoyle on its cover leering up at Simon through a fine layer of dust. Picking up the book, he shook Alice's shoulder lightly, but she didn't respond; so he put the book into her coat pocket and cautiously pulled her to her feet, uncomfortable touching even her hands but knowing that they needed to start walking. Her eyes opened when she stood, but they remained vacant.

It was growing cold. No, it was already cold and growing colder. Simon guided Alice down from the ledge onto the lower ledge, the rocks still wet from the river's surge. Then they descended farther until they reached the road below, which was littered with debris but still walkable. Simon glanced over the edge into the river but could see little water. It was all draining away, the destruction of the landslide leaving the river barren and blocked, the world strangely silent without the constant presence of its powerful flow.

Nothing looked familiar to Simon. He had recognized places along the canyon while walking with Dana, but now everywhere he looked seemed different. He didn't know where they were. We need to stop somewhere, but we can't stop here.

Dana, the only woman I've ever cared for in that way, is gone. Isn't there something I can do to get her back? Anything? I'd dig through the mountain if I could. No. Alice's stupid shadows. Too numb to be angry.

They reached a point where the hill to the side lowered and flattened into a wide field, the road turning toward it and leaving the canyon behind. Simon heard a noise, then, which he didn't recognize until spinning blades appeared above the trees and he saw a helicopter flying behind the hill that bordered the far side.

Instinctively, he ran after it, shouting and waving his arms though it was now too dim for the helicopter to see him. He tripped over something in the middle of the field, fell down, and lay there, the dirt cold and wet in his mouth, as the noise faded away. Then he realized that he didn't care. What does it matter now that she is gone? Dana has been taken from me.

Simon sat up and spit the dirt out of his mouth. We could be safe in a cabin right now—Dana could be safe in a cabin right now. He remembered Alice, then, Dana's Alice, and he forced himself onto his feet to find her. Looking back toward the road, he couldn't see her in the growing darkness and he thought briefly of just leaving her there—stupid murderous shadows—but Dana wouldn't want that. Dana would want me to find her. Or would she? Wouldn't Alice be safer away from me? No, she would freeze; there's no one else. Dana would want me to find her.

He wandered through the field, eventually coming to its edge, a hill rising behind, where he found Alice sitting beneath a tree. She was rocking again, quietly this time, his hiking pack beside her—I must have dropped it earlier.

There was an old fire pit beside the tree, probably made by hikers earlier that summer. It's as good a place as anywhere else. Following routine, Simon set up the camp, putting up the tent and placing the single sleeping bag inside. Dana was taken from me. Dana is dead.

Only one sleeping bag. Simon stared at it. It will freeze tonight, Simon. Are you supposed to freeze, too? I can't share it with her. Should you die too, like Dana? If I have to. Nothing will happen, Simon, not tonight. You are dead. Dana is dead and you are dead. I can't share it with her. I shouldn't even be alone with her. Nothing will happen, Simon, not tonight. I can't share it with her.

Neither Simon nor Alice hungry, Simon turned on the lantern and remembered the first night they all had spent together, when the lantern had guided Dana back to their camp. He shivered as he stared out into the darkness, leaning closer to the light as if it could warm him. Would Dana follow the lantern tonight? Would he see her step into the light, smiling, happy to have found him? No, because Dana is dead.

Simon turned away from false hope and stared at the silent ground. Alice was in the tent, probably already sleeping. He was exhausted; he needed to sleep; yet he was restless. Rising to his feet, he started pacing around the camp.

Nothing will happen, Simon. It is cold. Nothing will happen.

Simon pulled the hood of his coat tighter around his head and continued walking, straying farther from the camp, passing through waist-high grass, shaking his head, not wanting to be there, not knowing what he wanted, afraid of his thoughts, afraid of how the cold was twisting them.

You are going to freeze.

That doesn't matter. Nothing matters.

If nothing matters, then why don't you share it?

Because I can't.

You are dead—nothing will happen.

I can't.

Then Simon stumbled, falling through the tall grass onto the hard, wet earth. He lay there a moment before sitting up and looking back at what had tripped him, the lantern's dim light revealing an old worn-out tarp covering a lump on the ground. He pulled the tarp away, exposing a large bundle of firewood kept dry under the tarp.

Simon stared at the firewood for a moment—dry firewood—his mind unable to comprehend the chances of him finding it there. I will have a fire tonight.

He carried some of the wood back to the old fire pit, grabbed paper and matches, and arranged it all as he had on the other nights; but tonight the firewood was dry, and tonight the fire started.

The warmth felt so good after being cold for so long, and Simon piled on more wood, building the fire higher. Its light now overpowered the lantern, which he turned off. Then he sat down before the flames, baking in their heat.

Lie down for a little bit, Simon—just to warm yourself.

And Simon did, although he felt as if he was forgetting something he needed to do. But, not wanting to concentrate enough to remember, he let it go, thinking, as he drifted, how wonderful it would be to wake and find Dana there in the tent, the whole day having been only a dream.

Chapter Thirteen

S IMON WOKE TO THE SOUND OF A HELICOPTER. FILLED with excitement, he couldn't wait to tell Dana that help had arrived. But he felt the cold, hard ground beneath him, and then he remembered. His body slack, he simply lay there, not caring. What good is a helicopter if it can't bring Dana back? he thought, not wanting to move until the pain went away. They would find him or they would not. He stared at the fire's ashes, which swirled in the early morning breeze. The sound of the helicopter faded away as he fell back asleep.

a flash of blonde hair, wearing a blue jacket.

He woke later to find that the sun had broken through the clouds, casting long shadows on the ground. It was the first time he could remember seeing the sun in days, or had it been weeks? The light shone on the grass, the plants, the trees; but Simon focused instead on their shadows, resenting the beauty shown by the sun. With Dana gone, what does it matter? he said to himself.

She was taken from you, Simon.

Then, though habit urged Simon to do what to him was more than only a morning routine, he ignored its call, angry at the sight of the world all around him, a world revealed clearly in the morning's crisp sunlight, a world without Dana. He tried to not notice, to not even think.

Alice wasn't stirring in the tent. Simon called her name as he sat up. She didn't answer.

"What's wrong with her?" he said and then he rose slowly, walked to the tent, and looked inside, checking that she was still alive. He couldn't see her face, but he could tell she was breathing. She gave no response, however, when he asked if she was hungry.

Anger filled him, then, at Alice for getting Dana killed. Why did she have to force us to hike down the mountain? he thought. Dana could be safe in a cabin right now. Help would have arrived already. So stupid. This has all been so stupid.

He dropped the tent's flap and stormed away, returning to the river canyon and peering over its side. He was surprised to see most of the water gone. It reminded him of something he had told Dana, but he shut the memory down, not wanting to think about it right then.

"All I wanted was to be a man who could be with Dana, and what was my answer?" he asked before telling himself: she was taken from me—that was my answer.

Simon felt betrayed. There is no point in asking for anything, he thought, because I don't receive anything I need. But that's just the real world, isn't it? Isn't that what life is really all about—disappointment?

Then the thought occurred to him: but isn't there more? Hasn't my life taught me that? Didn't Dana show me that there could be more?

But he felt the cold wind, reminding him of what had come to Dana in the end. Cold, yes, just like life, he thought. Disappointment, disappointment and pain—that's all there is, isn't it? All those hopes that I hoped, all of that supposed help . . .

"Was it just a fantasy?" he asked himself. He didn't dare give an answer.

And standing there above the river channel, Simon felt his footing suddenly give way as the edge of the ground broke off and fell down into the canyon. He fell back, landing on his side, and stared at the small gap in front of him that used to be stable ground.

"Nothing stands forever," he said.

The sky darkened, the sun hiding once more, and Simon returned to camp to find Alice still in the tent and not moving. He wasn't sure what to do about her, and he didn't know if he cared. Not about her, not about himself, not about anything. What is waiting for me at home anyway? he thought, imagining his future life: every day the same, working and then going home, no one for me to care about, no one to care about me.

"Every day the same as the one before," he said. "All of them meaningless and empty."

He heard a helicopter again, far away but somewhere around the mountain. He scanned the trees that surrounded the valley; but the helicopter never appeared, and he was eventually left in silence once more.

walking along the trail, her hair in a ponytail, hands in her jacket's front pockets, looking up, they were singing to her, of course they were singing to her.

It was uncomfortable for Simon to be alone and so close to Alice even though she was in the tent and he was outside. Not uncomfortable due to want, for he felt nothing, but uncomfortable due to habit—uncomfortable because he knew it was a bad idea. So he left the camp, putting distance between himself and Alice but staying close enough to keep an eye on the tent—he was unsure of her mental state and didn't want her to wander off and get lost.

And there among the trees, he sat and looked out at the tent, the road, the canyon, the missing river. I'll just wait here until help arrives, he told himself, believing that the helicopter would return later that day. It was stupid of me not to flag it down this morning, he thought. But at the time, he just couldn't. Even now, memories weighed down on him, making it hard to care. And Simon sat and Simon wandered, the absence of Dana always with him.

"She shouldn't have gone back to check," he said. "I shouldn't have let her. I should have gone myself."

"I knew something felt wrong," he told himself. "I knew something would happen."

But he hadn't known, not really. He had been worried but not enough to tell her to stay.

And he thought of all the time he had spent with her, of all the things he had shared with her, of all the dreams he had had for her, dreams now dying one by one as the reality hardened that she was really, truly gone.

"Why didn't I stop her? Why did I let her go?"

And then he thought: Why wasn't I warned? Why wasn't I warned that this would happen? I could have stopped her if I'd been warned—or I could have gone myself. It should be me under there, not her. Dana deserved better than that. How could this happen to her?

And he thought of going back. What if I was wrong? What if she survived somehow? He wanted to go back because he wanted to believe it hadn't happened. He wanted to go back and see that the mountain hadn't fallen after all. He wanted to go back to find Dana just sitting there waiting for him.

But he knew it was only false hope. He had seen the mountain fall. He had seen Dana buried. She was lost to him—taken from him.

The first time he had met her—Simon remembered that day. He had been sitting under a tree. He remembered the excitement at seeing her, the thrill of that first greeting. But the excitement and the thrill were gone, gone as if they had never been. He smashed the memory, pushing it away though it tried to return again and again.

And Simon sat and Simon wandered; but no help came that day, and evening arrived before he realized how much time he had wasted. Alice hadn't stirred the entire day. Simon still wasn't sure what to do about it. Finally, with night approaching, he returned to the camp and convinced her to eat a little food and drink a little water, her first meal in over a day. At least she's not going to die on me, he thought after she had eaten. He wondered what Alice would do once he got her home.

"Probably find a new nanny she can get killed," he muttered, knowing it was unfair to blame her but finding it hard not to.

He lit a fire again as the light turned to darkness and the cold turned more bitter. The pile of firewood was much smaller than it had been the night before. I should have saved more for tonight, he thought. But he hadn't been planning ahead, nor was he really planning right now.

"There isn't enough to last all night," he said as he examined how much was left, "but it will have to do."

Or I share the sleeping bag with Alice, he said to himself before quickly rejecting the thought, knowing it was a bad idea. Except, when he thought it, he felt nothing: neither want nor desire. And the lack made him wonder if perhaps he might have been wrong about attraction never going away.

Could what had happened yesterday serve as a stepping stone for my life? he asked himself. Something had triggered it all to start, so why couldn't something trigger it to stop? Like a phase that I grew out of? Maybe I don't have to worry about it anymore. Maybe I don't have to freeze tonight. Maybe I can throw all those silly rules away.

"What good do they do me, anyway?" he said, and he thought: Dana is dead. If the rules can't keep her alive, what are they worth? Nothing.

But a wave of concern slammed into him in response to his thoughts. He knew what he had neglected to do—he felt what his neglect was doing to him—but what did he have to say? I can't do that now, not when I feel this way, he thought. And why should I bother when this is the result? Except, something worse could happen if I don't. Maybe if I don't, I might—

Then a sudden chill made him shiver, reminding him how cold the night had become. He threw more wood onto the fire and scooted closer, focusing on the pleasant warmth it gave him, forgetting his earlier concern and nursing his growing bitterness as time passed in silence. Then, after adding the last piece of wood to the flames, he laid down before the fire and stared at the strange shapes leaping within. He pulled his hood tighter, the ground hard beneath him, wishing the fire could warm his back as well.

You cannot help the girl tomorrow if you die of cold tonight.

I can't help her tomorrow if I screw up, either.

No, you are done with all that now. You won't feel anything inappropriate—not after everything you have been through. You have it all under control.

No, I can't do that. Better to be cold.

Then get the girl's coat at least. It will help keep you warm. The girl won't need it in the sleeping bag.

But a feeling of warning burned within him at the thought of entering the tent, a feeling he didn't want to think about right then. He knew he was straying. But not far, he told himself as he lay in front of the fire. I can mend it easily, just not now, not after what happened to Dana. I need more time.

And the flames slowly dwindled.

> *He saw a flash of blonde hair before she turned the corner and came into view, walking along the trail, wearing a blue jacket, her hair in a ponytail, hands in her jacket's front pockets, looking up, staring at birds in the tree above where Simon sat unnoticed. "Hello," he said to her. He'd never been so bold, not with a woman so pretty. The birds were singing to her. They were singing to her. She almost tripped, only a stumble. Why was she here alone? Well, why was he? The birds were singing to her. Of course they were singing to her. She smiled at him and said, "Hello."*

Chapter Fourteen

FOG SURROUNDED SIMON WHEN HE WOKE, HIS BODY SORE and face numb, the fire cold ashes, white and dead—as gloomy as the fog all around, the same fog he had seen the morning before Dana was lost. A mountain had fallen that day—what will fall today? Simon wondered. What is left to be taken from me?

He sat up, sniffing and rubbing his hands briskly over his cheeks, a momentary fear of frostbite vanishing as feeling returned. Then he coughed, the noise sounding muffled in the haze; and he stood and looked at the impenetrable wall of white nothingness all around the camp. The tent, the nearby tree, and the cold fire pit were the only things left in his world, and even those were fuzzy, everything a little less clear than it had been the day before.

Shaking his head, Simon went to check on Alice. He unzipped the tent flap and crouched to peak in. She was turned away from him, long red hair spilling out of the sleeping bag, curls spreading out softly upon the ground.

You have seen hair like that before—

Simon killed the thought immediately, recognizing it as dangerous, but he stared at the sleeping bag another moment until he saw it move with Alice's breathing. Then, satisfied she was still alive, he zipped the tent back up and sat down outside.

He felt uneasy, as though everything were unstable: his foundation, his bridge, his rules, his decisions. And sitting there, surrounded by fog, he felt like the only man in the world, no one else to judge, no one else to help—good and evil, right and wrong, everything swaying, everything bending. Uneasy, unstable—but isn't it natural for a man to feel this way when he's all alone? Simon asked himself. Every man feels lost when separated from society. That's just the way it is. I just have to endure it, he thought, reasoning that there was nothing special about him or his situation.

And, though he ate a little, there was an emptiness inside of him that food would not fill. Maybe I need to rest more, he thought, but then he answered: No, I've wasted too much time already. I can't sit around and do nothing like I did yesterday.

Except, he wasn't sure what he should do. The idea of hiking down the mountain alone with Alice made him nervous. It seemed safer to just wait for help to find them now that he knew someone was looking. Because why else would a helicopter be flying around? he said to himself. But what if they don't find us in time? Maybe guiding Alice the rest of the way by myself would be smarter than waiting.

And then he remembered his thoughts from the day before and wondered again if he could have been wrong about attraction never going away. Could it really be gone? he asked himself. After what happened to Dana . . . could that have drained it away forever?

He wasn't sure, but thinking of Dana awakened the rawness inside of him, chasing away his motivation, and he lost the will to even stand.

No, I can't waste another day! he told himself, shoving the pain downward and burying his memories. I can't think about that right now. I can't think about any of it. However, the uneasiness didn't leave, and Simon wondered what he should do about it.

You need more time, Simon. There is no need to worry about that now. Not so soon after Dana was taken from you. Not after such a betrayal.

And the words clouded Simon's uneasiness with bitterness. It all makes no sense, he thought. Life was fine when I was alone. Maybe I wasn't completely happy, but at least I was content. Why did I even meet Dana if she was just going to be taken away from me? What kind of a plan is that? And he answered: a sadistic one, that's how it seems to me.

And that is how it has always been for you, isn't it? First cursed with an attraction you never asked for, and now cursed with lifelong loneliness. Don't you deserve to be happy, Simon? You resisted for so long—now, don't you deserve some happiness? Or will you choose misery your entire life?

Uneasiness turned into warning as bitterness tightened into anger, the memories of Dana and the pain all flooding through Simon. But he pushed it all down—pain and anger, worry and warning, everything mixed together and churning in a confused ball—he buried it all, surrounding it with numbness and inattention, hiding it deep within himself.

Then Simon heard the helicopter. He stood to look for it, hopeful that his trial might soon be at an end, but fog still covered them—he couldn't even tell where the sound was coming from. It never sounded very close, and soon it was gone. Perhaps they'll come back later when the fog has lifted, he thought, but a doubt lingered.

"What if they don't find us in time?" he said. "Maybe we should start walking."

Then he asked himself how much longer they had to walk, trying to remember this field and when he had passed it on his way up the mountain. The entire time walking with Dana he had assumed the road ran by the river until it reached the town, but he had forgotten this part, where the road left the canyon and wound around the other side of the mountain instead, meeting up with the river miles later before finally entering the town.

How much time is that going to add? he asked himself. I was dropped off at the edge of town and then . . . then it was a day's hike until my first camp, he remembered, a camp in a field beside a tree. And looking at the tree and the old fire pit, Simon recognized it all from before.

"It was here, wasn't it?" he said. "This was where I camped that first night."

He walked over to the tarp he had discarded after first finding the firewood. Could it be the one I lost? he asked himself. Picking it up, he looked it over. The color is right, but a tarp is a tarp, so who knows, he thought, but I guess it might be. I do remember gathering a lot of wood that night, so maybe it was me that left it here.

But if he was right, then that meant they had at least a day's hike to get off the mountain, at a fast pace too—something he wasn't sure Alice would be able to manage. It's too bad the road doesn't continue following the canyon, he thought, because then it wouldn't take even half as long.

But the riverbed is dry, Simon. You could walk in it and climb back onto the road later. That would save hours of walking.

And it'd also be incredibly dangerous, Simon thought. What a horrible idea. But it did make him curious. He walked over to the edge of the canyon to see what was left of the river. The fog had partially lifted, leaving everything damp but allowing him to see down to the bottom, where the water was mostly gone, lingering only in pockets and small pools. A rock shelf sloped down from the top of the canyon to the bottom, like a carved path. We could walk right down into it, he thought. A memory of something he had told Dana bubbled to the surface, but he shoved the memory back down with the rest, unwilling to feel anything right then.

He listened, wishing to hear the helicopter again but hearing nothing. Anxious to get moving, he decided to check on Alice again, considering as he walked back if it would be wise to start moving now while they still had a chance to make it on the road. As long as I can keep her moving fast, he said to himself. But if not . . .

He unzipped the tent and looked inside at Alice, her red hair so familiar, her body breathing in and out. Tired of being cold, he could almost feel the warmth of the sleeping bag. But if not, he finished his thought from earlier, if not then we'll be stuck camping on the mountain again. Alone. Would I be able to make a fire tonight? Simon doubted it. The wood will still be wet and there will be no more hidden bundles for me to stumble over. No, if we have to camp again overnight, then the only source of warmth for both of us will be that sleeping bag.

And why would that be so bad? Why should you freeze when you don't have to? Will you waste the rest of your life choosing misery over comfort?

The sleeping bag moved up and down with the girl's breathing, every breath feeding the terror growing within Simon as he felt the old desire flow through him again—the unwanted want that had never really left, for it never really did. Recoiling from the attraction, Simon dropped the tent flap and fled in despair, running back to the canyon's edge, tempted for a moment to just keep going, to end it all right then with one final, justified leap. But he stopped, collapsing instead by the edge, his face next to the gap created when the ground had fallen into the canyon the day before. Nothing stands forever.

Is this it then? he thought, filled with shame and hopelessness. Is this really going to be my lot for the rest of my life? Always feeling this desire? Everything working against me, even my own mind? For it already was—thoughts stretching out within it until he shoved them off to one side.

After everything that has happened, after Dana and after losing her, I still think of this? he said to himself, groaning. Still, the thoughts persisted, dodging defenses grown weak with neglect. And Simon felt fear then, fear that he would never escape this, fear that eventually he would fall, fear that in the end his only choice would be to surrender.

So why not just give in now, Simon? Who is here to judge you? Who is here to stop you?

"No!" Simon said. "I'm a good man."

Why?

"Because I'm supposed to be a good man—because I want to be a good man."

Supposed to be? Miserable—that is what you are supposed to be. Because you want? Want what? More pain and disappointment?

And warning bubbled up within Simon, breaking through the numbness and filling him; but it was coated with his bitterness, and Simon did not want to listen, not now.

And why? Who do you do it for? For society? They would spit on you if they knew what you wanted. All of their wants can be fulfilled every day. But yours? Never. Why do anything for them? They will never do anything for you.

For Dana, Simon thought, the memories of her returning—I'll be a good man for Dana! I can't let her down like this. Everyone else can burn for all I care, but I won't let Dana down.

"I'll be a good man for her," he said. "She'd want me to be a good man, an honorable man. I'll be a good man for her."

And the thoughts retreated, bowing to his determination. The warning, however, remained. It called to him, reminding him to not walk this way alone. But it was poisoned by his anger, the mixture of emotion making it hard to hear. I need more time, Simon thought. I'll fix that, but I need more time. Dana will be enough for now. For now, I'll do it for her. And I won't be alone—I'll have her memories with me. I'll be a good man because of Dana.

But what would a good man do now? Simon thought, sitting up beside the edge. Would it be better for me to just leave the girl here? I could hike to town myself and send back help for her. But, no, I can't just leave her here all alone by herself. Who knows what would happen if I did? But I can't be alone with her either, not again, not another night.

So why not just give in now?

No, I'll be a good man. I'll be a responsible man. Except, Simon thought, wouldn't a responsible man seek the help he needed in order to be good? But he ignored that thought, not wanting to face his anger. And what about my bridge? he asked himself. I built it to stay strong at times like this.

Then he answered: I'll use a different bridge. The memory of Dana will be enough. I'll be a good man for her. With the loss so fresh, that will be enough—at least for now.

But if I can't leave the girl, and I can't be alone with her, then what then? Just wait for help? Sit around and do nothing until someone else comes? He didn't like the idea, but he couldn't think of a better one. To even walk along the road with her seemed like too much of a risk. His thoughts were too bendable now. He was afraid of what would happen when they started to twist.

"And what if they don't come?" he said.

"They will," he answered. "They have to."

"But what if they don't?"

"Then I'll decide then."

So he waited, sitting there beside the edge, listening in hope for the sound of an engine—a car, a helicopter, anything. But nothing came. And Simon felt the day wear away, the fog long gone, his eyes constantly checking the sky, his ears straining to hear salvation.

The girl emerged from the tent as he kept his vigil. She sat down by the dead fire pit, not leaving the camp. Simon kept her in the edge of his vision, watching enough to know that she wasn't wandering off but not enough to encourage the thoughts that fought against him.

"I probably need to go talk to her soon," Simon told himself. "Otherwise she might think I left her."

But what are we going to do? he asked himself. There's no guarantee that anyone will come, and I can't be alone with her at night again. We can't just sit here any longer. But we've wasted too much time already; night will fall long before we make it back by the road. And then what? Just keep walking through the darkness? And what if the girl can't keep walking, then what? Carrying her definitely isn't an option, he told himself, worrying it was inevitable that taking the road now would mean spending another night along it as well.

"Unless help sees us while we're walking on the road," he said.

And what if no one comes for you?

"There's no other option."

Yes there is. You know the other option.

"No, that's a horrible idea. We can't risk that."

More dangerous than you spending a night alone with the girl? It will be quick, a matter of hours, and you will be back on the road and almost to town.

But somehow the road seemed safer, and Simon felt a vague assurance that help would find them on it.

And you trust that?

I have to trust something, Simon told himself, sighing and standing up. He brushed the dirt off his pants and braced himself as he looked at the girl, holding his mind blank, not wanting to feel the guilt of any thoughts that might wander through it; he walked over to her, struggling to not think as he approached.

"I'm sorry," the girl told him.

"What?" Simon asked, surprised.

"I'm sorry for killing Dana."

And her expression reminded him of so many faces he had seen as he sat pathetic in front of his uncle's computer, the memories trying to return though he fought to hold them back, a flurry of emotions erupting within him, his thoughts starting to twist, starting to twist him. And he told himself: I can't do it, not alone with her like this.

But I don't have to be alone, he reminded himself.

No, I'm not ready to mend that yet, he thought, anger rising as he remembered what was taken from him. And I'm not alone, he said to himself, I have my memories of Dana.

Except, he knew it wouldn't be enough, not to stand against this. No, the road isn't going to work, he thought, because I can't risk being alone with the girl another night, and there's no guarantee someone will find us before dark. She isn't safe with me, not when I'm alone, not when my thoughts are trying to break me—because I can't be sure that I'll always be me, not if I'm alone with her for much longer.

There is another way, Simon. And if you go that way, you will reach the town before dark.

But it was a horrible idea—to walk down into the dry riverbed—the very thought filled Simon with a warning of danger.

Sometimes you have to do a horrible thing, Simon, to keep from doing something even worse.

And Simon listened, the reasoning seeming sound to him as he stood there alone. Yes, this is how I can do it, he told himself, relying on his own judgment to make the decision. Just a quick trip down the canyon and then we'll get to the town, he thought. And I'll be a good man, a good man for Dana. Just a few hours. I only need to be strong for a few hours. That's reasonable. I can do that. I can do that for Dana.

His mind decided, Simon told the girl they needed to go. She stood silently and waited, not giving any complaint. Thoughts rose within Simon at the sight, but he shut them down and packed up the camp quickly, attaching the sleeping bag and tent to his pack and swinging his pack onto his back. Then, standing, he looked for his walking stick before remembering he had lost it beneath the mountain—the same place he had lost Dana.

"Let's go," Simon told the girl, refusing to think about his loss, and she followed quietly as he led her toward the horrible thing that he thought would keep him from doing something worse, the girl not protesting as they started down the rock shelf, each of them keeping one hand along the canyon wall to steady themselves on the slick stone.

It was a greater descent than he had expected, the two of them walking carefully down the rock path that sloped dozens of feet to the canyon floor, Simon doubting for a moment if they should go on but, afraid to turn back, continuing downward. Then, at the bottom, the ledge stopped before reaching the ground. It was not too far for Simon to jump, but it was too far for the girl to get down without help. Seeing no way to avoid it, Simon held the girl's hand and helped her down, but he let go as soon as he could and killed the thought the contact had created, not giving it a chance to get comfortable in his mind.

Why can't you think it? What harm is a thought?

Because I can't. Because thoughts have the power to change my path, and I need to be a good man.

They walked along the dammed river bed in silence. Water was trapped here and there in small pools, and the dirt was all mud, but the ground was littered with rocks and debris for them to step on. Simon missed his walking stick as he tried to balance from one rock to another; and the girl kept slipping, which slowed them down, but he didn't dare hold her hand again. He kept a careful watch, but only from the corner of his eye because looking directly at the girl was too difficult right now, the thoughts louder and more insistent.

I need to be a good man for Dana, he told himself. I need to keep myself in check.

In check for what, Simon? A lifetime of denial? You are choosing the path to permanent misery. Lifelong chastity? That isn't even healthy. There will never be another woman like Dana—you know that, don't you?

And Simon wondered if it really was a good idea for him to deny himself for the rest of his life. Could it affect my health? But to not deny himself was out of the question. He needed to be a good man.

Of course, there is always the substitute, Simon, with so much variety and novelty to keep you satisfied—for now.

No, that would be wrong, Simon told himself. But then he reconsidered. That would be wrong, but would doing something wrong keep me from doing something worse? I couldn't look at the same things as before, of course, but I'll bet there is plenty out there that is close enough and also legal. Most men look, don't they? And they seem okay; well, most of them do; well, at least they claim to be okay. But then his thoughts were interrupted by the girl stumbling and falling toward a rock, forcing Simon to catch her elbow. He pulled her back to her feet before quickly letting go.

No, I can't look at anything like that, he thought. I don't want to be like that. Besides, I wouldn't stop at just looking, he told himself, shaking his head to kill the thoughts worming around in his mind. No, I can't even think about things like that. It's up to me to keep myself out of trouble, and the first step is to stop thinking about things like that. And I'm not going to fall for the "just one time" trick either.

Then he realized: aren't all these thoughts just tricks? It reminded him of what he had told Dana about *The Screwtape Letters*: "It's happening all around us." That's what is happening to me right now, isn't it? Simon said to himself. Not just my own thoughts and weaknesses but something darker working against me as well. He tried to remember the methods the book had warned about, but then an image came to him—as though he were looking down from above, he saw the girl walking next to him to one side, and on the other side, a cartoon devil, with goat horns and a tail, dressed all in red, whispering things in his ear. The suddenness and strangeness of the image tickled his memory in warning, but the warning was overwhelmed by a feeling of how ridiculous the whole idea seemed. And Simon shook his head, unwilling to waste any time thinking about the book.

"If it didn't save Dana, then what's the point?" he said to himself.

"What?" the girl asked, looking up at him.

"Never mind," he said.

They continued along the riverbed and had walked for an hour when Simon was surprised to see sunlight upon the canyon's walls. He looked up to see that the sun had broken through the clouds, its rays now spilling partway into the canyon though not yet reaching him and the girl as they walked along the bottom.

Could the storm finally be over? Simon wondered.

He wished that it had never happened, that they were all back in their cabins still, that he would wake up there, go outside in the morning, and find Dana on one of the trails. It was stupid for us to hike down the mountain, he thought. It would have been better if we'd never tried. It would have been better if I'd never spoken to her. She would have never even seen me. She would have just kept walking on by. She would be alive today.

Simon heard the helicopter then, the distant sound coming down into the canyon. He wondered where it was. Somewhere along the road? he asked himself. Would we be rescued now if we had taken the safer way? He shook his head. So many mistakes, he thought, but it's too late to turn back now. Maybe they'll find us when we get back up onto the road in another hour or so.

As they walked onward, the girl complained of being tired, and Simon could see she was moving more slowly, stumbling more, so he decided they should rest. He set down his pack next to where the girl sat. The canyon was narrower here, its walls lower but still sheer, straight cliffs from top to bottom; and Simon wondered for the first time if there would be a path out of the riverbed when they were ready to return to the road. I should have thought about that before we came down here, he said to himself. But it was too late to worry about it, so he walked a few feet back in the direction they had come and looked up at the walls of the canyon, wondering how long the river had taken to dig this deep, and wondering how much water had been flowing through it before it was dammed. He touched the canyon wall before turning back, his shadow falling upon the rock wall, the sun now overhead.

Simon looked at the girl for a moment before he realized what he was doing and forced himself to look away. The girl had pulled out *The Screwtape Letters* but hadn't opened it, the gargoyle on the book's cover watching Simon and the girl with interest.

There is no harm in you looking, is there? That is better than doing something else, isn't it?

Yes, there is, Simon thought, because it doesn't work that way, not for me. It would just lead to more and more.

And why does that matter?

Because it does. Because I'm going to be a good man for Dana and that means I need to keep myself in check.

Then the thought returned to Simon that he didn't have to do it alone, but he pushed it down, not ready to face it yet.

Yes, you are better alone.

The girl screamed and pointed behind Simon with a shaking hand. Something had followed them into the riverbed.

Twisting to look, Simon froze halfway, chilled by the sight of a man behind him, tall and dark, close enough to touch. Simon shrank from the presence and, seeing movement, raised his arms in fear, expecting to be attacked. He stepped back onto a rock but slipped, his foot sinking into the mud. Then he looked up, fearing what might be there—and saw nothing but his own dark shadow on the wall.

"Idiot girl!" Simon yelled. "That's what got Dana killed!"

Pulling his foot from the mud, he flew toward the girl, grabbed her shoulders and yanked her to her feet. He stared into her scared eyes as color drained from her face.

You have seen this before, Simon—remember how much you liked it.

And, his judgment clouded by anger, Simon didn't shove the thought away as he had before. Instead he let it linger. But then he noticed that the girl's pale face wasn't looking at him. No, her eyes—wide with terror—were looking over his shoulder. And the canyon was no longer silent.

Simon let go of the girl's shoulders as a sound he recognized—a sound he should have expected from the moment they climbed down into the canyon—grew behind him. And turning, he saw it: the swelling river rushing toward him, broken through its temporary dam, reclaiming what it had never really left.

You were always such a fool, Simon.

The water charged forward in a growing mass, slowed by dirt and debris but moving with unstoppable force, pulling up rocks to join the surge, filling the canyon with a triumphant roar, the river dark and full of destruction.

"Run, Alice!"

Chapter Fifteen

THE RIVER HAD NEVER GONE AWAY. NO, IT HAD POOLED behind the earthen dam created when the mountain fell, the water forming a large reservoir—but a temporary one—the reservoir eventually cresting above the piled earth, spilling over in a trickle that quickly built into a stream, tearing more and more dirt from the dam, water gathering at its base, filling the deeper pools and starting to move downstream, more and more water spilling over the dam, every drop draining more strength—allowing more and more drops to follow—the stream now a flood, weighed down by debris but gathering force, more and more power pouring down the dam and flowing into the riverbed, the entire reservoir starting to empty, ready to fill the canyon—but not yet.

The leading surge spread from wall to wall. Froth formed upon the brown water's surface where it crashed against the sides, the water dragging along stray rocks and reclaiming dropped branches, the flood now enough to drown a man—but nothing compared to what was building upstream. The water reached Simon's abandoned hiking pack and lifted it upon its waves before the pack sank into the flood, spinning and turning and vanishing. *The Screwtape Letters,* dropped and forgotten in the mud, was quickly hidden underneath the dark flow.

And the flood charged on, chasing the two of them as they ran down the canyon, sheer cliffs on both sides—no way to escape, no way to outrun the river. We're not going to make it, Simon thought, swiveling his head from side to side in search of higher ground as the noise grew closer. We're going to drown.

Then they turned a corner, and Simon saw a small ledge partway up the cliff to the left with a solitary tree growing on it. But the cliff rose straight above the ledge, offering no escape. He looked farther down the canyon, knowing the surge would turn the corner any second, and there he saw a vertical ridge of rock protruding from the cliff's face, like a spine running from the top of the canyon down to a large boulder, the base of which was littered with drying debris. It was their only chance.

"There!" Simon yelled, running toward it.

But, hearing a cry, he turned around and saw that Alice had stumbled and fallen to the ground. The first splash of water turned the corner behind them.

"Move!" he yelled.

But Alice just lay there gasping for breath, eyes closed, tears running down her cheeks. And Simon feared that she was broken. After everything she had been through—the landslides, the shadows, losing Dana, and now sensing her own death—Alice was broken.

There is no time, Simon. Save yourself.

"No," Simon said, running back to Alice. "I won't leave her."

He bent down and picked her up, cradling her in his arms. Then he stood and stumbled away, but the water had come too close and it was moving much too fast. No time to reach the boulder, he ran to the ledge instead. Slower with the added burden but still able to reach the wall in time, he lifted her high to grab the ledge.

"Climb up!" he told her.

She did. And he scrambled after her, the water rushing beneath him as he scurried up onto the ledge. A massive branch banged into the wall below like a battering ram as the murky waters reclaimed the canyon, splashing against rocks, debris floating and sinking, the flood's noise filling the air.

Simon stood on the ledge and looked down at the water below. He could already feel what was coming; the flood inched higher to meet them. He knew how much water must have built up and how much would soon rush down the canyon. It would carry them away. We have to get out of here, he thought. But, turning to the cliff, he saw what he had feared he would see—a bare wall, no hand holds, no way to climb. There was nowhere for them to go.

Wood groaned as a large tree was dragged along the opposite side of the canyon, its stripped branches spinning as the current turned the tree over and over. It scraped along the bottom, then struggled into the middle before bouncing back against the opposite wall, farther down the canyon now, the flow already strong and swift, the current growing.

You are going to drown, Simon.

Simon looked from one side of the ledge to the other. There was nowhere to go. He looked farther downstream at the boulder he had hoped to reach. Water had carved a line in the cliff face from the ledge to the top of the boulder. The work of years, the line ran straight for more than two dozen feet. And above the boulder, the ridge reached all the way up to the top of the canyon, teasing him with the opportunity of escape. If only we could have made it there instead, he thought. But we can't reach it now.

You are going to die, Simon. You have little time left.

Simon looked at the tree beside him on the ledge. Its trunk was thick and strong enough to hold them, but its branches were too high to reach, and climbing would do no good anyway: the cliff was as bare at the tree's top as at its bottom, and he knew the flood would reach even higher. They were trapped.

All your rules and all your struggles, all your resistance, and now you simply die. None of it mattered, Simon. None of it.

Simon looked upstream, dreading what was coming. The water had grown closer, now only feet below the ledge. It moved with a feigned calm, the truth beneath its surface only betrayed by the erratic movement of anything unfortunate enough to be carried along. Soon that will be us, Simon thought.

Could we swim to the boulder? he wondered, not wanting to give up; then he saw the mash of branches and debris that pressed against the boulder, pieces constantly breaking off to spin violently into the flow, replaced by other branches that floated from upstream. There's no way we'd make it there, he thought. The current would catch us if the debris didn't smash us first.

"Of all the luck," Simon muttered, the words sounding like a whine.

He walked to the wall, flattening his hand against it, and looked up for any sign of hope. He found none. The water was higher now, the current reaching closer.

First Dana and now this. You will die here, Simon. And when you die, you will die with nothing. Your life has been meaningless.

Simon looked at the tree again. He could claw his way up if he had to, but that would only delay the inevitable. He listened to the roar of the water. After everything, this is what happens, he thought. Was there even a point to anything? He felt too young to die.

You have been cheated out of your life, Simon. Think of all the things other men get to feel and experience. All of that has been taken from you. Your entire life will pass in just the next few minutes. Everything you want to experience has to happen in just the next few minutes.

Simon had wanted to live so much longer. He had wanted to do so much more. He turned back to the flood, so close now to the ledge. Soon. He felt unprepared, the rift he had created with his negligence separating him from what he needed most, a rift his bitterness wouldn't allow him to mend. But as he looked from cliff to tree to boulder and back again, the reality of the growing flood replaced his petty anger with fear and panic. He knew what he needed to do—he needed help—and he knew what he needed to do to get it.

How pathetic and insincere, Simon. Now, when you are about to die, suddenly you will ask for help? You are worthless, Simon. You deserve nothing.

And Simon felt unworthy to ask, the action itself seeming alien and uncomfortable to him after he'd avoided it these past few days. Standing there beside the tree, he leaned his head against the trunk. I can't do it, he thought. That help isn't available to me anymore. I chose to walk alone. Now I guess I'll have to die alone as well. The water below had crept higher. Only a matter of time. The rest of my life will be spent in the next few moments, he thought. So little time.

But still time for something, Simon. Still time to feel something—to feel love. Do not waste your last minutes looking for hope that does not exist. Take advantage of the short time you have left. The girl is right there, Simon. No one else is around. You know that others call it love, so many others. Why can't you, now, at the end? Are you wiser than they? Are you better than they?

In his growing panic, Simon had forgotten about Alice. But the idea was wrong, very wrong. Who cares what others call love, he said to himself. Besides, no one calls it love at her age.

Age? That is just a number, Simon. When biology itself has been ruled to provide no rational basis, do you actually expect an arbitrary number to be compelling enough to stand? No, Simon, do not be so naive. The future will judge that tradition to be nothing but an artifact of a time—a time that has passed. Why follow a standard you know will be crushed by the stampede of future progress?

Because doing that is wrong!

Who are you to say it is wrong, Simon? When history marches away from you, will you claim it is moving in the wrong direction? What arrogance. When millions stand against you, will you insist it is you who is right and the millions who are wrong? What arrogance indeed! Do not pretend to be so wise, Simon. You are no smarter than those who will disagree with you. Let go of your arrogance and accept what is coming. Accept what you can have, Simon. Accept it in the little time you have left!

Simon shook his head, dismissing the twisted logic, but he had turned to look at Alice; and the river—which had never really gone away—rose, swelling into its familiar channel. The girl sat only feet away from him, her face on her knees, her whole body trembling, frozen in fear, staring at nothing, broken; and memories slammed into Simon: every memory of everything he had seen—every face, every act—the scenes staggering him as they replayed in his mind; and he remembered what he had thought as he looked; and he remembered what he had felt as he looked—and he remembered what he had wanted . . .

And why not, Simon? In a few minutes, you will be dead. Do not waste the time you have left. Use it to feel what was stolen from you. It is only love, Simon! Everyone else knows it is only love. And what if they are right? Shouldn't you feel love now before the end?

No, Simon told himself, shaking his head. That's not love and that's not what I want. Pretending it is love does not make it right.

But his bridge had fallen, collapsed upon his crumbling foundation, leaving him at the mercy of the river, Simon abandoned even by social constraints now that death had become certain. But he didn't want to give in. No, he thought, I'll be a good man. And he remembered what he had told himself before: I'll be a good man for Dana. I'll do the right thing for her. But the river slowly rose, the memories dancing before him, and Simon took one step toward the girl.

You have been so strong, Simon. Think of all you have been through. Shouldn't you get what you want—just this one time—here at the end? Other men get what they want. Why not you? Other men marry a wife and indulge their wants every night! How is that fair, Simon? Why can't *you* get what *you* want? Are you not as good as they?

And the river continued to rise, Simon listening to the logic, bitterness swelling inside of him as he thought: What hypocrites! Expecting me to starve while allowing themselves to feast! He let the false feeling of injustice soak into him, the river growing, intention forming in his mind, one more step toward the girl; but then he checked himself, fighting the thoughts that threatened to overwhelm him, reminding himself that he needed to be a good man. It doesn't matter what others have and I don't, he told himself. I will be a good man. Dana would want me to be a good man.

You are going to die, Simon. Will you die before getting what you deserve? That is not fair. But you can make it fair. You can make it fair now. You can take what you want. Stop wasting the little time that remains. You can do nothing to prevent the inevitable, but you can take what is yours in the minutes you have left. No one is here to stop you. No one is here to judge you. Take it, Simon! Take what you deserve!

No, Simon thought; but the river had risen too high, stronger than it had ever been, faces and actions swirling before him; he took another step. No, he thought again. I can't do this. It is wrong. I must be a good man. I can't let Dana down.

Dana is dead, Simon. Everyone is just a corpse that has not learned to rot yet. Seize any pleasure you can take while your fingers are able to grasp. Dana is dead. She cannot see you. You are alone.

And Simon, truly, was alone, his world nothing but darkness, darkness and the river. Too close to the girl now, the river churning and singing to him—mocking the meaning he had found in life, telling him to take what he deserved, telling him that no man should deny himself, telling him to feel pleasure one last time before the end. And Simon listened to its call, raising his foot to take one step closer—

"They want him to forget."

Such shame as he had never known. Dana's words drove Simon to his knees as the wrongness of the act washed over him, driving out the whines of his unwanted want. What a fool I am! he thought. How could I have forgotten? And now, to die like this? Here at the end, when my thoughts should be guided by honor, they are centered on pleasure instead—stupid, pointless pleasure. How pathetic I am. What a monster I am.

Yes, Simon, a monster, and it is too late to turn back now—you have already gone too far. You have nothing more to lose. Be what you are, Simon. Be what you have already become. Take what is yours. There is little time left!

Where is my honor? Simon asked himself. Is pleasure worth losing my honor? And what of the girl? Must she die in fear and confusion, hurt by someone in their selfishness? But the river's pull was overwhelming, and Simon would soon be carried away. I can't resist it much longer, he thought in despair.

You cannot resist, Simon, for you cannot deny what you are. Be what you are! Take what is yours!

No, this is not what I want.

Yes, Simon, it is what you have always wanted. Stop denying yourself!

No! This is not what I want!

But the river was too powerful and the girl was too close. Simon could not resist alone. He felt the cold, hard rock beneath his knees; his face was buried in his hands.

There is no point in that, Simon. You deserve no help. You chose to walk alone, and now you will eat the fruit of your choice. And you will eat it alone.

But, though unworthy of help, Simon asked for it anyway, pleading on his knees for the strength to resist, for the ability to stand—to be a man. He could not do this alone. He asked to not be alone. He asked for help. He asked for guidance. He asked for strength. Then he opened his eyes and stared at the ground below him. He could feel the pull of the river—strong and demanding. The girl, Alice, was right there. The choice was his to make.

And Simon stood.

"I will end how I choose to end," he said, and he turned away from Alice, once again searching for an escape. If I die then I'm going to die trying, he told himself.

He thought of the tree, but he brushed the thought aside, knowing they couldn't climb it. The water hovered inches below the ledge, the river not rising higher but still moving strongly. Simon could sense Alice sitting behind him, but he pushed the feeling away, keeping his focus on escaping the ledge.

Again he thought of the tree. This time he glanced at it, looking up at its branches. Too high to climb, he told himself. Then he wondered: but could I help Alice climb up to safety?

No, he decided after considering the idea, the lower branches are too thin to hold her weight and the thicker branches are too high for me to lift her. All this time, the river was singing to him. But Simon's mind was occupied with purpose.

There is still time, Simon. This is what you are! Why deny yourself? No one else has to deny themselves!

But Simon only shook his head, not listening any longer. He scanned the cliff above the ledge, sure that there must be some way out he hadn't noticed yet. I won't give in today, he told himself. Not today. And tomorrow? he wondered, but then he reminded himself: Every day is today. And today I'll be a man.

He thought of the tree once again. Stop wasting time! he told himself; and the river mocked his useless efforts—the river was there, always there. Turning from the cliff to the tree, Simon kicked it in frustration; and the tree moved with his blow, Simon losing his balance and stumbling toward the flood but catching his footing just in time. The water below moved swiftly. It was creeping higher.

Simon looked at the newly exposed roots of the tree, the remaining soil loose and falling away from the tree's base. The floodwater from the storm must have stripped it, he thought. It looks like I could just push it over now. He was amazed at the possibility. But push it where? he asked himself.

He looked first in the direction the tree was leaning: the other side of the canyon. But Simon didn't think the tree was tall enough to reach the opposite wall—and that side offered no escape anyway. Then he looked downstream, remembering the boulder and the ridge that rose above it. He considered the distance from the tree to the boulder. The tree might be tall enough, he thought, but do we have time? The water had almost reached them. Its waves would soon splash onto the ledge.

Stop wasting time, Simon. You still have a chance. No one is here. No one would know. Feel something good for a change. Take pleasure before the end!

No, not today, Simon thought, finding steady footing and pushing at the tree. It shook but did not move.

This is what you want, Simon. Take what you want!

Please, not today, Simon thought, shoving at the tree again. It moved this time, but only barely. The river was screaming at him, the water reaching higher.

This is what you are, Simon! Stop denying what you are!

"No! Not today!" Simon yelled, putting all his weight into one hard push.

And the tree gave way, its roots losing their grip, the entire trunk falling toward the boulder; but Simon fell with it as well, his momentum carrying him into the water, the icy chill sweeping away everything but shock and panic. Instinctively, he wrapped his arms around the tree's trunk, desperately trying to grab hold, but the fierce current found his legs immediately, twisting his body and pulling him downstream, and his fingers slipped along the wet bark. A sharp tug pulled him under, and his muscles tightened in the cold, everything dark; he threw a hand up and caught hold of the trunk as the current tried to pull him away from the tree. If I let go, then I'll drown. He needed to get his head above water. But as he tried to pull himself up, his grip came loose and he slipped along the tree again, his fingers sliding, finding nothing to hold. The current tore him away and he floated motionless in the water. His lungs ached. I'm going to drown! He flailed as the water pulled him, his hands desperately grasping, grasping at nothing, grasping until the nothing was something and he caught hold. Grabbing with both hands, he heaved himself out of the water, gasping for breath. He was caught in the branches not far from the trunk. Turning himself toward the tree, he kicked a leg up over it, sliding his body until he lay atop the trunk, one hand hugging the tree, the other still clinging to what had saved him from drowning.

The water flowed strongly along his thighs, his feet pulled back behind him by the current. He tucked them tightly against the trunk, his teeth chattering and body shaking in the cold air. Then he looked down, wondering what he held in his hand, and saw a hint of white beneath the dark water. He tried to lift it out, but it was caught in the branches and wouldn't move. Twisting it back and forth, he untangled it and pulled it out of the water: Dana's walking stick, scratched and scuffed, there in his hand. He sat up, unable to believe it could be there. He had seen it buried under the landslide.

Then he jerked his head up and looked back at the ledge, half-expecting to see Dana; but she wasn't there, only Alice, yelling and crying by the tree's upturned roots. The water was spilling onto the ledge now. We have no more time, he thought. He looked behind him and saw that the tree had reached the boulder. We have a chance but we have to move fast, he told himself.

Simon crawled along the overturned tree toward Alice, but the water worked against him and he moved slowly, hugging the trunk to keep from slipping, his feet tight against the tree to avoid the current's pull.

Then, almost to the ledge, he held out the walking stick to Alice, gripping the carvings firmly. He told Alice to grab hold of the carved handgrip and follow him across. But she didn't move.

"Come on, Alice!" Simon told her. "There isn't time!"

Panic and fear were in her eyes, water brushing against her shoes, everything weighing down on her; and Simon was afraid she couldn't do it. Looking at her, he saw the same dullness she had shown since he first met her. Alice had been broken.

But then there was a shift, a flicker of life shining, retreating, returning, Alice battling within herself. She looked down and saw what was in front of her.

"That's Dana's walking stick!" she said.

And hope flooded into her face, the dullness falling away until Simon could see the life that Dana must have always seen in her.

"Grab on!" he said. "We need to move across. We can climb up over there."

No longer hesitating, Alice held tight to the carving and climbed out onto the tree, its trunk now halfway submerged. She grimaced at the initial cold and exclaimed in surprise as the current caught her and pushed her toward Simon.

"Just hold on tight," he said, and he loosened his legs' grip on the trunk, letting the current do most of the work as he shimmied backwards to the top of the tree, avoiding the branches that stood in the way, the whole time watching Alice, who frowned at the current though hope shone in her eyes whenever she looked at Dana's walking stick.

Then Simon's foot hit rock. He scurried quickly up onto the boulder, navigating carefully through the tangle of branches at the top of the tree and helping Alice up after him. The water now covered the ledge and almost covered the tree as well. Soon it would reach the top of the boulder where they stood.

"That's Dana's walking stick!" Alice repeated in excitement.

"Not now," Simon said. He grabbed hold of her shoulders and directed her to the ridge that ran up the cliff. "Climb!"

Then he looked back anxiously, afraid that a flood of water would strike them now when they were so close to escaping. It seemed like something bad should happen given how everything else kept going so wrong. But the water wasn't rising fast enough to catch them, and Simon reminded himself that, while so much had gone wrong, much had also gone right. More than I deserved, he thought, looking down at the tree that had allowed their escape from the ledge, and the walking stick that had saved him from the river.

Then he turned his attention back on Alice, who was climbing up the ridge carefully, moving from handhold to handhold with an alertness and energy she hadn't shown since he had met her, never even slipping once. Simon followed after, tucking Dana's walking stick under one arm as he climbed. It made him slow and clumsy, but he refused to leave it behind. What could it mean, finding it here? he wondered as he advanced up the ridge, his body cold and shaking. Then his foot slipped, and the other barely caught his weight. Simon looked down at the boulder dozens of feet below. Water almost covered it now, and most of the tree was submerged. Then he looked up and continued on, setting aside his hopes for now and focusing only on the climb, moving higher grip by grip.

Alice had disappeared over the top of the canyon; then Simon saw her face looking down at him. She watched him climb the last few feet before pulling himself up over the edge. He collapsed upon the ground and stared up at the sky. He couldn't believe they had made it. Above, the dark clouds had parted and the sun was spilling through, radiating a hint of warmth, although his body still shook with fear and cold. He rolled over onto his side and looked down into the canyon. The tree, now buried in water, quivered as the current tugged at it. It rocked side to side, letting go of the boulder but still held to the ledge by its roots for a moment. Then the roots came loose and the tree pulled away, carried within the deep flows of the dark river.

Chapter Sixteen

SIMON ROLLED BACK FROM THE CANYON'S EDGE AS ALICE sat down beside him. She picked up the walking stick and ran a finger along its scratched carvings.

"See, I told you it was Dana's!" she said, her voice overflowing with excitement.

"Yes," Simon told her.

He lay on his back and looked up at the sky. A strange feeling. He hadn't expected to live. The sun shone down on him, dark clouds retreating. A strange feeling. His earlier fear was going away, leaving everything else jumbled together: relief and shame, disbelief and gratitude, even a little hope.

"But if this is here, then Dana could be alive too!" Alice said.

"No." And Simon thought: I saw her buried.

"But—"

"No!" Simon sat up. "I can't lose her again!" And he rose to his feet, chilled by the cool air.

His clothing soaked and weighing down on him, Simon shook with the cold. But I am alive, he reminded himself, and he expressed his gratitude silently. Gratitude that they had made it. Gratitude that Alice was unharmed. But the fact that I didn't hurt her is no reason for congratulations, he told himself. No, the fact that I came so close is a reason for shame. I shouldn't have let my thoughts twist me like that. I shouldn't have been so foolish. How could I have forgotten? I can't resist alone. I know that. I've known that for years! But I let myself forget. What a fool. I can't ever make that mistake again.

There was a guardrail a few feet in front of them, separating the road from the river canyon, the road continuing on down the mountain, its pavement dry from the sun. They had hours to go before they'd reach the town.

And behind Simon, the flood roared through the canyon, the water rising higher—but not high enough. No, those waters will never reach me now, Simon said to himself. But there's more than one way to drown; and although the right is often obvious, the wrong is always appealing. I can't ever let myself forget again. Never again.

His hiking pack was gone, all their food, water, and supplies lost in the canyon. But with this cool air, their wet clothes were a bigger problem.

"We need to get walking," he told Alice. "We'll freeze like this if we don't get to town before dark."

Alice stood, pulling herself up with Dana's walking stick; but then she held the walking stick out for Simon.

"Here, you should have it," she told him.

Not expecting the offer, Simon looked from the walking stick to Alice in surprise. There was a change in Alice's face. He had caught a hint of it in the canyon but hadn't had time to really think about it then. And now it was obvious: Alice looked different, as if something had lost its hold on her. Maybe her fears lost their power compared to what she just went through? Simon wondered. Or is it hope? he asked himself. The hope that Dana might be alive?

Whatever it was, it showed on her face. And that only made Simon's shame deepen. To think that he could have willingly hurt her. Who would even consider such a thing? he asked himself.

Still, she held out the walking stick for him, waiting for him to take it. And Simon did want to have it, this last memory of Dana—last memory, unless . . .

No, I saw her buried, he reminded himself, and this is all I have left of her.

But do I deserve to have it? he asked himself, remembering why he had chosen it for Dana. I came so close, he thought. What kind of a man would even let himself come close? But I can see peace in Alice's face now, and excitement, and hope. And none of that would be there if I'd given in. Yes, I resisted. I ignored my want. I kept the darkness outside. And isn't that what Dana told me was important? To keep it outside? And I didn't let it in. In the end, I didn't surrender to my attraction.

While his words made him feel a little better, Simon wasn't totally convinced that he deserved to have the walking stick, but he accepted it anyway. Alice then checked her coat pockets.

"I think I lost my book," she said, looking back into the canyon. "I must have forgotten it when we started running."

"We all forget things sometimes," Simon told her.

He took off his coat. The air was chilly, but his wet coat only made it worse. He draped it over one arm, walked to the guardrail, and stepped over, Alice following by his side. Then they were on pavement again, heading down the road. Simon shivered; Alice was silent. Most of the mountains were behind them now, the canyon was to their right, and a wide field rolled away to their left with trees lining a small rise in the distance. The town was somewhere in front of them, and each step took them a little bit closer.

Simon kept a small distance between himself and Alice as they walked, the separation driven both by shame as well as caution. He had neglected his bridge and had walked along the river's bottom, where he had almost drowned. But, even after going through all of that, he still worried he might do it again because, as long as he was isolated on the mountain with Alice, thoughts had too much power to twist him. He wished he were a stronger man. He clung to what strength he had been given. It had to be enough.

But Simon could feel the river. Always there, the lifelong challenge threatening to overwhelm him. *Can I really resist this want forever?* he asked himself. *How can I do that when even a small gap in my armor makes me vulnerable? Every time I am weak, every time I am doubtful, it will always be there, ready to pull me under. How can I stand against that?*

You will fall eventually, Simon. It is inevitable. Why waste time trying to fight when your cause is hopeless? Just give in now and get your failure over with.

No, Simon told himself, deflecting the hopelessness. I won't give in, not today. And I can rebuild my bridge. It only fell because of my neglect. I can build it again. I don't have to give in. Not today. And every day is today. If I can remember that, humbly asking for and accepting the help I need, then I can stand.

But his shame deepened as he was struck by the memory of how close he had come to hurting Alice. He had thought about doing it, he had actually considered it, he had taken steps toward her. What kind of a man would even think about that? he asked himself.

You went too far, Simon, and you cannot erase that. To think what you thought, to want what you wanted, such things can never be undone. You have already disgraced yourself, Simon—you might as well finish the job. You will never be better than this. There is no point in trying. You will never escape the guilt. This is what you are, Simon. Your attraction is what you are. Be what you—

No! My attraction is *not* who I am. It's just something I have to deal with, Simon told himself. What I want isn't who I am. I am who I choose to be! And Simon reined in his shame. He knew he deserved to feel it, but he couldn't let it overpower him, knowing that shame, just like hopelessness, could be used against him—one more weapon to bring him down. And Simon wasn't going to let that happen.

Not today, he thought. Not today—words used by many people struggling with many different challenges—words used by Simon now. He took the memory of how close he had come and the thought of how weak he was, and he attached them to his bridge, fusing the shame and regret into place, his bridge regaining strength. Not today, he repeated to himself. Not today.

The sun wasn't warm enough to dry his clothes, and Simon shook with the cold. He increased their pace, leaning on Dana's walking stick. If her walking stick is here, then couldn't she have survived? he wondered. But he ignored the thought. He had lost her once. He couldn't do that again. She had been buried by the mountain and he had seen it. She is gone, he told himself. But . . .

No, she is gone, he repeated.

They made good progress along the road, the thick sound of the river all around, the reservoir draining into the canyon below. And as he walked, Simon kept repeating the same words to himself, continually brushing aside the stray thoughts that tried to sneak their way into his mind. The thoughts came faster and faster, seeming to sense that the window of opportunity was closing; they threw themselves at him desperately: that because of this, this because of that. No logical connection from one thought to the next, only a single motivation: that he should surrender, that he should not resist. But Simon knew better, and he batted each one to the side. I won't do that today, he told himself. Not today. I am who I choose to be. I won't do that today. His defenses back in place, Simon would not be swayed. Thoughts had no power when he ignored them, and Simon would not be swayed. Not today.

Alice didn't speak as they made their way toward town, but she didn't have to—her excitement and hope were clear in the way she walked, the way she looked up at the sky, the small smile that never left her face. Simon knew what she was hoping for, and the hope started to grow within him as well. What if Dana really were alive? he asked himself, not knowing how she could be, but also not knowing how her walking stick had found its way to him. Could there be a way? he wondered. He wasn't ready to let himself believe the hope, but his dreams for a life with her were returning. Once Alice is safe, I will come back to look for Dana, he decided. I know I won't find her, but just in case . . .

Then Simon remembered what he had done, or what he had almost done. Even if Dana were alive, we could never be together, he told himself. Not after how close I came. That isn't something she could ever forgive or learn to live with. It doesn't matter that I did nothing in the end. I thought about doing something. I took steps toward Alice. I went too far. No, alive or dead, Dana will never be mine. I'll still return to look for her; but it will be for her sake, not for mine. I can never have her as my own.

The pain threatened to raise thoughts within him, but he smashed them unformed, adding the emotion to his bridge and throwing out the nagging feeling of unfairness before it could grab hold of him. I have what I have, others have what others have, and envy is nothing but a sign of ingratitude, he told himself. I should be grateful I didn't drown in the flood. I should be grateful I didn't drown in the river. It was my choices that led me to stray as far as I did, and I will accept the consequences.

Simon viewed his lonely future with calm determination, blocking all twisting thoughts with the words "Not today." His mind thus occupied, he was surprised when Alice grabbed his elbow to stop him from walking. Then he noticed the dust swirling in front of him and the sound of a helicopter, louder even than the river, starting to land a little way down the road.

He dropped his coat to the pavement and rested both hands on the walking stick, feeling suddenly weak. Could it really be over? he asked himself. Could I really have made it? Already the unwanted thoughts had quieted, the loss of isolation robbing them of the ability to press him so directly. They would not fully leave, of course, but their approach would have to be more subtle now, a trickle rather than a tidal wave. Simon raised a hand to shield his eyes from the dust as he watched the helicopter descend. Before it had even landed, a man jumped out, ducking below the spinning blades and running toward them.

"Dad!" Alice yelled, bursting forward to meet him.

And Simon watched their happy embrace: Alice's father picking her up and spinning her around, Alice laughing, all stress vanished from her face, both of them beaming, both of them crying. Simon thought of what Dana had told him about Alice's father—this immoral senator, this imperfect man, this father who loves his daughter. Truly, we are much more than just our shortcomings, Simon thought, and the realization gave him strength for his own struggles. He memorized the image, wanting to always remember this happy reunion between father and daughter, the father finding his daughter safe and unharmed. Simon didn't want to ever stand in the way of that. He added the image to his bridge. The river flowed dark below, but already his bridge was feeling strong again. His foundation, however, would need more work after such neglect. But I'll give it the attention it needs, he promised himself.

Then Simon saw a flash of blonde hair as a woman stepped out of the helicopter. Alice's mother, he assumed, not looking at her. He was a little surprised that she would even be here, with what he knew about her. But

Simon had no desire to see her, so he leaned his head upon his hands on top of the walking stick instead, resting for a moment and enjoying the feeling of relief that washed over him. He had done it. He had truly done it. But not alone. No, never alone again.

"Dana!"

Simon froze, his head still down. No, it can't be, he told himself, afraid to even look up. Then hope rose within him, and he needed to see; but hope was followed by guilt as he remembered what had happened so shortly before. If it is her, how can I face her? he asked himself. But he simply had to see. He raised his head.

A woman was walking toward Alice, her head bent slightly beneath the helicopter blades, her blonde hair flowing in the wind, tangled but beautiful, her slim body hidden under a man's bulky coat. She was limping and had a small bandage on her forehead, but there was a wide smile on her face. It was Dana. It really was Dana. She leaned down and caught Alice in a tight embrace.

Simon stared, unable to believe what he was seeing. It didn't seem real. He had seen the mountain fall on her. How could she be here? He heard their voices. Dana laughing. Something about a cave and another opening. He had seen no cave. Alice was telling Dana how they almost drowned in the river, waving her hands widely as she told Dana about Simon pushing over the tree. How could this be real?

Then a man was in front of Simon, Alice's father, the senator, shaking Simon's hand vigorously, thanking Simon and giving him an awkward hug, the fake friendliness so common to politicians overshadowed by honest emotional warmth. The senator's hair was ruffled perfection, but multiple days of stubble showed on his face, almost enough to match Simon's own. The senator's clothes looked like he'd slept in them—a button-up shirt and khaki trousers. It must have been him in the helicopter the whole time, Simon guessed. The weariness in the senator's eyes hinted at that. Now, though, the weariness was lightened by excitement.

"Why, you're freezing!" Senator Miller said. "We need to get you dried off and warmed up!"

He leaned over and picked up Simon's coat from the ground. Then he threw his arm thickly around Simon's shoulders and dragged him toward the others. Alice was still talking about their time in the canyon, a bright smile on her face despite the darkness of the story. But Dana was staring at Simon, one hand on Alice's shoulder as she listened, her expression blank and unreadable. And regret sank into Simon at how far he had allowed himself to go, Simon almost wishing he had drowned in the flood instead of having to face Dana like this.

The sun shone bright on Dana's face, beautiful yet tired. There was a questioning look in her eyes. She walked toward Simon, Alice beside her, Alice looking at Simon and chattering to him about a cave and how Dana climbed on top of the mountain to look for them and how she slipped and how her walking stick fell into the canyon and how Simon found it and how her father found Dana on the road and how her father and Dana had been looking all day for Alice and Simon but hadn't looked in the canyon.

They all stopped a few feet apart, Alice holding Dana's hand and swinging it back and forth, a huge smile on Alice's face as she hugged her father again, her father laughing and wiping a tear from his eye. But Dana just stood there and looked at Simon, not saying a word. Simon wanted to reach out and touch her, but he couldn't. He felt unworthy to even be standing this close. He looked at the ground instead, the shame cutting too deep with her so near. He had believed she was lost after the mountain collapsed, but now he understood the true meaning of loss: to have her here yet to know he could never have her. Such bitter regret.

"Alice, your pants are soaked!" Senator Miller said, and he turned her toward the helicopter. "We better get you dry!"

Hand in hand, father and daughter walked away, leaving Simon alone to face Dana, who hadn't said a word to him yet.

Then he felt a soft hand rest on his own, which was still holding tightly to the carved grip of the walking stick.

"I didn't expect you to walk in the riverbed, Simon."

He raised his head, forcing himself to meet her stare. I deserve to hear this, he told himself. I deserve to feel this. I'll add the regret to my bridge. This must never be forgotten.

"I thought out of anyone you would know better than to take that risk," Dana said, and she glanced at the walking stick he held in his hand.

Simon only nodded. There was nothing he could say to justify himself.

"But what else did you forget, Simon?" Dana asked, her hand leaving his to lightly touch the scratched carvings above it.

And, hearing the worry in her voice, Simon couldn't answer her; the shame was just too great. He looked down again, and they were both silent for a moment.

Then Dana's finger traced from the carving down to the top of his hand. Simon was thrilled by the light contact but wanted to recoil from it at the same time, feeling unworthy to have her even touch him.

"But you wouldn't feel right carrying this, would you?" she said. "Not if you hadn't remembered in time."

Her voice had lost some of its worry, but too much of it remained. Simon dropped the walking stick, letting it fall into Dana's hand as his arm fell limply to his side.

"I came so close," he confessed, hanging his head in shame. "Too close. I'm so sorry, Dana. I almost . . . I'm so sorry I let you down. Everything became so twisted and I almost . . . I'm sorry, Dana. I'm so sorry."

Simon felt the weight of Dana's eyes upon him. He was on the scale now, and Dana was rendering judgment. The verdict, however, was already obvious, at least to him. He would accept it as well as he could. This would never be forgotten.

"But what about Simon?" Dana whispered, as if carrying on an internal debate. Then she said to him: "But you didn't do anything, Simon. Maybe part of you wanted to, but you chose not to. Maybe you fought on the inside, maybe you almost fell on the inside, but on the outside—you chose to resist. Even when you thought I was dead—and you probably felt cheated, didn't you?—even then, even when you'd been alone with Alice for days, even when it looked like you were going to die, even then, even when you had no hope and there was no one to see you and no one to judge you, even then, even then you—you, Simon, you—you made the right choice."

She spoke more softly, then, as if only to herself: "But what about Simon? Are the brave brave because they never fight fear, or are the brave brave because they never choose cowardice?"

And she paused, as if considering what she had just said. Then she spoke to him again: "What we choose shows who we are, Simon.

Attraction is attraction, and none of it matters. Our choices are what matter. And in the end, you chose to do what was right."

Simon looked up, surprised at the lack of scorn in her voice. But he heard the river in the canyon below, and he felt it inside himself, filling him with hopelessness. It will always be a part of me, he reminded himself. It will always be trying to lure me in. Dana deserves someone better than me. She deserves someone stable, someone who she knows will be the same from day to day.

But hopelessness was dangerous, so he steeled himself and threw it away, not wanting to ever be weak again—never again. I will tend to my bridge, he told himself. I will care for my foundation. I will never forget again.

He gathered his strength as he looked at Dana. I will accept the rejection, he told himself. I will face the consequence of my shortcomings, and I won't let them drag me down. But he was stung by regret and disappointment that he could never be strong enough for a woman like Dana. She had praised his final choice, but he knew how fragile his decision had been.

"Today, maybe," he told her, fighting to keep his voice from shaking. "Maybe I did the right thing today. But that's it. And that's as far as I'm able to go."

Simon stood silently and accepted what he had lost. On his own, but not on his own. Alone, but not alone—no, never alone again. And, hardened by his mistakes, Simon was filled with determination to never repeat them. He was ready to face the solitary road ahead—his bridge already being repaired and his foundation strengthening within him— he would keep his focus solely on being strong for today, only today. And today he would resist. Today he would be a man.

But any expectation of loneliness was shattered when Dana rushed forward and embraced him, her body tight against his own, her kiss light upon his cheek, her whisper soft into his ear.

"Every day is today, Simon. Every day is today."

www.ingramcontent.com/pod-product-compliance
Lightning Source LLC
Chambersburg PA
CBHW031950170626
46807CB00006B/2424